THE GRASS IS ALWAYS GREENER

a BELLES novel

THE GRASS IS ALWAYS GREENER

a BELLES novel

by Jen Calonita

poppy

LITTLE, BROWN AND COMPANY

New York   Boston

Copyright © 2013 by Jen Calonita
Excerpt from *Summer State of Mind* copyright © 2014 by Jen Calonita

Poppy

Hachette Book Group
237 Park Avenue, New York, NY 10017
Visit us at lb-teens.com

Poppy is an imprint of Little, Brown and Company.
The Poppy name and logo are trademarks of Hachette Book Group, Inc.

The publisher is not responsible for websites (or their content) that are not owned by the publisher.

First Paperback Edition: April 2014
First published in hardcover in April 2013 by Little, Brown and Company

Library of Congress Cataloging-in-Publication Data

Calonita, Jen.
    The grass is always greener / by Jen Calonita.—First edition.
        pages cm.—(Belles ; 3)
    "Poppy."
    Summary: Amid preparations for their preppy Southern town's Founders Day celebration and their own shared sweet sixteen, sisters Isabelle Scott and Mirabelle Monroe long to break free from the tight constraints that come with being the daughters of a prominent public figure.
        ISBN 978-0-316-09110-7 (hc) — ISBN 978-0-316-09109-1 (pb)
    [1. Sisters—Fiction.   2. Family life—North Carolina—Fiction.   3. Social classes—Fiction.   4. North Carolina—Fiction.]   I. Title.
    PZ7.C1364Gr 2013
    [Fic]—dc23

                                                                                    2012032534

10 9 8 7 6 5 4 3 2 1

RRD-C

Printed in the United States of America

Other novels by Jen Calonita

The **BELLES** series:

Belles

Winter White

The Grass Is Always Greener

The **SECRETS OF MY HOLLYWOOD LIFE** series:

Secrets of My Hollywood Life

On Location

Family Affairs

Paparazzi Princess

Broadway Lights

There's No Place Like Home

SLEEPAWAY GIRLS

SUMMER STATE OF MIND

RealityCheck

For Andrew (and Heather, Rick, and Ryan) Foy. Thanks for giving up your bunk bed for me. This one's for you.

One

"Izzie?"

"Iz?"

"Izzie, wake up!"

Isabelle Scott could hear someone calling her name, but
she ignored her. Izzie was napping, and when it came to naps,
the rule was you didn't wake her unless you absolutely had to.
Like if the house was on fire, or she was missing Ryan Lochte
about to win some Olympic gold.

Unfortunately, Mirabelle Monroe didn't seem to remember Izzie's rules.

"Izzie!" Mira's voice rose to a shrill as she shook her sister
gently by the shoulders. "Get up! We're going to be late!"

Apparently, the time allowed for a soothing awakening
was over. "Come on, it's Saturday!" Izzie said with a yawn.

Isn't it? Her brain felt kind of foggy. She squinted to read the hula-girl alarm clock on her nightstand. "What time is it?" The room was so dark it had to be the middle of the night. Her eyes narrowed. "Did you wake me up to watch another E! *True Hollywood Story?*"

"No." Mira rolled her eyes. "I have one DVR'd for when we get back," she added quickly, and tugged on one of the custom-made window treatments Izzie's aunt had ordered for Izzie's room. The Roman shade retracted, flooding the room with sunlight. "And it's not the middle of the night. It's one thirty *in the afternoon.*"

Izzie pulled her comforter over her head to block out the light. "So? A person can sleep in once in a while, can't they?" Mira grabbed the blanket and the sisters glared at each other. Izzie could tell by Mira's outfit (Go-to sweater set. Check! Slim-fitting cords. Check! Riding boots. Check!) that she had someplace to go. Her long, curly brown hair was equally watch-me-world ready. Izzie felt tired just looking at her. "I don't have the energy to get dressed," she admitted.

Mira's face softened. "Iz, I know this is hard to deal with, but it's been a month. We have to talk about this."

"No, we don't." Izzie's voice was hoarse. As far as she was concerned, there was nothing left to say. She had accepted as many condolences as a person could. She'd eaten from a dozen fruit baskets from Antonio at the Harborside grocery mart. But no amount of eating or talking made her feel any better.

2

Grams was gone, and she wasn't coming back.

Mira was still hovering. "You've missed almost three weeks of school. Isn't it time you rejoined the world of the living?"

Izzie closed her eyes and tried to drown out her sister's lecture, but deep down she knew Mira was right. Sleeping her life away wasn't going to fix anything.

"I heard Mom on the phone with school," Mira added. "They say if you don't come back this week, you'll get an incomplete for the semester, and the semester just started a month ago."

School. How could she even think of going back to Emerald Prep? Sure, her friends Violet and Nicole were there, but so were Savannah and her minions, who did nothing but whisper behind Izzie's back. In just six months, she had gone from living with her grandmother in the less-than-desirable town of Harborside (known for having the highest crime rate in the county) to residing in exclusive Emerald Cove. Along with the new zip code came a family that included her state senator father (who, for half a second, had claimed to be her uncle), her aunt Maureen, her sister Mira, and two brothers. After a rocky start, Izzie had made peace with her new, privileged life. Her grandmother had been in the finest rehabilitation center in the state, she had a family that loved her, and Brayden was officially hers (and out from Savannah's perfectly manicured clutches).

"Is this about Zoe?" Mira's voice was tentative. Even

though Izzie had turned to face the wall, she could picture Mira playing with her pearl necklace.

"This has nothing to do with Zoe." Izzie squeezed her worn Lambie blanket like it was a stress ball.

But it was about Zoe, because ever since she arrived, Izzie felt like her life had started to unravel. Her mother, who died when Izzie was nine, had a younger sister. A *sister*! And everyone had kept her a secret. Izzie only found out about Zoe when Grams's health went downhill fast and her aunt showed up on the Monroes' doorstep. The real punch to the gut came later, when Zoe made a confession on Grams's deathbed: Grams had asked her to be Izzie's guardian last year when she got sick, and Zoe had said no.

Izzie had nothing to say to Zoe after that.

There was barely time to ask Grams why she didn't tell her about Zoe. There was only time to say good-bye to the woman who'd raised her. Grams passed away in early January and took all her secrets with her. Izzie was angry with her grandmother for that. Angry and mad at Zoe, her mom, the world. It was just easier to sleep than to deal with her emotions.

"Zoe's been calling a lot, but Dad won't let her talk to you," Mira said quietly. "He said she needs to give you space."

Izzie wished there was an ocean between them like there had been before. She'd overheard Zoe telling someone at the funeral that she'd been in Africa photographing a celebrity for

Vanity Fair when she found out Grams had taken a turn for the worse. Zoe was apparently a famed celebrity photographer, but Izzie hadn't wasted time Googling her to find out for sure. "I don't care what Zoe does."

"If you're not upset about Zoe, then why won't you get up?" Mira finally snapped. Izzie's sister hated a problem she couldn't fix. "Don't you miss the swim team?"

"Yes," Izzie realized. Badly. Being in the water was almost as necessary to her as air.

"Well, if you don't come back to school soon, Savannah is going to be all over Brayden again *and* be the star of the swim team," Mira felt the need to say. "Is that what you want to happen?"

Over my dead body. Mira's reminder was all it took for Izzie to finally swing her legs over the side of her bed and get up. *When was the last time I was out of this room?* she wondered. Aunt Maureen had been bringing her food for weeks— some she ate, some she didn't. Her TV had cable and she shared an adjoining bathroom with Mira, so there was no need even to go downstairs. Izzie scratched her itchy green pajama pants. Could the last time she left have been Grams's funeral a few weeks ago? She shut her eyes, trying to block out the memory. She could still see Aunt Maureen and her dad leading her away from Zoe at the grave site. *You weren't there for Grams or me before, and I don't want you here now!* "Now that I'm up, where are you dragging me?" Izzie stretched her arms. They looked thinner than she remembered. "Are you taking me to EP to make up some homework?"

Mira gave her a look. "I should, but no, this is supposed to be fun." She gave Izzie's disheveled appearance a once-over and pushed her toward the bathroom. "But first, you need a long, hot shower and some new clothes." She threw a towel at her. "I already put a cute outfit in the bathroom. Don't worry," Mira added before Izzie could start her inquisition. (If it wasn't a pair of jeans and a comfy T, she wasn't wearing it.) "They're your own clothes. Now go! We're leaving at two thirty." Mira shut the bathroom door behind her.

For a moment, Izzie just stood in the bathroom, letting the grief wash over her again. Sometimes it came on so strong it seemed like a choke hold. She felt so alone without her grandmother or mother in the world. Then she forced herself to remember she wasn't alone. She had family now, and one of them was waiting on the other side of the door with a hair dryer and expensive gel.

By two fifteen, she was ready, and even though she wouldn't say it, getting out of her pajamas felt good. What felt even better was seeing Brayden waiting at the bottom of the stairs. When she reached the bottom step, he pulled her into a tight embrace.

"Hey, you," he whispered after kissing her softly. "It's good to see you up." She buried her face in his neck and didn't want to let go. How did he always manage to smell this good? Was he wearing new jeans? Was his hair longer?

How many times had Brayden seen her the past few weeks looking like a train wreck with smudged makeup, smelly clothes, and bed head? She could only imagine how she looked—hollow eyes, cheekbones that only looked worse when Mira put blush on them. But Brayden was still staring at her with those magnetic blue-green eyes like she was the winner of *America's Next Top Model*. She smoothed a crease in his T. "It feels weird to be out of bed."

Brayden's eyes stayed locked on hers. "Baby steps."

"Baby steps," Izzie repeated as if this were a foreign concept.

Mira rushed past on the phone. "I have her and we're leaving in five," she reported to someone on the other end.

"Where is she taking me?" Izzie leaned into Brayden's chest. It felt familiar and safe. "I can't handle a spa day or a manicure/pedicure trip."

Brayden's laugh echoed through the two-story foyer. "Mira and I cooked this up together, so you can relax. You'll like where we're going."

Mira appeared by his side. "Ready?"

Izzie looked warily at the front door. "I don't know. Maybe we shouldn't go out this afternoon. I'm feeling a little tired."

Brayden eyed Mira as he rubbed Izzie's shoulders. "Sometimes doing nothing can make you more tired. Maybe you just need a little push. What did your mom always say?" he reminded Izzie gently.

Izzie's voice was barely audible. "No guts, no glory." They had her there. It was time to let go, figuratively and in real life. She let them pull her out the door.

~

It didn't take a genius to figure out where they were headed. When Brayden's Jeep turned onto the highway between Emerald Cove and Harborside, it was a dead giveaway. But the more sea grass and dunes they passed, the more anxious Izzie felt. *Please don't pass Grams's old house*, she thought. It hurt too much to see it. The only piece of her grandmother still in Harborside was in her safe-deposit box at TD Bank. The lawyer for Grams's estate said her grandmother had left something in there for her, and Zoe had agreed to pay for the box until Izzie was ready to see what was inside.

No, Brayden knew better than to take her past her grandmother's recently sold house. So where were they headed? The community center? The Pit Stop? When Brayden parked near a ramp leading to the desolate boardwalk, Izzie grew even more curious. Every shop on that stretch of planks was closed till at least April. "Can someone please clue me in?"

Brayden's mouth twitched as he opened her door. "You'll know soon enough."

The sky was a dreary gray, which fit her mood, and the wind was whipping pretty good as they pushed against it to walk up to the boardwalk. Just as she'd suspected, the area was deserted and the buildings were dark. All except for one.

"Shore Life Arcade?" Izzie asked as they walked toward the brightly lit building. She could already hear the video games inside, and just seeing the place put a smile on her face. Izzie had been going there since she was a toddler. The arcade was where her mom had taught her how to master the crane game. It was where Grams had taught her the secret to Skee-Ball. And it was where she had wound up most weekends when she lived in Harborside. She had a thing for air hockey.

The crowd waiting inside startled her even before they yelled "surprise." *But my birthday isn't till March*, she thought, then realized they meant surprise as in, "We're here to force a smile out of you if it kills you."

Her dad and Aunt Maureen were there along with her little brother, Connor. Kylie, her best friend from Harborside, was standing on top of the air-hockey table they usually dominated, and Hayden, Izzie's older brother, was standing nearby with Violet and Nicole. Several other familiar faces from both Harborside and Emerald Cove were there as well. It was a tad overwhelming because they were clapping and cheering as if she'd won some sort of pageant. All she'd done was finally leave her room. She thought about bolting for Brayden's car, but her dad quickly put a hand on her shoulder.

"What do you think, Isabelle?" he asked. "Up for an afternoon of arcade games with all your favorite people?" Her dad seemed so pleased with himself she didn't have the heart to tell him her answer was no.

"How did you guys know about this place?" she said instead.

Kylie jumped off the air-hockey table with the help of Hayden. "Me, of course." She gave her a squeeze. "B and Mira said they were trying to coax you out of bed, and I said the surest way to do that was to get you back by the sea air." Her eyes twinkled mischievously. "Since you can't swim outdoors this time of year, I figured the next best thing was to give you a challenge. You've never said no to an air-hockey match."

That was true.

"You haven't heard the best part." Her dad sounded like a kid. "We've got the rest of the afternoon, but at five the community center is bringing over kids to play for free for an hour."

Her father made such an effort to include the things she loved into their lives. For some reason that sentiment made her teary. A lot of things made her teary lately. Even that LEGO commercial with the dad taking time to play with his son made her cry.

Aunt Maureen put an arm around her. "I didn't know your grandmother well, but I know she would want you to enjoy your life. You've done your crying—and I'm not saying there won't be more tears—but it's time to have fun again.

You're not honoring her memory if you don't. So what do you say?"

Izzie looked from the bright, blinking lights and video screens to the wall behind them. Somewhere on there was a faded picture of her and Grams. They'd held the Skee-Ball high score for a while and Grams had loved this place as much as Izzie had. She could almost feel her grandmother egging her on. "Do we have any tokens?"

"Do we have tokens?" her dad repeated, and handed her a heavy bucket full of coins. "I expect you to play me at that pirate game later."

"Deal." Izzie grinned and looked at Brayden. "Up for a friendly game of Skee-Ball?"

"Is that a challenge? You're on." Brayden took another bucket of tokens from the row lined up on the prize counter. "But don't get too cocky. I'm not going to let you win just because you're my girlfriend." Both of them were übercompetitive.

"I don't expect you to *let* me win. I *am* going to win." Izzie dropped the first token in the slot, and nine balls came rolling down the ramp. She sent the first one up the ramp, and the ball jumped into one of the two hard-to-reach one-hundred-point slots.

"Show-off." Brayden sent his first ball up the ramp and scored fifty points.

"Watch yourself, surfer boy," Kylie said, coming up behind

them. Hayden was with her. "Iz used to spend more time in here than the owner."

"So did you," Izzie pointed out before sending another ball into the hundred slot.

"Hey, would I ever leave your side?" she asked. Izzie knew the answer. Kylie was always there for her. "Besties for life." Kylie hip-checked her, then looked at Brayden. "Did she tell you she holds the arcade's high-score record for Skee-Ball?"

Brayden pretended to look outraged. "You were going to hustle me!" Izzie laughed.

"All is fair in love and arcade games," Hayden told him. He turned to Kylie. "What about you? You up for a challenge, too?"

"Aren't I always?" she asked, which struck Izzie as a strange thing for her to say to Hayden. "Winner of four straight games buys lunch at Corky's."

Hayden looked at her intently. "You like to lose, don't you?"

Four games later, Izzie and Brayden were tied (maybe she was getting rusty) while Hayden had whipped Kylie, which surprised Izzie. Kylie never lost.

"Who's up for air hockey?" Kylie asked.

"I am," Izzie said, feeling looser and calmer than she had in weeks.

"Prepare for war, my friend," Kylie said as Mira, Violet, and Nicole walked over to watch the game alongside Brayden and Hayden. "Just because Grams kicked the bucket, doesn't mean I'm going to go easy on you." Izzie's friends looked up in surprise.

"I don't expect you to be." Izzie tried not to be self-conscious. Kylie's bluntness was one of the things she loved most about her. She just wasn't used to experiencing it around her Emerald Cove friends.

Mira waited till Izzie scored the first point to start her Operation Cheer Up Izzie routine again. "So are you having fun? It's nice to be out and see everyone, right?"

If Izzie weren't intent on winning the match, she might have given Mira a look. Instead she kept her eye on the board and the blur of the puck. "Yeah, it's fun."

"Good. So you'll come back to school on Monday?" Mira asked brightly.

Kylie started to laugh. "Mira, haven't you learned by now? The perkiness route gets you nowhere with Iz-Whiz. She hated when her social workers did it. Be firm."

Mira nodded and cleared her throat. "You *will* come back to school on Monday!"

Everyone laughed, including Izzie. She was having a good time, but that didn't mean she was willing to give up her comfy bed just yet. "Nah."

"Headmaster Heller will hold you back." Mira stumbled over her words.

"Who cares about Headmaster Whoever?" Kylie said in a

serious tone, but Izzie saw her eyes were playful. "Don't you miss the metal detectors in Harborside?"

"Miss the metal detectors?" Violet asked with more than a touch of scorn.

"Vi?" Hayden said. "Just a hunch, but I think Kylie's joking."

"Oh!" Violet's oval eyes flooded with relief. "For a minute there, I thought she was actually suggesting Izzie ditch Emerald Prep for Harborside."

Kylie looked at Violet, and Izzie scored. "What's wrong with Harborside?"

"Nothing." Hayden nudged Kylie, and she seemed to relax. "But if you think we're giving Izzie back to you already, you're mistaken. Even bribing me with a chance to drive the Charger wouldn't change my mind." He turned to Izzie. "Don't you miss that snazzy uniform of yours?" Izzie smiled. "Admit it. Despite how warped EP can be, you kind of miss it."

"Maybe." Izzie thought about the swim team. She shot the puck across the board, and it became airborne. "I just dread the 'I'm sorry about your grandmother' comments." Her brow creased. "If I took the semester off, no one would remember come fall."

Nicole leaned over the air-hockey table and her blond hair blew all around. "Do you think anyone forgets anything in Emerald Cove? Just go back and get it over with."

"If you don't go back till fall, you'll be a grade behind us,"

Brayden said, as if she needed reminding. "We'd graduate first and you'd be all alone. How fun would that be?"

"No fun," Hayden replied as if she didn't know the answer already.

Izzie put her hockey piece down. "I'm tired, okay? Going to class, talking to people, getting dressed. It's too much."

Kylie scored and started to cheer. Violet glared at her. "Sorry. Competitive nature." Kylie looked at Izzie. "You may not be ready, but I don't think you have a choice. It's time to go back to snobville."

"Baby steps," Brayden reminded her. "We'll all be there to help you."

"Besides, you don't want to miss Founders Day," Mira added. "The Butterflies plan a huge part of the two-week-long celebration."

This did not surprise her. Emerald Cove didn't do anything small scale.

"Please come back so I don't have to take orders from Savannah in Butterflies meetings anymore," Violet begged. "If I get another e-mail from that girl—"

Izzie's eyes narrowed. "What e-mails?"

"Aren't you checking e-mail?" Nicole asked. "I sent you a funny YouTube clip—"

"Oh, Savannah's doing more than e-mailing." Violet cut Nicole off and ignored Mira, who was furiously shaking her head. "She's pitching ideas for the Founders Day festivities

15

so she can get them approved before you get back to school."

"What?" Izzie cried, starting to turn red. Savannah fired her up in a way few things could. "She can't take over the whole club! We're cochairs."

"You're only cochairs if you go to Emerald Prep...." Brayden started to smile.

Izzie could feel her blood pumping through her veins. She was alive. She had to remember that. The others were right: It was time to get back to her life. She could hear Grams's snappish voice in her head. *You're here and I'm not. So do something about that girl. Get her good for me, toots.*

"No one is taking my chair just yet." Izzie picked up the air-hockey piece again and ricocheted the puck toward Kylie. "Someone better warn Savannah I'm coming back." The group cheered. If Izzie had her way, Savannah would not be the only one in charge for long.

Two

Mira pressed the full-body-massage button on her pedicure chair. As the massager moved up and down her back, she placed her feet in the bubbling footbath and sighed. There was nothing better than a mani-pedi on a Sunday afternoon.

"If Mr. Preston taught biology class at the nail salon, I would definitely remember the full life cycle of an amoeba," Charlotte said from the chair beside Mira's. Her eyes took on a mischievous glow. "Maybe I should ask my dad to donate funds for a spa classroom at EP."

"Yes, please! I'd like to take *all* my classes in this chair." Mira flinched as the technician used a scrub brush on the bottom of her foot. "I'm glad you talked me into this today. It's nice to not think for a little while."

"Yeah. Your life has been all drama lately!" Charlotte's

voice vibrated slightly as the massage rollers pounded her back. "Izzie's finally coming back to school after losing her grandmama; Kellen is leaving; your dad is still getting killed in the media. I would be holed up in our shore house crying my eyes out."

"Don't think I haven't considered it," Mira said with a sigh. She was glad she and Charlotte had hit it off during cotillion. After a huge fight left her friendless, Mira had felt like a champagne bottle ready to explode with just one tiny twist. Now she felt like she had someone to confide in again. "But disappearing would make things worse. I want to be with Kellen as much as I can before he goes. And it's not like he's leaving for forever. He says he'll be back all the time."

Charlotte leaned forward to see Mira better, and her long, red hair touched her knees. She looked skeptical. "He *is* moving several states away," she reminded her. "I guess that's why every time I see you, he's glued to your side by your locker, you're kissing in the cafeteria, or you're hanging out. Does he live with you now, too?"

"No." Mira watched the woman drizzle brown-sugar scrub and lemon on her legs. "We're just trying to do as much together as we can. Last weekend his mom drove us to Raleigh and we had dinner at this Italian restaurant while she went shopping. Next Saturday we're having a movie marathon, and Sunday we're going to sneak into the school art lab and paint each other something." She blushed. "Is that lame?"

"Lame?" Charlotte repeated. "You're going to make me throw up from all the over-the-top cuteness you two have going on. Be careful you don't overdo it," she warned. "The last thing you need is to fall in love with him right before goes." Mira didn't say anything, and Charlotte's eyes widened. "*No! Tell me you did not fall in love with him.*"

"I didn't." Mira swallowed hard, feeling the lump in her throat. Just because they weren't in love didn't mean she didn't like him a lot. "That would be stupid. He's leaving right after Valentine's Day."

She and Kellen had barely been together a month, but they had hung out for a while before that. He had helped her through her breakup with Taylor Covington, and persuaded her to give painting a real shot by signing up for classes at EP. Kellen was the push she needed to be herself and not follow people who dragged her down (like Savannah). Now he was leaving. Just when she was getting to know herself and him.

"He won't be here for Founders Day or the annual summer clambake," Mira realized aloud. "We had so many plans and now we won't get to do any of them." She was not going to cry at the nail salon. It seemed so uncivilized. Like wearing sweatpants out to dinner at Buona Terra. "We've talked about taking a class together at Emerald Arts for months, and now it won't happen."

"You don't need a silly boy for an art class. I'll take one with you instead." Charlotte popped a piece of gum into her mouth and offered some to Mira. Her new friend was almost never without gum or a mint.

Mira watched Charlotte's mouth try to work the gum into a bubble. "You will? I didn't know you were into art classes."

Charlotte's bubble quickly popped. "I'm not, but I guess it's time to get into them." She flashed Mira a huge smile. "If I want to become a world-famous fashion designer by the time I'm twenty-one, my sketches could use some improvement."

Charlotte was crazy. Her dress sketches were gorgeous! Still, Mira wouldn't turn down her friend's offer. Charlotte was right. Just because Kellen wasn't going to be here didn't mean she couldn't take a class. "Okay, I'll swing by Emerald Arts after this and get us registration forms." She felt more upbeat already. "Some of the classes require art submissions to be considered, but it's nothing we can't handle."

"Of course not!" Charlotte sounded insulted at the thought. "Once we become amazing artists, you'll forget all about Kellen. Yes, he is darling, and he actually knows how to treat a girl, unlike most of the goons at our school, but I will *not* let you spend all spring crying over him. There are lots of guys out there who would die for a chance to go out with Mirabelle Monroe."

Mira tried not to laugh. Her friend tried to act fierce, but she was so petite and delicate that sometimes it was hard to take her seriously. "Like who? More guys like Taylor Covington? I'm over being a trophy girlfriend, and that's what most of the guys at EP are looking for," she said, getting wound up. "I want a guy who cares about my standing mani/pedi date with you and who will watch *Project Runway* with me...."

Charlotte frowned. "You might have a tough time finding a guy who will do that."

Mira ignored her. "I want a guy who will give me five minutes to talk about what I painted or will listen to why I'm dying to spend the night in the Museum of Modern Art." Her list was getting long, and she knew why. She already knew "that guy."

"You're describing Kellen, and Kellen is no longer for sale," Charlotte said quietly. "But by your birthday you'll have a new Kellen, and that one will be even better." She bit her lip. "But maybe we shouldn't call him the new Kellen. It sounds bad."

Mira's laugh came out garbled since the shiatsu setting on the massage chair had jumped to high speed. "My birthday isn't until the end of May, so I guess I have some time. I still need to come up with a theme, though! My mom is going to be overwhelmed. She lives for big parties, but she has two this spring between me and Izzie. Her birthday is in March."

Charlotte held up her Vitaminwater in a toast. "Well, it's time to get cracking. Here's to a spring full of hot guys, awesome parties, and zero drama."

Mira clinked Vitaminwaters with her. She would certainly drink to that.

A fresh manicure and pink pedicure had a way of changing Mira's perspective. So did the weather. February was just days away and already North Carolina was warming up. Snow was a figment of the imagination; scarves and gloves had all but disappeared. At fifty degrees, Emerald Cove felt almost springlike. Mira wanted to wander around all afternoon in this weather. She could get an iced coffee or see what clothes had come in at Prepsters, her favorite boutique. But first she had a date with her new favorite haunt—and it had nothing to do with clothes or shoes.

Pushing the door open to Emerald Arts, Mira felt her heart pump an extra beat at the sight of all those art supplies. She had passed the store a zillion times in her life and had never gone in till that past fall, when the art bug had bitten her. Now there wasn't a week that went by that she didn't pop in for something.

"Mira, darling!" Clarissa Cage, Emerald Arts's owner, gave a little wave from behind the register. "What could you possibly still need, sugar?"

Mira had dropped a large portion of her Christmas money at Emerald Arts the day before. "Actually I'm here about classes. Is it too late to sign up for the next session? My friend and I want to take one together."

Clarissa grabbed a green flyer from the counter. "It's not too late, but you better get going on your submission piece if you want to be considered for the best class. Selma Simmons's is the one everyone wants." Mira's eyes widened. "She's a tough cookie, but I guarantee you'll learn a boatload." Clarissa passed Mira the class flyer.

WARNING:

If you're looking for an intro to painting that comes with a lot of hand-holding, this is not the class for you.
But if you're ready to take your painting skills to a whole new level, then Emerald Cove artist **Selma Simmons** is the person to take you there. Open to painters age 14 and up, Selma's class is by **INVITATION** only.
To be considered for the spring semester, applicants must submit a contemporary painting by February 21.

February 21 was only a few weeks away. That didn't give her much time to wow one of the most well-known artists in North Carolina. "I'm in," Mira said, feeling excited by the challenge. This was exactly what she needed to take her mind off Kellen's leaving and to kick her paint skills up another notch. "I can't believe she's teaching here."

"Third time back," Clarissa said. "Selma's class and Art Equals Love are the two most popular programs we have at this store."

"What is Art Equals Love?" Mira asked with curiosity.

"An art therapy program for children," Clarissa explained.

"It's gotten quite popular. We have four classes a week now. Teen volunteers with an art background help the children with their work. If you ever have some extra time, we could always use some more volunteers."

Mira had a feeling she would like working with kids. It had never occurred to her that art could be used as therapy, but it made sense. "Thanks. I'll get back to you about that," Mira said, glancing at the schedule for dates. She smiled. "But I guess since I'm here now, it couldn't hurt to look around to see if I need anything."

Clarissa laughed. "You go right ahead!"

Mira quickly disappeared down the first aisle determined to find palette cups for her easel. She was so busy scanning the shelves that she bumped into another shopper and sent her items spiraling to the ground. She reached down to pick up a wetting agent for a darkroom. "I'm so sorry!"

"It's my fault." The woman loaded the items in her arms. She smelled like Mira's favorite perfume. "I have some photography projects I'm working on and I guess I grabbed more than I could carry. I feel like I'm here on a daily basis."

"Me, too. I live in this store." As Mira handed her a package of photo enlargement paper, she made eye contact, and her breath got stuck in her throat. "Zoe."

"Mira! I didn't recognize you," Zoe said. "Cute coat. Jen Aniston has one like it."

Mira's coat was charcoal and had amazing buttons, but

24

she was too busy staring to say thank you for the compliment. She never could get past how much Izzie looked like her aunt Zoe, and how much Zoe looked like the pictures she had seen of Izzie's mom. Zoe's hair was much longer and straighter than Izzie's, but there was no denying they were related. The only difference Mira could see between them was body type. Izzie was more muscular, and that probably had a lot to do with her being a swimmer. Zoe looked almost fragile, like one of those expensive china dolls Mira used to have on a shelf in her bedroom. The kind you looked at but didn't dare play with.

"Jen is a sweetheart," Zoe said, still chatting about Jennifer Aniston. "She's always giving me free clothes, like this coat." Zoe pointed to the trendy raincoat she was wearing. "She is so generous. So is the other Jen, who always flies me down to Miami."

"J.Lo?" Mira was flabbergasted.

Zoe laughed. "She doesn't actually call herself that, but yeah, the one and only." She leaned in conspiratorially. "She's even prettier in person. Unfair, but true. They're not all like that, though. If I told you about the case of acne one star has, you would flip."

"I can't believe you hang out with celebrities." Mira was in awe.

"It's cool." Zoe did not even attempt to be modest. "People are always flying me somewhere to hang or take pictures. I can't stand Paris." She wrinkled her nose. "Crowded and overrated."

"I can't wait to travel," Mira said. "My parents have taken us all over the U.S. and to the Caribbean, but we haven't done Europe. We're waiting until Connor's a little older."

Zoe nodded. "Younger siblings can be a real drag. At least I was."

Mira wasn't sure how to respond.

"I'm teasing," Zoe said. "Sort of. I got under Chloe's skin." Her brow wrinkled at the memory. "I had to be wherever she was, which my mother shouldn't have allowed, but I would have done anything to get out of that house and that town and…" She slapped her own cheek. "God, I totally forgot to ask! How is Isabelle?"

Mira had been wondering when Zoe would get around to asking about her niece. "Izzie is doing better."

"Great!" Zoe looked relieved. "Maybe she'll let me stop by and see her, then. I'm not sure how much longer I can afford this hotel. I'm not used to paying!" She stared at Mira's art supplies. "So you're a painter?"

"Oh, it's just a hobby," Mira said, "for now." She thought about Selma's career.

Zoe eyed her with interest. "Well, if painting doesn't pan out, have you ever thought about modeling? That's how I finally got out of Harborside." Zoe circled her. "Someone offered me a contract to go to New York, and I never looked back." Mira felt like she was at the tailor being measured for a gown. "You've got a great look."

Mira tried not to get excited by Zoe's vote of confidence. "Thanks. Someone gave me a name at *Justine* to call about modeling, but I haven't done it. I feel silly."

"I'll call *Justine* personally and tell them to use you if you want," Zoe said. "But don't stop there. You should be in *Marie Claire* and *Glamour* and do runway work, too. I can't believe no one has ever told you that before."

Mira felt like she might fall over. "I've never seen myself as a model, but…"

Zoe was clearly no longer listening. She frowned at a text message on her phone. "I should jet. We'll talk modeling again soon. Great running into you."

"You, too, Zoe." Mira was disappointed to see Zoe go so abruptly, but she was also upset with herself for *being* disappointed. If Izzie knew Mira had been speaking to her aunt, she'd be furious. But as Mira watched Zoe walk away, she still couldn't help hoping she'd bump into her again.

Three

Was Emerald Prep always this big?

That's what Izzie wondered the first day back after her "extended" winter break.

It turned out the most torturous part of being back was not dealing with the clique of girls who thought the universe worshipped them. It was the major upper- and lower-body workout she got racing from building to building. She felt like a Ping-Pong ball as she bounced from her final class to the Bill Monroe Sports Complex to talk to Coach Greff, and then to the administration building for a Social Butterflies meeting. And she had only a half hour to do it all. Thankfully Brayden was up for a jog.

"What did Coach Greff say?" Brayden asked as they took off again. He had been waiting for her outside the sports complex with a bottle of raspberry iced tea and a giant black-and-white cookie. She thought it was sweet that he had brought her favorite snacks to lessen the blow in case her coach didn't forgive her for missing almost a month of swim meets.

But it turned out that Izzie didn't need a pick-me-up. "I'm not suspended," she said with a grin, and Brayden hugged her. "I have to swim in the first heat till I prove myself again, but other than that, I'm still on the team." The first heat was the slowest, but Izzie was just happy she hadn't been benched.

"It seems fair to say you survived your first day back," Brayden said, turning up the corners of his fleece to block the light wind. Gardeners were planting bulbs and cleaning up flower beds along the path students took to the administration building. Spring was coming early in North Carolina, which meant summer weather was right behind it, and being on the beach meant Izzie had something to look forward to.

"I'm not sure if that makes me feel any better," she said, and Brayden looked at her strangely. "Look at them." Izzie pointed out students walking past on their way to club meetings or practices. "Their lives are exactly the same as they were a month ago, while mine's … How am I supposed to act as if nothing in my life has changed when everything has?" Izzie felt like there was a void left inside her by Grams's death and she wasn't sure it would ever be filled.

"You just need some time," Brayden said.

Izzie pulled her phone out of her pocket. She had felt it

vibrate. She didn't recognize the number, and she frowned when she read the text.

> ZOE'S CELL: Hi Isabelle! This is Zoe. Sorry for the text, but didn't know if I should call. Would love to see you and talk. Want to meet me for dinner?

No. Izzie hit Delete and put the phone back in her jacket. "Zoe."

"What did she want?" Brayden's voice was full of concern. She loved how protective he could be.

"To have dinner. Like that would happen." Her face was dark. "Did you know Grams asked her to be my guardian before we knew about my dad and she said *no?*"

"Mira mentioned it." Brayden looked uncomfortable. "Did she have a reason?"

"Whatever her reason is, it was wrong." Izzie took a giant bite of cookie. She could feel the anger bubbling up inside her. "She didn't want to help me, and that's all I need to know."

They stopped in front of the administration building. She'd already told her club adviser, Mrs. Fitz, that she would be a little late. Brayden pulled her toward him, his muscular arms enveloping her in a tight hug. "Forget her, then. You have me."

Izzie prayed crumbs weren't all over her lips as he leaned in to kiss her. When he did, all thoughts of Zoe went out the window. "Thanks for that. And the cookie."

"Any time." He turned back to the sports complex for his baseball practice, which started right after the period for club meetings and extra help. She couldn't believe he was doing that walk twice just to spend time with her. "Play nice with the Butterflies," he teased.

Izzie gave him a wry grin. "All but one in particular." She didn't expect the meeting to be in full swing when she got to the classroom, but there was Savannah at the whiteboard, her blond hair so long that it covered her plaid uniform skirt. (Savannah wouldn't be caught dead wearing the optional khaki pants that Izzie had chosen that morning.) Izzie slipped into the back row near Violet and Nicole before Savannah noticed her.

"The Founders Day celebration is coming up," Savannah reminded the group in her thick Southern drawl, "so we really need to put our best Butterflies' foot…er…wing forward. There is lots to do between the parade float and the booth at the street fair, and this is not the time for us to slack off," she practically threatened with a smile on her porcelain face. "That's why I think we need to—"

"Look who's back, everyone!" Violet interrupted. "Izzie's here!"

People stopped paying attention to Savannah and immediately rushed to see Izzie, which really surprised her. Maybe she wasn't the only one who hated lectures from Savannah.

Mrs. Fitz muscled her way over. "It's wonderful to see you,

Isabelle," their adviser said, oblivious to the strained smile on Savannah's face. "I was so sorry to hear about your grandmother, dear."

"Thanks." Izzie quickly looked around for a distraction. Savannah's whiteboard presentation, which used green swirly fonts and lots of flowers, was hard to miss. "It's good to be back to help with Founders Day."

"It's a lot of work and it's coming up pretty quickly," Savannah said. She was still standing at the front of the room. "Do you think you can handle it after all you've been through?" She glanced at Mrs. Fitz worriedly. "If Izzie is too distraught, I think I've proven I can manage this event on my own."

Savannah did her best stab at fake modesty, but Izzie wasn't buying it. She was back and there was no way she was letting EC's self-professed princess push her out of the castle that easily. "It's nice of you to be concerned, but I'm ready to be cochair again," Izzie told Mrs. Fitz and Savannah.

Mrs. Fitz actually looked relieved as she dabbed at her brow with a hankie. The only other person Izzie'd ever seen use a hankie was her grandmother. "Wonderful! We're so happy to have you on board again."

"Definitely!" Savannah said with a tad too much enthusiasm. "I was worried about you, but, of course, I could use the help. Lord knows there is enough to do between the parade and the street fair and the annual costume ball."

"Right." Izzie nodded. "Because how would EC survive without another over-the-top ball?" Unfortunately, no one laughed. *They take these things seriously*, she thought.

"You shouldn't joke about the Crystal Ball." Savannah sounded ruffled. She glanced at her yes-men—Lea Price, Millie Lennon, and Lauren Salbrook—for backup.

"It's the highlight of Founders Day," explained Lauren as she played with her hair. "We celebrate with reenactments, historical readings and tours, a parade, and a street fair reminiscent of the ones they had in the eighteen hundreds."

"But none of those things compare to the ball," Savannah added. "The Junior League plans a lot, but the Butterflies are a very important part of the fair and the parade. We cannot mess this up. Founders Day is the most important event of the year."

"I'll let Christmas know it's been pushed to second place," Izzie said. Again, no one laughed, and Izzie started to suspect they all had lost their sense of humor.

"How can Izzie be trusted to help us when all she does is make jokes?" Lea snapped.

Violet rolled her eyes. "Spare us the drama, Lea. How hard can it be to glue glitter on a parade float?"

"Who cares if she knows how to handle a glue gun?" Lauren snapped. "Savannah's been coming up with Founders Day ideas

33

for weeks, and now *she* shows up and acts like Founders Day is a laughing matter." She narrowed her eyes at Izzie.

Everyone started bickering, which was as much a club tradition as saying the Butterflies' pledge. Violet came back at Lauren, and Nicole at Lea, while Savannah moaned to anyone who would listen and poor Mrs. Fitz tried in vain to gain order.

Izzie tried not to smirk. How twisted did a person have to be to enjoy this? Somehow she did. Being back on the swim team, walking across the ginormous quad with Brayden, wearing those oppressive uniforms, and tangoing with Savannah was getting her blood flowing again. Izzie placed two fingers in her mouth and whistled as loud as she could. Savannah jumped.

"Let's all just calm down!" Izzie shouted, and they looked at her. "Savannah and Lauren are right. We have a lot of planning to do, and I've been out of the loop. I shouldn't make jokes when Savannah is trying so hard." Izzie took out a notebook and a pen and motioned to Savannah. "I'd like to hear what she's come up with." It killed her to say some of this stuff, but when in EC, act like an ECer.

Savannah's mouth was open so wide it could have doubled as a fly trap. "Okay, then." She turned to the whiteboard and looked like she'd forgotten how to work it. Finally she clicked the remote, and pictures of Savannah and her friends on elaborate floats filled the screen. Mira was in all of them. "We all know the highlight of Founders Day is the Crystal Ball because the Emerald Cove community reenacts the sounds and styles of 1888, the year Emerald Cove was founded. What you guys don't know is that this year, the Junior League has decided we can attend as guests instead of as volunteers." An excitement Izzie didn't understand rippled through the room. The girls were acting as if they'd never been to a dance before, which was funny considering most of them had just gotten their cotillion gowns back from the dry cleaner's.

"And since this is a year of change, I thought it would be nice if we retired our usual float and fair booth ideas and came up with new ones." The girls mumbled in agreement as Savannah jumped to a new page on the screen that had the word *suggestions* written in pink. "The festival parade and fair need to speak to the time and place of the first Founders Day. So how do you think we should do that?" She looked from one girl to the next.

Izzie leaned over to Mira as Savannah continued to question the group. "*This* is the toiling work she's done while I've been gone?" she whispered in Mira's ear, almost choking on the scent of her flowery perfume.

"Be nice," Mira warned. "You stole her boyfriend and her date to cotillion, and she hasn't killed you yet. Go with it."

Izzie sighed.

"Maybe we could have a bake sale and sell green bagels," Izzie heard Millie suggest as Savannah's smile turned into a frown. "You know, green, like emeralds?"

Lame. What could they do for Founders Day that was exciting but also had to do with EC traditions? Izzie didn't know many traditions yet, but she did remember the ones she had with Grams. Always wear a football jersey on a game day, keep salt in the freezer for luck...."What if we did something that had to do with our club mission?" Izzie said, out of turn. "Whatever we come up with benefits the same charity that the Junior League picks for Founders Day." Everyone looked stumped. "Founders Day does benefit a charity, right? Every event this town has benefits a charity." Mrs. Fitz blushed.

"Not Founders Day," Lauren told her. "Admission to everything is free, except for the gala."

How is this town not poor? Izzie wondered. "But I thought the Butterflies only took on missions that helped others."

Lea pulled a strand of her too-glossy-to-be-true hair in front of her mouth to avoid anyone seeing her lips moving. "Here she goes again."

"Guys, this is a no-brainer." This was one point Izzie was not willing to negotiate. "We aren't Butterflies if we don't turn a profit to help a charity close to the town's heart."

"How about the EC Children's Hospital?" Charlotte suggested from the back of the room, where she was doodling skirt sketches in her notebook. She was an even newer Butterfly than Izzie. She'd signed up after cotillion. Maybe that was why she didn't fear Savannah's wrath.

"That is an excellent idea," Mrs. Fitz said, jotting it down in her planner. "What do you think, girls?"

"I like it," Mira said. "We could even do a kids' theme for our booth to tie into the hospital. Like a craft or spin art."

"Spin art?" Savannah sounded less than enthused. A picture of her and Mira in happier days shone bright on the whiteboard behind her head. "How does that have anything to do with our history? If we're going to do this, then it has to tie in with the theme." Even Izzie had to agree with that. "What is EC known for?"

Millie raised her hand like they were in class. "The bay."

"Money!" said Lauren.

"Main Street shopping!" offered Nicole.

"Mining," Violet said with a shrug.

Mining. That gave Izzie an idea. "Have you guys ever seen those carnival mining booths? The ones where you dig through sand to find jewels? The kids love that booth on the boardwalk," she told the group. "I know the guy who runs it, and he charges six bucks for them to fill up a bag with colored rocks." She looked at Savannah. "We could ask for donations to dig for emeralds. Fake ones, but you get the idea."

"My family did that at the state fair!" said Millie. "My brother loved it."

"We could easily make a mining booth," Charlotte seconded.

"I bet Mira could paint a cave on a tent and we could have the mining station set up inside and…"

The room was buzzing with ideas. Everyone had suggestions on how to build a wooden mining station, where to buy fake jewels, and how to find kids' mining hats.

"Girls, this is fantastic!" Mrs. Fitz marveled. "We've made more progress in fifteen minutes than we have in weeks." Savannah smiled weakly, then almost blanched when Mrs. Fitz pulled her and Izzie into a group hug. "With the two of you in charge, the Butterflies are going to have their finest appearance at the Founders Day celebrations yet! Wait till I tell Headmaster Heller," she added. "The children's hospital. Genius."

"Make sure you tell him it was a group idea," Savannah called after Mrs. Fitz as she walked away. "I'm the one who called this meeting!"

"Good idea!" Izzie said drily. "Maybe the headmaster will give you extra credit." Savannah obviously didn't appreciate her comment. When no one was looking, she yanked Izzie out of the classroom. "Hey!" Izzie shouted.

Savannah dragged Izzie around the corner using what could only be described as sudden superhuman strength. When she turned around, she looked like she was going to pull a giant clump of brown hair out of Izzie's head. "And here I was trying to be nice to you because of your grandmother!" she snapped, sounding more like her old self.

Izzie was unfazed. "If that was nice, I'd hate to see you on a bad day."

That comment only ticked Savannah off more. "You and I both know we can't stand being in the same room together," she said, sounding shrill, "especially after all that happened, so why—*why*—do you insist on torturing me by being a Butterfly?"

Izzie shrugged. "I like it. The fact that you hate me being there is a bonus."

Savannah became unhinged in a way Izzie had never seen her. "This is not funny. You stole my boyfriend and turned my best friend against me, and you have half of my town smitten with you." Her voice didn't have its fake sweetness or even its perfected biting venom. "You are *not* taking the Butterflies, too!" Izzie opened her mouth to protest. "I won't let you ruin Founders Day with your ridiculous ideas. We're stuck with the children's hospital," she said as if helping sick kids was the worst idea in the world, "but I know what EC needs, so we'll go with *my* suggestions, because if you don't . . ."

Izzie didn't do well with being threatened, especially when it was by a girl who had tried to take so much from her already. "If I don't, you'll what? Steal my boyfriend back? You tried that and it didn't work." Savannah looked ready to breathe fire. "You may scare most of the girls in that room, but you don't scare me. I like the Butterflies and I'm staying, whether you like it or not. I have as much of a say as you do."

An eerie calmness suddenly came over Savannah (possibly because others had started to trickle out of the room and she didn't want to cause a scene). She smiled, but the gesture was anything but sincere. "You want a say?" she said. "Fine. You got one. See you at our first tête-à-tête." She started to walk away.

"When is that going to be?" Izzie asked.

Savannah didn't look back. "When I feel like e-mailing you."

Izzie watched as Savannah sashayed down the hall as if it were a catwalk and she owned it.

Four

Mira poked her head out of the Social Butterflies' meeting room with trepidation. Violet and Nicole were hovering over her shoulder. "Is she gone?"

"Oh yeah, she's gone." Izzie looked down the long, empty hall. She half expected there to be a cold chill or a big gust of wind now that the witch had left the building. Her sister and friends trickled out of the classroom. "Thanks for the backup."

Violet punched Izzie's shoulder lightly. "We knew you had it covered." Izzie made an indistinguishable noise.

"Was she *that* upset?" Mira asked, adjusting her signature plaid headband. "She seemed so nice to you during the meeting." Izzie glared at her. "Okay, so maybe she was a tad fake, but who cares? You can handle her. You're so much better at leading the Butterflies than I was." She knew she was laying it on a bit thick, but it was the truth. When it came to do-gooding, she could think of no one better at it than Izzie. She was more of a natural than half the lifelong Junior League members in EC. That's why she had asked Mrs. Fitz to replace her as cochair with Izzie.

"When I agreed to take over for you, I didn't realize I'd be signing on to a semester of hell with the devil herself!" Izzie complained. "Savannah is taking this Founders Day stuff a bit seriously, isn't she?" she asked the others. "It's just another ridiculous EC event."

Everyone in the group gasped.

"Rule number one for planning Founders Day: Don't speak badly of Founders Day." Nicole shook her head at her. "It's sacred."

"You guys think every tradition EC has is sacred." Izzie sounded frustrated. "How many can one town have?"

"At least a dozen," Violet said knowingly. "The year I moved here, I counted, and the celebrations that are part of Founders Day are the most revered of them all. It's actually fun seeing pictures of the town in the early nineteen hundreds and doing things that have been done for over a hundred years. I think you'll like it, Iz. It's not some swanky five-star affair. It's normal." Violet thought for a moment. "Well, normal for Emerald Cove."

Izzie hung her head, as if the thought of what she was going to have to deal with was weighing her down already. "This town is so *not* normal."

"Why don't we go to Corky's and we'll give you the low-down on all the events that are part of Founders Day?" Nicole put an arm around her. "You'll be fine after we get some sweet-potato fries in you. I'm starving!"

"Actually, I am meeting Kylie there in a half hour," Izzie said, looking at her watch. "We agreed to meet up so I could vent about my first day back. Do you guys want to all go together?"

"Sure," Mira said. She noticed Nicole give Violet a look. Mira knew Violet and Nicole hadn't warmed up to Kylie yet, but she was sure they would once they got to know her. Izzie's best friend was brassy, but so was Izzie, and Mira liked how Kylie didn't shy away from the truth. Hopefully the girls would grow to like her, too.

~

A short trolley ride later and they were at Corky's, waiting to be seated. A waitress grabbed menus and began roller-skating over to their table, but halfway there, Izzie stopped short and Mira crashed into her.

"What's..." Mira followed Izzie's eye line over to the window. "Oh my." Hayden was kissing a girl they both knew.

Izzie's face was hard to read, but her action wasn't. She pushed past her and headed to the table. "Kylie?"

Kylie and Hayden looked up, startled, and practically jumped out of the booth.

"Iz-Whiz!" Kylie's cheeks were flushed. "I thought you said four thirty."

"It *is* four thirty." Izzie looked from Hayden to Kylie for some sort of explanation, but neither offered one. "What's going on? Are you two…together now?"

Kylie pretended not to hear the question. She looked at Violet and Nicole instead. "You brought your friends. Cool. Hey. Wow. You guys actually leave school wearing those nerd costumes, huh?"

Violet bristled. "Oh, you know us Emerald Prep girls, always making a fashion statement." She looked Kylie up and down and then scratched her chin. "At least we don't have to worry about getting holes in our jeans." Kylie's were purposefully ripped at both knees, and she had Sharpied a design over one whole leg.

Mira felt herself tense. Sensing friction among girls was like a sixth sense. It was needed to be friends with someone like Savannah. Right now she could feel the drama building between Violet and Kylie while Izzie seemed to be preoccupied with the Kylie-and-Hayden situation.

Hayden did what he always did—attempted to crack a joke to cut the tension. "Well, as fun as this has been, I think I'm going to leave you girls to do what you do best—debate Peeta versus Gale and determine which lip gloss has the best shine."

Violet stepped in front of him. "Not so fast." She flashed him a wicked grin. "You didn't answer Izzie's question—how long have you two been hanging out? From the look of things, I'd say you've been keeping it from Izzie for a while, right?"

Kylie quickly walked into Violet's personal space before anyone could react.

"This doesn't concern you," Izzie's best friend said darkly.

Sometimes Violet couldn't mind her own business. "Really? Last I checked, Izzie was my friend, and friends look out for each other."

"Violet, I can handle this." Izzie's face twisted sadly as she looked from Kylie to Hayden for answers. "So how long have you guys been lying to me?"

Kylie exhaled sharply as if she'd been holding the information in for far too long. "I love you to pieces, but we didn't know how to tell you about us."

"When did this happen?" Izzie sputtered. "You guys hardly know each other."

Hayden and Kylie looked at each other guiltily. "We hit it off that day we went to Corky's in the Charger," Hayden explained. "I Facebooked her, and we talked some more, and then we started hanging out right before…" He trailed off when he saw Izzie's somber expression. "We weren't sure how you would react, so we decided to wait." Kylie nodded. "It seemed like bad timing."

"What was bad timing?" Izzie asked. "Grams's death or the fact that you two hooked up at her funeral?"

"Izzie," Mira admonished. "That's not fair."

"Mira's right." Kylie gave Izzie the evil eye. "That's a low blow, my friend. We were trying to protect you."

"You did a great job protecting her," Violet spoke up. Mira was going to have to muzzle both of them soon if they were going to get through this.

"I'm warning you," Kylie growled at Violet. "Stay out of this." Her tone was softer when she turned to Izzie. "I know you're still mourning, but you can't hide behind Grams's death forever." Violet made a face, and Mira saw that Izzie didn't fail to notice. "Life goes on. We like each other, so we started hanging out. What's the big deal?"

"If it's no big deal, then why did you hide it from me?" Izzie pressed. "I'll tell you why. Because it's weird and you know it. He's my brother, and you're my best friend."

"So?" Kylie was getting agitated herself. "Technically, he's not even your brother, so I don't owe you an explanation."

That was taking things too far. Mira wasn't surprised when Izzie headed for the door. "Real nice," Violet said. "Who says something like that?"

"The only person who can," Kylie shot back. "Her best friend. You don't know her the way I do. She's fine."

"Oh yeah?" Violet questioned. "Then why did she just leave, 'best friend'?"

Kylie's confidence seemed to waver. She touched Hayden's arm. "Crap. I put my foot in my mouth, didn't I? I should go after her."

"No, let me," Mira said, hoping to stop a fight from breaking out on Main Street. "The rest of you stay here. And don't talk to one another," she added as she rushed out.

Thankfully Izzie hadn't gone far. She was pacing in front of the restaurant. Mira approached slowly as if she were greeting a stray dog whose temperament had yet to be determined. "Are you okay?"

"No! I know I was harsh, but what were they thinking?" Izzie said to Mira.

Mira watched her wear out the sidewalk. "I don't know. But is it really that bad? You love both of them. Maybe they'll be good for each other."

Izzie gave her a look. "They won't be."

She wasn't usually this irrational. "Why?" Mira asked. "And don't say because she's from Harborside and Hayden's from EC. You paved the way for that scenario."

Izzie sighed. "I know. It's just she's my best friend and Hayden's my brother." Her face was pained. "What happens if they break up? I can't choose between them."

"No one is going to make you choose." Mira put an arm around her. "You have no say in their relationship anyway, so why make yourself crazy about this?"

"I guess you're right." Izzie stared at the trolley as it

whizzed by. Mira had a feeling there was more to Izzie's fears than a breakup, but she didn't push it. Izzie was so fragile lately. "You're going to say I should go back in there, aren't you?"

Mira nodded. "Yep. Maybe a milk shake will make you feel better."

Izzie laughed. "You think milk shakes make everything better." Mira was glad to see the color return to Izzie's cheeks. She looked more like her old self again.

"Hey, ladies. What's so funny?"

They both turned around. Kellen was standing behind them. It drove Mira crazy that Kellen seemed to get cuter as the time for him to leave got closer. His sandy-blond hair looked softer, his green eyes somehow brighter. His peacoat made him look Abercrombie-catalog-ready. Maybe she was just studying him more closely now.

"I'll meet you inside," Izzie said as if she could sense they wanted time alone, which Mira always did. "Later, Kellen."

Kellen kept his eyes on Mira. "I missed you today."

Mira leaned into him. "I missed you, too. I can't believe Ms. Marks took your class on an all-day field trip when you're only here a few more weeks," she joked.

"Someone should suspend her." Kellen gave her a lopsided smile. "She did get us back in time to order Valentine's boosters, though." Every Valentine's Day, EP's school newspaper added an insert called the Book of Love in which students could write each other love notes. Hate notes were highly discouraged.

"Oh?" Mira cocked her head. "Get one for anyone special?"

"Yep. You." He wrapped his arms around her. "Not to give too much away, but mine has clues about our last date."

Last. She tried not to hang on that word. "Sleuthing. I like that."

"Good." Kellen grinned. "I promise the night will be full of surprises."

"I don't care what we're doing just as long as we're together," Mira said, and he leaned down to kiss her. Her stomach growled.

Kellen pulled away. "Is your stomach trying to tell me something?"

"It has bad timing! Are you hungry?" Mira gestured to Corky's. "Hayden, Izzie, and her friends are in there." She bit her lip. "On second thought, let's go someplace else. The scene was getting ugly."

Kellen looked curiously at Corky's glass doors. "While I'm always up for drama, I actually have to go home and pack. I was on my way to buy more boxes when I saw you."

"I'll go with you." Mira didn't hesitate. She didn't want to let him out of her sight.

"Are you sure?" Kellen frowned. "I don't want you to leave on my account."

"They'll survive without me. I'll text Izzie to let her know I had a change of plans." She slipped her arm into his, and Kellen led her down the street. "I have time to hang out with them." *It's you I don't,* she thought sadly.

Five

Izzie was used to seeing people stream in and out of the Monroe house. It wasn't unusual to run into people with her dad's campaign in the living room, or to find his personal assistant at the kitchen island jabbering on the phone about fundraising efforts. With her dad back in the race for the state's open U.S. Senate seat and primaries coming up in May, the Monroes' house had turned into campaign central.

Which was why she was surprised to come home one day and find her dad and Aunt Maureen alone in the kitchen while Connor played with LEGOs in the adjoining family room. She couldn't remember the last time the house had been that quiet.

"Hi, gang. How was your day?" their dad asked as if it were completely normal to find him at the island drinking coffee without an entourage. "How was swim?" he asked Izzie as Hayden and Mira trickled in behind her. "Are you back in the final heat yet?"

Izzie dropped her book bag. "I wish." She eyed one of her aunt's homemade chocolate-chip cookies. She was training, so she tried to resist their allure. "It's been torture having to watch Savannah swim the last heat of the one-hundred-meter-freestyle medley."

"For you or for her?" Hayden joked, and took a cookie from the plate.

"Hopefully you'll be back where you belong by next week's meet." Her dad removed his reading glasses and placed them on the newspaper in front of him. "Your aunt and I have been looking forward to coming out to cheer you on."

"He cleared his afternoon schedule for it," Aunt Maureen added. Izzie knew that was a big deal. Her dad didn't have enough time to even eat these days. Hayden joked he needed a second assistant just to feed him.

"I hope it will be worth it," Izzie said, her fingers inching toward the cookies. "I'd hate for you to waste valuable campaign time to watch Savannah swim in my spot."

"Ignore her," Mira told her parents. "She's having a Savannah situation."

Izzie took a cookie and stuffed it in her mouth to keep from saying anything about Savannah she would regret. She had texted Savannah twice about getting together to discuss

Founders Day, but the prima donna had texted back that she didn't feel it was appropriate to meet till Izzie had brushed up on her EC history. She even had the nerve to leave books about EC near Izzie's locker.

The most frustrating part was that Savannah could be right. Izzie didn't know much about the town she now called home. Until Savannah gave her that reading homework, she had no idea that the townswomen were some of the first to fight for suffrage. Or that, for a short period, the town's official symbol wasn't emeralds—it was cows. (No wonder they buried that fact on page 168 of the book she was reading. Cows didn't seem trendy enough for Emerald Cove.)

The crash course in EC history was helping, but Izzie hoped Savannah didn't think she could give her a pop quiz before they discussed Founders Day again. Their meeting with Mrs. Fitz was next Tuesday, and this weekend was Valentine's Day. Savannah wouldn't want to celebrate the day of love with her. Izzie had to nail her to a meeting.

"Speaking of thorns like the Ingrams," their dad said, "I have some news."

Mira immediately panicked. "Did they get to Charles?" Charles Abrams was their dad's new campaign manager. Their dad had hired him only last week. He had gone through so many it was a running joke now.

In less than six months, Lucas Hale, Callista Foster, and Savannah's father had all tried to take Bill and his campaign down. For a minute, it looked like their dad was going to drop out of the race, but after he cleared his name, he had come back from the holidays in fighting form. Izzie admired that. She felt like she had to prove herself every day, too.

"Nothing's happened to Charles," Aunt Maureen soothed. "Your dad likes him."

"Now that all background checks are clear, I *really* like him," their dad joked. "I promise you, no one in this campaign is going to mess with our family again."

Good. Izzie didn't think she could handle another month of newspaper stories that chronicled whether she was really Bill Monroe's daughter (she was) or how her dad had used taxpayer dollars to take their family to New York over Thanksgiving (he hadn't) or how he had messed up some environmental bill (it was never even on the table).

"My poll numbers are up and I seem to be making strides in several counties," their dad continued. "If this keeps up, Charles says, I have a real shot of getting the nomination for the Democratic Party." Everyone grinned. "*But* it also means we are still going to be in the public eye the next few months. I'll need you to attend fund-raisers, make appearances at key public events, and do interviews. We want to control the information out there." His face darkened. "We don't want to give Grayson Reynolds any ammunition," he said, referring to the sleazy reporter at the *North Carolina Gazette* who was on a one-man mission to destroy their dad's reputation and political future.

"So what you're saying is don't go tagging school property, keying any cars, or robbing area banks," Hayden translated. "Come on! I live for that stuff."

His mom pulled the second cookie he was taking out of reach. "Very funny."

"Look, you don't need me to tell you how to act," their dad said. "You are great kids. Act the way you normally would. Just remember the world—especially Grayson Reynolds—will be watching and waiting for you to screw up."

"That's encouraging," Izzie said. When people waited for her to mess up, she usually did.

Their dad grimaced. "I know, but I said no more secrets and I am keeping my word even if the news isn't great." He looked warily at Izzie. "Which is why, with full disclosure in mind, I should mention that we're having an unexpected guest for dinner tonight." He looked at his wife. "Why don't you tell her, Maureen. It was your idea."

Her aunt shot him a look, which Izzie wasn't used to seeing. "Yes, well, since she will be here any minute, I should." Aunt Maureen suddenly looked anxious and started pulling at her pearls, which she did only when she was about to let a bomb drop like...

"Oh no. You didn't!" Izzie backed away from the table like

she was going to make a run for it. She was so loud that Connor looked up from his LEGOs. "Why?" she moaned, her tone alternating between pained and angry. "I thought you said I didn't have to see her if I didn't want to."

"Zoe is coming?" Hayden asked. "Mom! Not cool." Izzie and Hayden still hadn't discussed what was going on with him and Kylie. She figured they were both too afraid to bring it up. She didn't want to make things weird—even if they already were. Kylie seemed to be using the same approach. Every time they spoke, they talked about only safe subjects, like Harborside and Izzie cochairing with Savannah. What else could Izzie really say? *I don't want you to date my brother?* No, she had to think this through, and right now the bigger problem was Zoe dropping in on her doorstep again.

"I invited Zoe to give Isabelle some closure," Aunt Maureen explained to the mutinous group. "Zoe is part of Isabelle's family, and we need to give her a chance."

"Being related to me does not make her family," Izzie countered. Her shoulders were stiff, which made her swim-team jacket look like it had shoulder pads. "She hasn't acted like family."

"You're right," Aunt Maureen agreed. "But she's stuck around, and that's because she wants to make things right with you. If you haven't noticed, she's not going away." Izzie didn't say anything. "Maybe she will if you let her explain."

"I already know what she's going to say." Izzie was huffy.

"She's sorry. Who cares? She doesn't want to get to know me. She's just sticking around because she feels guilty."

"I didn't think this dinner was a good idea, either, but Maureen is right about one thing: You deserve the truth," her dad said. "Don't let her be a coward. Make her be honest with you. If you don't like what she has to say, then I promise you never have to see her again."

His response surprised Izzie in a good way, but it also made her wonder: How well did he know Zoe? She'd never thought to ask him.

Aunt Maureen looked flustered. "I know I overstepped by inviting her, but I don't want you to regret not getting to know her while you have the chance. Don't you want to ask her what your mom was like when she was your age?"

Izzie was quiet for a moment. Grams had taught her it was important to live without regrets. It was just one dinner. "Okay, fine. I'll stay, but I am not changing out of my gym clothes," she decided. Aunt Maureen smiled in relief, but was it Izzie's imagination or did her dad look disappointed that she had caved?

Aunt Maureen squeezed Izzie like a lemon just as the doorbell rang. "We'll be with you the whole time, and dinner will be over before you know it!" she said before heading to the front door. "I guess we should go greet our guest." The group slowly followed her.

"This might be the first time I've ever been anywhere on

time!" Izzie heard Zoe say as she kissed Aunt Maureen and handed her flowers. "I am always late."

Well, that was one thing they had in common. Scotts were never on time.

Zoe looked so much like her mom that she had to remind herself she wasn't seeing a ghost. It was Zoe's clothes that reminded Izzie that it wasn't her. Izzie's mom wouldn't have known a designer label if she had been handed a dress by the designer himself. All she cared about was whether the thrift-store jeans fit. Zoe, on the other hand, was clearly a clotheshorse. A thin royal-blue scarf lay over her bright green sweater, which she had paired with jeans and snakeskin heels.

Zoe finally noticed Izzie lurking in the doorway. "Hey!" She headed toward her, and Izzie froze. "Thanks for agreeing to have dinner with me."

"It was my aunt's idea," Izzie said, and Aunt Maureen gave Izzie a pained smile.

Zoe's laugh made her even sound like Izzie's mom. "I'm not surprised, but hey, I'll take whatever in I can get." She held a bottle of wine out to Izzie's dad. "This is my peace offering for you, Bill. It's Pindar. Remember that vineyard on Long Island?"

"Of course. Thank you." He sounded stiff.

Izzie and Mira exchanged looks. Peace offerings? Their dad acting less than friendly? What exactly was the story with these two?

Her dad looked at the label. "As I recall, this was *your* favorite."

"Guilty!" Zoe laughed again. "Still is. Now that I can afford it, I order it by the case. I thought it might be a good icebreaker if we all had a glass." Izzie felt her foot start to tap. There was no way the Monroes were going to serve them wine at dinner.

Her dad surprised her with his response. "I guess they can each have a sip." He looked at Izzie. "Especially since this was the wine your mom and I had on our first date."

Izzie loved learning details about their relationship. Suddenly she wished she had paid closer attention to that label. She watched her dad carry the wine, as if he were holding a piece of her mom.

"Why don't we head into the dining room?" Aunt Maureen suggested, switching into hostess mode. "There is no need to stand here and make introductions when you've already met everybody."

"She hasn't met me!" Connor squeezed around the side of his mother. Connor hadn't gone to Grams's wake or funeral because he was so young. He stared at Zoe. "Hey, you came to see our Christmas lights!"

Zoe leaned down. "That's right. It's nice to see you, Connor. I guess I should introduce myself. I'm Isabelle's…" She glanced briefly at Izzie, who tensed at the mere thought of Zoe using the word *aunt*. "I'm Isabelle's friend."

"Oh." Connor looked confused. "You look a little old to be her friend."

"Oh, Connor!" Aunt Maureen said with a forced laugh. She steered Connor to the opposite end of the table. "Zoe, please sit where you like."

Normally Mira and Izzie sat across from each other, but as soon as Zoe slipped into Mira's usual seat, Mira took the one next to Izzie and Hayden took the chair on the other side, flanking her as if they were her bodyguards. Their dad sat next to Zoe. If Zoe was bothered by the seating arrangement, she didn't show it.

"So, Mira," Zoe said, folding her napkin on her lap. "Have you been back to Emerald Arts since I saw you? They're having a sale on acrylic paints."

"Really? Till when?" Mira was unable to hide her excitement.

Izzie bristled. "When did you run into each other at Emerald Arts?"

Mira avoided making eye contact. "It was only for, like, a second."

"A few weeks ago," Zoe clarified. "We chatted about all the places I've been and with which celebrities." She glanced at Aunt Maureen. "I've pretty much been around the globe on Hollywood's dime. People are always impressed by that."

"Love the modesty," Hayden mumbled. Izzie coughed to cover her grin.

"How did you get into that line of work?" Aunt Maureen asked politely.

Zoe took a scoop of mashed potatoes without passing them around the table. "I briefly modeled before I decided to see what it was like on the other side of the camera." She smiled at Mira. "I told Mira she would be a great model. I can see her face on the cover of *Teen Vogue*. Shoot! I was supposed to call *Justine* for you, wasn't I? I will as soon as I get back from New York." She shook her head. "Since word got out I was still on the East Coast, the phone has not stopped ringing. Everyone wants to shoot with me!"

Hayden passed the crystal salad bowl high to cover their faces. "I hope you made an appointment to talk to her, Iz, because it sounds like she might not be able to squeeze you in." This time Izzie started to laugh out loud.

"Hayden?" Aunt Maureen's voice was strained. "Something you wanted to add?"

Hayden feigned innocence. "Nope. Sorry. Tell us more about your amazing life, Zoe." Izzie thought she heard Mira kick him under the table.

"I think Mira knows there are better avenues ahead of her than modeling," Bill chimed in. He slung the mashed potatoes down on his plate a little too hard and the serving spoon made a sharp sound. "You know better than anyone how superficial that world can be."

"Oh, Bill! Some people never change," Zoe said, glancing

61

at Izzie. "You never saw modeling as a legitimate career. That's why you didn't want Chloe to become one."

This is getting interesting, Izzie thought. Her dad was clearly unnerved by Zoe, not that she noticed. At the moment, she was scrolling through messages on her iPhone.

"So, Zoe, did you say you're going to New York soon?" Aunt Maureen asked, trying not to sound perturbed that Zoe had her phone at the dinner table. Even Bill wasn't allowed to have one there. "We took the kids this Thanksgiving and they loved it."

"The LEGO store is huge, but so is the park with all the rocks," said Connor.

"That place is pretty great," Zoe told him. "New York is the only place to be as far as I'm concerned. Other than Southern California, of course."

"North Carolina has a lot going for it, too, as you might recall." Her dad was cutting his steak with increasing vigor.

Zoe ignored the comment. "Remember those pictures I took of you and Chloe at the Central Park boathouse, Bill?"

Her dad put down his knife and smiled for the first time since Zoe arrived. "Of course. We were Zoe's guinea pigs," he told Izzie. "She had just purchased her first Nikon and was trying to figure out how to use the lenses." He laughed. "In some of the shots, we look like circus performers, but I think you managed to fire off one or two good pictures."

"I should have the negatives back in Los Angeles somewhere," Zoe said. "Maybe you'd like to see the pictures, Isabelle."

It killed Izzie to admit it, but she would love to have a picture of her parents together. "That would be great."

"What a career you've had," Aunt Maureen marveled. She had clearly drunk the Kool-Aid. "Everyone in town has been talking about it."

"I'm not surprised." Zoe seemed a tad impressed with herself. "Most people like to hear what it's like to work with the Beckhams or the Jolie-Pitts."

"I take it working with celebrities is not the *pits*," Hayden deadpanned. "Get it?" Bill started to laugh and Aunt Maureen glowered at them.

"What made you want to model?" Mira asked to change the subject. Izzie was wondering the same thing.

"It was a way to get out of Harborside," Zoe said between bites. "The only thing I regretted was leaving your mom," she told Izzie. "Back then we were as thick as thieves. My mother and I, not so much. Chloe wound up following me after she finished junior college. I never even got a degree. The world is my college."

"I'm sure it is, but nothing trumps a good education," Aunt Maureen said, mostly for Hayden's benefit. He was a junior and she wanted him to start thinking about college.

Zoe shrugged. "When you have talent and guts, there is nothing you can't do." She obviously missed Aunt Maureen's point. "When I hated modeling, I got into photography and interned for free for a while, crashing at a friend's pad," she told the table. "Pretty soon I got a job as a photographer's assistant and was taking my own lessons with some of the most amazing photographers in the world. That's the spring Chloe came and stayed with me in New York and met Bill. She…"

Zoe had a way of storytelling that made it feel like she was talking only to you, and everyone wanted to listen to her. Zoe was magnetic, that was for sure, but Izzie had seen others like her. It was an act she wasn't going to fall for.

"…so of course, your mom was a nervous wreck," Zoe was saying. "She hated New York, but she couldn't find a job in Harborside, so I lined up a waitressing job for her in the city at this great restaurant that was known for attracting celebrities and sports stars." She winked at Izzie. "I'm the reason your parents even met."

Her dad's shoulders seemed to tense.

"Bill told Isabelle that New York grew on Chloe. Is that right?" Aunt Maureen asked. Izzie couldn't help being touched by Aunt Maureen's efforts. She had invited the sister of her husband's ex-girlfriend to dinner—all to help Izzie better know the mom she lost. It had to be weird hearing about her husband and a former girlfriend he had a child with, but she was doing this for her. Her aunt was a rock star.

"Once Chloe met Bill, she liked it more," Zoe said. "I

worked long hours, so it was weeks before I even knew the two of them were hanging out. You were so scrawny back then!" she teased Bill. "Always talking about bulking up and hitting the gym." Hayden stifled a laugh. "Chloe hated weight lifting, so they usually went to Far Rockaway to swim instead. She told him it would give him great upper-arm strength. By July Fourth, they were inseparable. Remember that rooftop party we went to in Brooklyn?"

As much as Izzie didn't want to listen, she had to. This was her parents' story.

"I do." Bill grinned. "Chloe got into an argument with a local politician about a community garden they wanted to tear down." They both laughed.

"She basically ran the guy out of there, then proceeded to call him daily till she changed his mind," Zoe added, taking a sip of her drink. "Our apartment turned into her command center! God, she racked up such a phone bill. She called every politician in the area twice!"

Izzie laughed despite herself. "She was always like that. Mom called till someone listened. Was she obsessed with infomercials back then, too?"

"Infomercials?" Mira questioned. "Really?"

"It's not what you think," Zoe said. "Chloe hated them. She was always rambling on about how they should be banned because they were such a sham. She would have made a great lawyer."

"Yes, she would have," her dad said. Izzie noticed it was the first time Bill had agreed with Zoe all evening.

"Isabelle has that gene in her," Aunt Maureen bragged as she buttered a roll for Connor. "She is a cochair for Emerald Prep's Social Butterflies club. Both the girls are members. The group does many community-service projects."

"You don't say." Zoe held her glass up in honor. "Your mom would have been really proud."

For some reason, the gesture hit Izzie the wrong way. Zoe talking about her mom as if she knew her—as if they had a relationship when she died—was too much for Izzie to handle. "How would you know what my mom would think?" Izzie suddenly snapped, and everyone looked startled. "You wanted nothing to do with us until you absolutely had to. You abandoned the whole family!" Zoe flinched, and Izzie realized she was shouting.

"It's okay, sweetheart," her dad said. "Maybe we should talk about something else."

"No," Zoe said sharply. "We should talk about what happened between your mom and me." Izzie looked at her. "I have spent a long time thinking about the mistakes in my life and figuring out ways to correct them," Zoe said softly. "I may not be Mother Teresa, but the Dalai Lama didn't call me his star pupil for nothing. I'm sorry I wasn't there for you and your mom. I was wrong to ignore you, but I have always lived life on my own terms. When your mom left me in New York, I thought, *Screw her. Who needs family?* We create our own family wherever we go, so I made mine in California. I have a great life there, but that doesn't mean I didn't regret what I had lost."

Izzie had no idea what caused her mom and aunt's falling out. All she knew was that her mom never spoke of having a sister. Whatever it was, it had to be pretty bad.

"I traveled so much those years and had so many addresses and phone numbers that it is no wonder no one was able to find me when she passed away." Her blue eyes glazed over. "Your grandmother was many things, but most of all she was prideful, and when I turned my back on her and your mom, they turned their backs on me, too. When your grandmother finally tracked me down years later, I was hurt to learn it wasn't to make amends. She needed something from me. I should have taken custody of you, but I was so angry at your grandmother that I couldn't see that it was you I needed to protect. I will always regret saying no, she said hoarsely. "I was so conflicted, I went straight to his Holiness to work on my inner beauty after that. When I was done, I came to find your grandmother and you." She smiled. "It wasn't hard. Your name is in every paper. You have sort of a Cinderella story thing going on."

Izzie wasn't sure what to say. She had spent so many weeks being angry about being abandoned by Zoe that she had never thought about how abandoned Zoe felt by her own family. Now she didn't know what to think.

"Your mom and I didn't end on good terms, but I have so many great memories of her that I'd like to share with you if you'll let me." Zoe sounded tentative. "And if I have the time."

"Time?" Aunt Maureen asked.

"Yes, it appears you can only book a hotel room for so long in Emerald Cove," Zoe said. "My room at the Sea Crest hotel is only available for another week. Something about an annual historical-society convention for Emerald Cove's Founders Day. Apparently every hotel in town is booked, and to be honest, I don't think I can afford to pay my mortgage back home and a hotel here much longer anyway. I have money, but no one has *that* much money. Except maybe you, Bill."

Izzie could feel her chest tighten. On the one hand, having Zoe as far away as possible would let her move on, but on the other...Aunt Maureen had been right. Zoe knew stories about her mom that no one else could tell her.

"We understand you can't stay here forever," Bill asked. "You can keep in touch with Isabelle by phone and—"

"Maybe my dad could help you find somewhere to stay," Izzie interrupted before she even thought about it. "So you could stay a little longer. If you wanted to." Her eyes met Aunt Maureen's. She understood.

"Zoe could stay here for a few weeks," Aunt Maureen offered.

"What?" Bill suddenly dropped his act, sounding incredulous.

"The guesthouse is empty in the winter," Aunt Maureen reminded him. "It has its own entrance and kitchen and bath, so Zoe would be on her own but still close enough for Isabelle and Zoe to continue to get to know each other." She gave him a meaningful look. "This would really help Isabelle, don't you think?"

Her dad looked resigned to the decision already. Izzie's aunt usually got her way. "Yes." He turned to Izzie. "If this is something you really want."

What she wanted was more time. Time to sort out her feelings, to learn why her mom and Zoe stopped speaking, to hear Zoe's side of the story. The only way those things were going to happen is if Zoe was still here to tell her. "I do."

"That would be fantastic," said Zoe. "People keep calling for photography sessions and I keep saying I don't know how long I'm staying. Now I do! I have to be back to Los Angeles in the spring, so I'll be out of your hair by April, I swear. My friends throw me an annual birthday party in Cabo that I can't miss."

"Izzie's birthday is in March," Mira offered. "Mine is in May. We're turning sixteen."

"Are you having a huge sweet sixteen?" Zoe asked.

"I am," Mira said. "Izzie hasn't decided yet. She's not a huge fan of parties."

"Mira," Izzie warned. Zoe didn't need to know everything about her.

Mira rolled her eyes. "Fine. I'll stop talking about it. But you're going to be sorry if you don't have one. Sweet sixteens are a lot of fun."

"Party or no party, I'm glad you'll be here for Isabelle's birthday," Aunt Maureen said. "Family is so important."

Zoe opened her mouth to say something, then seemed to think better of it. Instead she turned to Izzie. "Are you *sure* you're okay with this?"

Tonight's conversation had made Izzie realize one thing: A person's life could change with just one decision. She didn't want this to be one she regretted. "Yes," Izzie said, twisting the cloth napkin on her lap into a knot. "I'm not promising that this will make things better between us. What you did is still not okay. I don't forgive you yet." She breathed deeply. "But I'm willing to try."

Zoe smiled sadly. "That's all anyone can do: try."

Six

"'Happy V Day, Mira,'" Charlotte read from the just released Book of Love insert in the EP school newspaper. "'Your first clue about tonight's date: Don't bother wearing your favorite jeans or fancy shoes. Go with rain boots. Clue number two can be found where you lost your diamond earring last month. Kellen.'" Charlotte frowned at Mira. "*That's* what he writes in the only Valentine's booster he'll ever write you? *Don't bother wearing your favorite jeans tonight?*"

Mira swiped the pink pages from Charlotte and dropped them in her paisley bag along with the other four copies she had grabbed. *What if one got wrinkled?* "I think it's romantic." Mira tried to sound confident, even if she wasn't. *Rain boots? Really?*

"Why would you need rain boots?" Charlotte sounded

rattled. "It's not supposed to rain tonight! Where is he taking you? Fly-fishing?"

Mira gave a nervous laugh. "No!" She bit her lip. "He wouldn't, would he?" The only thing she did know was that they were celebrating a day early. Kellen was leaving tomorrow.

Charlotte wrinkled her nose. "God, I hope not. You'll reek for days."

"If that's what Kellen has planned, I'm going to say no," Mira declared. "Dad wants us to make an appearance at a food bank with him on Sunday. Smelling fishy would not be good for his poll numbers."

It looked like a bottle of Pepto-Bismol had exploded at Emerald Prep. The halls were a sea of pink decorations, and everyone had gotten into the Valentine's Day spirit. Many of the girls had accessorized their uniforms with light-up hearts, Savannah and her friends had on annoying red berets, Charlotte had made herself a pair of funky heart earrings, and Mira was wearing a pink headband. Why couldn't Kellen think pink? Clues were cute, but the rest of his message was flat, and now that Charlotte had mentioned it, their date sounded like it could involve cleaning fish at the dock. He didn't even spell out Valentine's Day. Who called Valentine's Day "V Day" anyway?

Charlotte checked her lip gloss in Mira's locker mirror. "Don't sweat it. I'm sure whatever Kellen has planned will be good. I'd be more worried about your good-byes." Charlotte pulled on her jacket, a cute bright green raincoat that she had designed herself. "That's going to be the worst part. How do you say good-bye for forever to a guy you like?"

"I don't know." Mira spun the bracelet on her wrist around and around, which was a nervous habit. "I hadn't thought about that part yet, because it's not really good-bye. He'll be back at Easter."

"Yeah, but that's just for a visit," Charlotte went on as she reapplied her mascara. "It's pretty much over between you guys. You can't do the long-distance thing when he's not coming back permanently and…" Her eyes caught Mira's misty ones in the locker mirror and she stopped herself. "Oh God, Mira. I'm a horrible friend!"

"No! You're being honest," Mira said. "I need that. It's not like I haven't thought about this stuff a zillion times myself."

"Okay, so let's think about something else." Charlotte slammed Mira's locker shut. "What are you doing for the art class submission? I'm torn between two designs: One is a gown for the First Lady and the other would be my dress for the Crystal Ball."

"I started two new portraits, but I'm not in love with either of them." Mira stared at the pink streamers and red hearts decorating the hallway. "It's hard to focus."

"It will be easier after tonight." Charlotte ran a comb through her red hair. "Any idea where Kellen's second clue is?"

Mira leaned against the locker next to Charlotte's. "I lost

my earring near the bus stop on Main Street when we were heading to Sup one afternoon." Mira frowned at the memory. The earrings were her favorite studs. Her dad had bought them for her thirteenth birthday. "If I'm right, the second clue should be there."

Izzie appeared out of nowhere. "Wear rain boots?" she asked Mira, and raised an eyebrow. "Does Kellen know who he's talking to?" Charlotte laughed.

Mira had no clue what Kellen was thinking, but at least he had given her one less thing to worry about: choosing the perfect outfit.

~

Mira walked to the trolley stop on Main Street at 6:40 PM and stared sulkily at her feet. It was a starry night, just like her Weather Channel app had predicted, and she had no need for her stupid rain boots. It killed her to swap out the outfit she already had planned for their last date—a mini-dress—for her least favorite pair of skinny jeans and a long, fitted sweater.

When the trolley pulled up a few minutes later, Kellen wasn't on it, and there wasn't a clue to be found near the bus stop. Stumped, Mira waited till everyone had gotten off. That's when she spotted a red envelope taped to the trolley-stop bench. It hadn't been there earlier, but there was no missing her name printed in big black letters on the front. Inside the envelope were ten dollars and a handwritten message:

Head to Bait, Tackle, and Reel 'Em In. Tell the guy behind the counter that Kellen Harper sent you. He'll give you the next clue.

Mira's shoulders slumped. They *were* going fly-fishing! She dragged herself the short distance to the tackle shop. She was so busy practicing fake enthusiasm for their outing that she barely noticed the guy behind the counter staring at her strangely.

"Hey." Mira gave him a less-than-peppy wave. "Kellen Harper sent me."

The guy placed a smelly carton on the counter. "That will be ten dollars."

Mira gave the container the evil eye as she forked over the ten-dollar bill. "What is in there?"

"Fish," he said as if it should be obvious.

"*Fish*," Mira repeated, and gingerly grabbed the container by the handle.

"I'm supposed to tell you to take the next trolley to the bay," he said, and handed her a plastic bag. She gratefully put the carton inside it. "Then he said something about meeting you on the pier. I think."

"You think?" Mira asked.

He shrugged. "Hey, I just sell bait. I don't usually coordinate people's dates."

And this had to be the oddest date ever. What could Kellen be thinking? He had to have his reasons. He paid attention to details, just like she usually did. As she walked to the pier from the trolley stop, she tried to figure out what he was up to.

"Do you have my fish?" Kellen called out, startling her. She looked around and saw him a few yards away. He had on a coat, jeans, boots, and an adorable skullcap.

Mira held the smelly bag out as she walked toward him. "Yes. I don't think anyone on the trolley appreciated the smell." He pulled her toward him and her grumpiness couldn't help but melt away. "You made me wear rain boots," she grumbled.

He grinned. "I like torturing fashionistas."

She gave him a look. "I can't believe you made me wear these for our last date, which is supposed to be romantic, considering it's the day before Valentine's Day. Or did you forget?"

Kellen looked like he was enjoying himself. "How could I forget when the guys were making fun of me all afternoon after reading your message: 'Live, laugh, love, today and always, near or far,'" he recited in a high voice.

"I was trying to get in the spirit of the holiday!" she said in mock indignation. "That's why I didn't write something totally dull like 'Go with rain boots,'" she said in a deep voice meant to sound like his. "Now I'm worried you're taking me fishing."

He laughed hard and held her tighter, blocking out the wind. "You can relax. Look over there." He pointed to a pretty Victorian house nearby. She recognized it as Harbor Shores, one of North Carolina's aquariums.

"We're going to the aquarium?" Mira felt relief wash over her. Anything beat outdoor fly-fishing! "I didn't know they were open at night."

"They're not. We're getting a private tour." Kellen led her to the building. "I have been racking my brain to figure out what to do for our last date, but nothing I came up with felt good enough. Hayden said I was trying too hard, while my mom said I wasn't trying hard enough." He gave her a crooked grin. "Being a guy who is good at dates is exhausting."

Now she felt bad. "No, stop. You did great. This looks fun." When she wiped her nose she got a whiff of fish. "I still don't get why I had to bring my own bait, though."

Kellen smirked and rang the aquarium door buzzer. "You'll know soon enough."

A voice crackled over the intercom. "Yeah?"

"It's Kellen," he yelled into the microphone box.

"Right on time," said the voice. "Come on back. You know the way." The buzzer sounded and the door unlocked.

77

Mira followed Kellen into the dank, dark lobby. It smelled pretty fishy, but it wasn't hard to ignore the smell when you saw how pretty the aquarium was. A long footbridge covering a pool with sand sharks was to her right, and a shallow stingray feeding pool was to her left. Everywhere else she looked, there were lit glass tanks showcasing octopuses, schools of fish, and other creatures. EC could have a great party in this place—if they could find a way to deal with the smell.

Kellen grabbed her hand, interrupting her thoughts. "Do you remember the first night we hung out? We both said we live near the water and we've never fished." Mira nodded. "Well, I figured it was about time we did something about that—and about your fear of being up close and personal with dolphins even though you love them." Mira froze. "I know we said we'd try a dolphin encounter this summer, but since I won't be here, I thought we needed a plan B."

"You might be," Mira said hopefully.

Kellen seemed pensive. "Maybe." She heard a small splash from the stingray tank and looked over. "If not, I think it would be cool if you remembered me as the guy who took you to meet some dolphins."

"Seriously?" Mira's voice echoed in the cavernous room. Here she'd thought Kellen's Valentine's message was weak at best, but now Kellen was giving her dolphins! "I didn't bring a bathing suit," Mira realized.

"Well, they don't actually let you swim with dolphins here, but you can feed them," Kellen told her. "I figured you'd like this better. You can't chicken out."

Now it made sense why she wasn't supposed to get dressed up. Wait till she told Charlotte.

"My cousin Jameson is a trainer here, so he arranged the night visit," Kellen said, guiding her forward. "He's waiting for us in the dolphin arena."

"And this is something you've never mentioned, why?" They passed a huge spiral fish tank with a small octopus inside. "Connor would love this."

"If I come back to town, we could come back here and bring Connor," Kellen suggested.

But what if he doesn't come back? Mira worried. She quickly forced herself to stop fretting about what-ifs. She wanted to enjoy tonight, and seeing the dolphins was enough to make her do just that. When they entered, two dolphins were swimming around in a pool with a floating platform.

"So this is the famous Mira." Kellen's cousin walked toward them in a head-to-toe wet suit. He put down a bucket of fish and held out his hand. "It's nice to meet you."

"It's nice to meet you, too." Mira tried not to think about what Jameson had just been handling when she shook his hand. *Fish guts.* "Thanks for letting us come tonight."

"Don't mention it. We do private tours for wedding

couples and dignitaries all the time, so my boss didn't mind me inviting family." Jameson looked at Mira. "I think your dad has even met Tom and Jerry."

"Tom and Jerry?" Mira repeated, eyeing the bucket again. In a few minutes, she would have to pick those fish up.

"Our dolphins," Jameson explained. "I'll introduce you once you've put on a wet suit."

"But I thought we weren't swimming." Mira's voice went up an octave.

"You're not, but those two are mischievous," Jameson said. "They've been known to knock visitors into the pool when they turn their backs on them. They buckle people's knees with their nose. It's funny as long as you're not wearing street clothes."

"I can just watch from the edge," Mira tried again. The dolphins looked big. Kellen gently nudged her toward the changing area. She could see there was no point arguing. Wet suit it was. Then she remembered something.

"Jameson has food here to feed Tom and Jerry, so why did I need to bring my own fish with me?" Mira asked Kellen.

He made a face. "You didn't *need* to. I just wanted to see how you handled having to carry bait on a trolley." He burst out laughing, and Mira glared at him. Jameson wisely steered her away to put on a wet suit, and then, before she knew it, she was standing near the edge of the pool.

The dolphins swam closer as she and Kellen stepped onto

the moving platform. She vaguely heard Jameson give them a few instructions: what to do, what not to do; how to pet, rub, and kiss them, and toss them their favorite toys. Then, suddenly, she was touching an actual dolphin. They didn't seem so frightening now that she was up close. Jameson snapped a few pictures of them with Tom and Jerry and promised to e-mail them later. Then, too soon, the encounter was over. The rest of the aquarium experience flew by. They fed stingrays (which made a weird slurping sound when eating sardines out of her hand) and had a picnic dinner in front of the shark tank.

"No final date will ever top this one. Tonight was incredible," Mira summed up later as they got off the trolley on Main Street and waited for Kellen's bus home. Mira's mom was picking her up in five minutes.

"*You're* incredible," Kellen told her.

Even if they never saw each other again, she knew this was a guy she'd always remember. "So this is it." Mira's voice wavered.

"I think so." Kellen's voice sounded strangled, too.

"I don't want it to be." Mira felt small. Her eyes were growing teary.

"Me, neither." He hugged her tightly. "Listen, these last few months have been better than all my time at Emerald Prep, and that's because of you."

"Mine, too," she said. Without Kellen, she never would have had the courage to start painting seriously. "So let's not say good-bye," she said determinedly as she heard the bus coming down the street. "It's not good-bye if you're coming back at Easter."

"I know, but..." Kellen hesitated. "I'm moving. This really is it."

The tears dripped down Mira's face, and she couldn't stop them. He was saying they were over. Through. Finished. But she didn't want to hear it.

Kellen brushed her tears away and kissed her. "I'll call you when I get there."

The bus pulled up in front of them and the doors opened. Kellen snuck in one last kiss before he got on. He turned around before he moved to his seat. "Bye, Mira," he said, saying good-bye even though she had hoped he wouldn't.

"Bye," Mira choked out as the doors closed. The tears dripped down her face. She had to see the bus drive out of sight to believe it. Kellen was gone, and this time it was for good.

Seven

Izzie did not want to cause a scene in the middle of EC's coffee shop/bakery/wine bar, but she couldn't take it anymore. She covered her face with her hands and screamed.

Savannah shot her a look of contempt from the seat across from her. "Was that really necessary?" she snapped in a thick drawl.

The phrase seemed to be a favorite of Savannah's lately. Savannah had used it when Izzie got mad at her because she kept putting off their meeting to discuss Founders Day. She'd used it again when Izzie snapped at her for changing their "absolute, definite" meeting time that Saturday morning to four thirty in the afternoon because of "prior engagements." And she used it a third time when Izzie obviously embarrassed her by screaming because it was five thirty on Valentine's Day and she was going to be late for her date with Brayden. But Izzie had had it. Every time she suggested an idea, Savannah shot it down.

"I'm done," Izzie said. The coffee shop was clearing out. The smoothie machine wasn't whirring, and the constant stream of people coming in and out for the past hour had slowed to a trickle. People were getting ready to go out for Valentine's Day, and Izzie wanted to be one of them.

"Something wrong?" Savannah sipped her second frozen mocha of the afternoon. Wearing a black tube dress with a bright pink tulle skirt, Savannah looked like she had someplace much more exciting to be. Strangely, she was in no hurry to get moving.

"You obviously hate any suggestion I make, so we might as well call things quits." Izzie rose from her seat. "Have a good Valentine's Day."

"Come on. Don't be like that," Savannah begged. "I'm sorry."

Pretend Nice Savannah was even more grating than Mean Girl Savannah. Izzie had a feeling she was up to something. The question was: What?

"I *want* to like your ideas, but none of them have anything to do with our town history. This is Founders Day!" she reminded her. "We need some culture. Some town lore! Didn't you read the books I gave you?"

Izzie didn't want to admit it, but she'd been studying

Emerald Cove's past the way she memorized facts for a biology exam. "A little."

"Good!" Savannah said, as if she were praising a dog for finally learning how to roll over. "What have you learned?"

"This isn't a quiz at EP, Savannah. I'm using what I learned to give you these ideas." She pointed to the long list in her notebook. Only two ideas weren't crossed out yet. "And you've hated all of them."

Savannah rolled her eyes to the ceiling, which was decorated with hanging hearts, just like every other shop in town. "It would be easier if you just let me do this myself."

Izzie picked up her drink and took a sip. "Not in a million years."

"Fine." Savannah opened her Vera Bradley notebook to the page with the sticky note on top. She took out the matching pen and smiled patronizingly at Izzie. "Then let's get back to brainstorming. Where were we? Float ideas?"

Izzie sat down and looked at her notebook again. "Okay, what if we tie the parade and booth idea together? Nicole had this idea of creating a 'Mr. Emerald' character." She laughed to herself just thinking about it. "You know, someone who dresses up as a giant emerald and tosses fake emeralds into the crowd at the parade."

Savannah looked horrified. "Social Butterflies don't *throw* things. And certainly not jewelry."

Izzie gripped the sides of the table and squeezed. "I give up. What do you have?"

"Is it finally my turn?" Savannah glanced at her short list. "My idea is to cover the float in green crystals and then we would dress up as characters from *The Wizard of Oz*. I would be Glinda, you could be the Wicked Witch, and Mira the Cowardly Lion." Izzie glared at her, but Savannah didn't notice. "The float would have a sign that says *The Emerald City*, but in this case the Emerald City is Emerald Cove."

Izzie frowned. She had suggested something similar the other day and Savannah had shot it down for being too much like the Butterflies' float from a few years back. "I thought you said we can't copy old ideas."

Savannah took a quick glance at her watch. It was almost six o'clock. "I did say that, didn't I?" She crossed it out. "Guess I forgot!"

Izzie's eyes narrowed. Savannah would never forget Butterflies history. It all made sense now. She had purposefully pushed the meeting till Valentine's Day, then switched the time till it would be dangerously close to someone going out on a date, and now she was stalling. There was only one reason Savannah would do that. "You're trying to make me late for my date with Brayden, aren't you?"

"What? Why would I do that?" Savannah asked innocently. Izzie continued to stare at her. "You mean because it's Valentine's Day?" She gave a little laugh. "Get over yourself. If you must know, I have a date tonight with a guy at St. Barnard's Prep who is so perfect, he might possibly be the future president of the United States." She adjusted her long, gold necklace. "Or have a career as a model. I'm not sure which, but the point is, I could care less about you and Brayden."

Izzie started to rise again. "Great. Then I guess you have to be going, too."

"Nope! My date isn't until eight, I'm already dressed, and he's meeting me here, so I have plenty of time." Savannah stared at the sweats Izzie had put on after an early afternoon swim at the sports complex. "You, on the other hand, didn't plan ahead. I'll let you go if you let me pick the idea for our float on my own."

"No!" Izzie's voice competed with the smoothie machine that had started up again. "I am not Mira. You cannot bribe me into going with whatever lame idea you've come up with." Savannah pursed her lips. "I have some great ideas here, which you probably killed just so no one would know I came up with them. But you're missing out." She waved her notebook in the air and a line that wasn't crossed out caught her eye. It was one of two ideas she hadn't mentioned yet. "This one is good. It involves putting a DJ on the float who would play songs that feature the word *green*. You know, for the town color." Savannah didn't automatically shoot her down so she went on. "Like 'A Little Bit of Green' by Elvis Presley, 'Green Light' by Beyoncé, 'Green Eyes' by Coldplay, 'This Green City' by the Cure…"

"Now, that's not a bad idea," Savannah admitted, "especially if we turned the float into a moving dance party. Have you ever seen one of those at Disney World?" Savannah waved her off. "Of course not. When would you have gone to Disney World?"

"Okay, I'm going to go now," Izzie said, and Savannah grabbed her arm.

"I'm sorry! Just listen. They have these moving dance parties that stop at different areas on the parade route." She leaned forward excitedly. "The characters jump off and dance with people and then get back on and move the party to the next stop. We could do the same thing."

"I actually like that. Then we're not just on a float, we're interacting with the crowd." Izzie sat down again. She couldn't believe she actually agreed with Savannah. "I have a list of fifteen songs that have the word *green* in the title alone. There must be others."

Savannah nodded. "We could put the music on a loop and all wear green and hop off at different corners…."

They had so many suggestions they talked for another half hour without arguing even once. It wasn't until Izzie went to scratch her arm that she noticed the time. "It's six fifteen! I have to go." Brayden was meeting her on Main Street in a half hour!

"You're meeting him at seven?" Savannah couldn't hide her glee. "Wow. You're not going to have time to go home to change."

88

She looked Izzie's messy appearance up and down. "That might be a problem if you're going to Buona Terra for their Valentine's Day seating. That's where he took me and I know they have a strict dress code that doesn't include sweats."

Izzie was too mad at herself to respond. One minute she could see why Mira had been so captivated with Savannah. When Savannah was passionate, she had a lot of smart things to say. But when she pulled the diva debutante routine, Izzie wanted to smack her over the head with her notebook. Instead, Izzie left without saying good-bye and walked outside to call Brayden.

"Hey!" Brayden picked up on the first ring, sounding happy but out of breath. "Are you on Main Street? I had a rip in my pants and I had to run home and change."

She bit her lip. *Just be honest,* she told herself. "No. I got held up by Savannah and I haven't even gone home from swim practice to change yet." She cringed when he didn't say anything. "I'm so sorry. If I'm late, am I going to ruin our plans?" Here a boy was doing something nice for her and she was blowing it.

"No, but how soon can you be ready?" Brayden asked.

She had to go home and get a ride back. This was not good. "An hour?"

"Okay." Izzie could tell he wasn't thrilled. "I'll see what I can do," he said. "Text me when you're on your way."

She hung up, closed her eyes, and banged her head on the coffee shop window.

"Isabelle?"

Izzie turned around. Zoe was carrying several shopping bags and a large iced coffee that looked so creamy it could have been a glass of milk. She hoped Zoe hadn't heard her whole conversation. "Hi."

"I thought you'd be on a hot Valentine's Day date by now," Zoe said with a smile. "Those who have dates have fun dressing up. The rest of us shop!" She held up her bags.

She sounded like Mira. "I'm supposed to be ready for my date." Izzie realized the time was only getting later and she still had no plan. "But I got held up, and I haven't even had time to go home and change yet." Now was Zoe's chance to make things up to her. "Is there any way you could drive me home, wait for me to get ready, then bring me back to Main Street to meet Brayden?"

Zoe frowned. "Oh! I wish I could, but I have plans right now. I'm meeting old friends for dinner and then we're going to this jazz club. I was just going to stash my shopping bags in my car."

So much for making things up to me. "Okay," Izzie said flatly. "I better go."

"Wait!" Izzie turned around. "I may not have time to get you home, but I might have the next best thing." Zoe held up her shopping bags. "I just bought these cute dresses at Prepsters, which is probably way too young for me to be shopping at anyway. Why don't you try them on in the bathroom and if one fits, you can wear it tonight."

Izzie wasn't sure what to say. This wasn't what she had in mind, but if she took Zoe up on her offer, it would save her a lot of time.

Zoe rummaged around in her oversize slouchy shoulder bag. "I even have hairspray, bobby pins, makeup, and body glitter with me." Izzie looked at her strangely. "I'm a photographer. I have to be ready for anything!"

This actually might work. Izzie couldn't help but smile. "Okay. Let's try it." They headed back inside to find the restroom. Savannah, Izzie noted, was long gone.

With the right tools, it didn't take Izzie long to get ready. Zoe was even able to turn Izzie's waves into curls with just a little water, her finger as a curler, and some spray gel. The body glitter gave her skin a nice shimmer, and the black tank dress Zoe had bought was surprisingly Izzie's taste. It looked great with a chunky silver necklace that Zoe lent her, too. They managed to have her ready in under twenty-five minutes.

Zoe spun her around to see the effect at all angles. "You are the best-looking Scott yet! Your guy is going to flip when he sees you. What is his name again?"

"Brayden." She'd only said his name a thousand times in the last half hour.

Zoe put her makeup back into her bag. "Well, go wow him! I have to get going, too. My friends got a reservation at Mumon, that new sushi place, and they only hold your table for fifteen minutes."

Izzie wasn't sure how to thank her for all she'd done. "I'll take your dress to the dry cleaner and have it back to you by the time you move into the pool house."

"Keep it." Zoe smiled. "It looks better on you than it did on me anyway. Besides, Michael Kors's people are supposed to send me a huge box of stuff from their new line. I'd rather wear their clothes than some local shop's off-the-rack knockoffs."

Mira made Izzie watch enough E! that she knew who Michael Kors was, but beyond that she had no idea how to respond. "Well, thanks. I guess I'll see you soon."

"Soon," Zoe agreed.

Izzie dashed out carrying only a small handbag Zoe had purchased that day. Thankfully her school flats had been in her messenger bag, so she had something to wear other than sneakers, and Zoe said she'd drop off Izzie's other clothes and messenger bag tomorrow. She'd already texted Brayden, who'd said to meet outside La Parma, the other Italian restaurant in town. (Take that, Savannah and Buona Terra!) "Hi!" she said, arriving out of breath. "Did I make it?"

"No, but you look so good it makes up for us missing our reservation." Brayden kissed her.

Izzie pulled away. "I'm sorry. I didn't mean to screw things up."

He didn't look so bad himself in a blue button-down shirt with a navy tie and navy khakis. "As soon as you said you were with Savannah, I knew." Brayden gave her a wry smile. "That's why I made alternative arrangements for dinner." He held up a brown bag. "I made us sandwiches."

She laughed. "Oh no! Now I feel terrible."

"Are you kidding? This is better." Brayden had a glint in his eyes. "Follow me if you don't want to be late again."

Izzie was confused. "I thought you said we lost our reservation?"

"Our *dinner* reservation. Not the important one." Brayden led her to the North Church, which had been in town since the late eighteen hundreds. A horse and carriage were waiting. "You've been trying so hard to study up on the history of Emerald Cove, but I thought it might be time for a tutor." The driver of the carriage jumped out and tipped his hat to Izzie. "These carriage rides aren't just a tour of the town; they also give you a history lesson with all these cool, little-known facts." She noticed Brayden had also brought a thermos and a warm blanket. He gave her a determined look. "Next time you see Savannah, you can knock her dead with your expertise on the history of the North Church. She'll be speechless."

Izzie kissed him again. "This is the best Valentine's Day present I've ever had."

It was also the only Valentine's Day present she'd ever had, but he didn't need to know that. Or that thanks to Zoe, she hadn't missed it.

Eight

After hours of painting, Mira had created three choices to submit to Selma Simmons for entrance into her art class. The question was: Which one would impress the notoriously prickly painter? The first painting featured a deliriously happy Connor on the tire swing in their backyard. The second was of a boy fishing on the pier she'd been on with Kellen only a week before. Kellen was always on her mind, which was why the third painting was a portrait of the two of them done in a slightly abstract way that was out of character for Mira. All three needed work, but she only had time to polish one of them. Mira plopped down on the floor of the empty pool house and tried to make a decision.

Her eyes kept being drawn back to the portrait of her and

Kellen. In it, she had created a darkened, desolate beach where an empty lifeguard stand loomed next to a beach blanket littered with belongings. A couple representing her and Kellen stood along the shoreline. What made the piece unusual—as far as Mira's paintings were concerned—was that she had painted the couple floating in the air, the wind pulling them out of their embrace. It didn't take a psychologist to know that this meant she missed him, even after only a few days. Talking on the phone and texting weren't nearly as satisfying as she'd thought they would be. And when Kellen said how much he liked seeing his new public school, it felt like a betrayal. But maybe she was just overanalyzing their conversations. Mira was so busy concentrating that she didn't hear the pool house door open till Zoe dropped a large box on the floor behind her. Mira jumped.

"Sorry! I didn't mean to scare you!" Zoe pulled her wheeled suitcase behind her.

"It's fine! I'm just glad I wasn't painting." Mira wiped the paint from her fingers onto her painter's jeans. "Sorry to invade your space. I didn't think you were coming till tomorrow and I needed some quiet."

"I hear ya," Zoe said, crouching down to look at the canvases. "Connor and some other kid were carrying on so loudly in the house I could barely hear your mom."

Mira began to clean her brushes. "Why do you think I

came out here? I'm trying to get into this art class, and we have to submit a piece, so I really needed to concentrate."

"You have a nice grasp on emotion," Zoe said, and Mira felt a tiny swell of pride. Zoe must know art. She was a famed photographer. "Which one are you going with?"

"That's just it," Mira said. "I can't decide. Any advice?"

Zoe stared hard at Mira's work. "Well, the one of the boy on the pier is nice, but kind of been there, done that," she said bluntly. "The Connor one is fun—the detail in his face is very nuanced—but I think I'd go with number three. It reminds me of Marc Chagall's *Birthday*," Zoe said, referring to the famous expressionist painting.

Mira was amazed by how Zoe got what she was thinking without her having to explain herself. "I wasn't trying to copy it, but when I started sketching, my thoughts went in that direction. Just darker." She frowned. "I wonder if Selma Simmons will think it's not original enough."

"Selma Simmons?" Zoe leaned on the wall. She was so tall and lean she looked like a giant string bean. "I know her. She can be a real pain when she wants to be, but she's always admired my photography. She once told me my work was so vivid it was like having a window into a person's soul." Zoe seemed pleased with herself. "I really do try to capture raw emotion in my subjects. Gwen Stefani is always telling me..."

Mira had noticed the other night at dinner that Zoe had a habit of talking about herself. Somehow all conversations led back to her own life.

"...Gwen's right. I get my best ideas when I'm bouncing thoughts off my friends," Zoe continued. "One time, Gwen said I should shoot with a lens that softens the focus, and it changed the way I photograph children." She rolled her eyes. "They're so squirmy it's annoying." She slapped her thigh. "Oh! I was supposed to call *Justine* for you, wasn't I?" Zoe got out her cell phone. "I've been completely overwhelmed." She gave Mira a devilish grin. "All these local families have started calling for shoots. Everyone wants their kid photographed by someone who has shot Heidi Klum's kids." Her eyes lit up. "You should assist me on a shoot to see what it is like!"

"That would be fun," Mira said. It also might take her mind off Kellen.

Zoe rummaged around in her bag. "And since I have you here now, we might as well take a few pictures to send to *Justine*, don't you think?" She pulled out her camera.

Mira touched her face in horror. "Not like this! I should touch up my makeup first, and I'm wearing this raggedy shirt and my painting jeans."

"It's very boho chic. That sea-green color is gorgeous on you." Zoe spun Mira around and sat her on the edge of one of the paisley couches in the living room before she could protest further. "And your makeup is perfect in this lighting." Mira looked in the mirror near the door. Maybe her makeup wasn't so bad. "Let's just try a few."

The pool house was perfect for a photo shoot. It was one big room with a kitchen area, a living room section, and a dining nook. Mira loved the open feel of the space. It let in the best light for painting, too. But that didn't mean she was ready to model. She had never posed before in her life. Zoe seemed to sense that and quickly put her at ease.

"I want you to relax," Zoe said, fixing Mira's hair slightly. "Leave it all in my capable hands. Emma Stone was nervous the first time I shot her, too."

"You shot Emma Stone?" Mira was excited but tried not to move.

"Before anyone knew who she was, and I gave her the same advice I am giving you—imagine I'm the hottest guy in school and you want me to adore you." Zoe shot off a test shot, adjusted some dials on the camera, and held a separate flash at her side and then above her head. "Nice. Ready for more? Follow my lead." She began clicking away before Mira could stop her. "Good! Drop your chin. That's it. Place your left hand behind your back and angle toward me. Yep. You got it!" She kept clicking. "Perfect!"

The flash was blinding at first, but after a minute or two, Mira didn't mind so much. Imagining Kellen was behind the camera worked. Mira couldn't help but smile and be engaging.

And she had to admit, it was fun being the center of attention.

"Oh! Sorry."

Mira and Zoe turned around. Izzie stood in the doorway holding a black dress in a dry cleaning bag. Her face was a mix of emotions. "Aunt Maureen said you were back here so I thought I'd return your dress, but I can see you're busy." The look Izzie shot her made Mira want to dive under the couch.

"No, stay! I'll go," Mira said hastily. "I didn't know Zoe was going to be here. She showed up while I was out here painting."

"Mira almost jumped out of her skin," Zoe said with a laugh. "I figured while we were both here we might as well take some test shots. Mira is going to be an amazing model, and having me shoot her head shots can't help but look good." Mira thought Zoe sounded conceited, but when you were that good, it was probably hard not to be.

"Well, I'll leave you guys to it." Izzie hung the dress on a hook near the door.

"Stay," Zoe said. "I want to hear all about your date. Was the dress a hit?"

"I think so." Izzie looked uncomfortable, and Mira noticed her toes begin to tap. "Thanks again. I don't know what I would have done if you hadn't shown up."

"Don't mention it." Zoe leaned on the edge of a chair. "I love helping people. My friends say I am always putting others' needs before my own." Mira and Izzie briefly locked eyes. "Are you sure you don't want to keep the dress?"

Izzie shook her head. "No, it's yours. Besides, no one wears a dress more than once in this town anyway. Right, Mira?" If Izzie was teasing, she couldn't be too mad.

Dress. Town. Time. "What time is it?" Mira panicked.

Zoe held up empty wrists, but Izzie had a watch on. "One fifteen. Why?"

Mira grabbed Izzie by the hand. "Zoe, can we finish up later? I'll come back and grab my art supplies. I forgot Izzie and I have someplace we need to be."

"We do?" Izzie asked as Mira dragged her along.

"Sure! I think I got a few good shots already." Zoe looked at the screen on her camera. "*Justine* is going to love you! I'll call them Monday. And I say go with the beach painting. It's a winner."

"Thanks." Mira grinned. "That means a lot coming from you." Mira could sense Izzie watching, and suddenly she felt funny. She had a feeling she was going to hear it when they got outside, and she did.

"Since when are you two friends?" Izzie had an edge to her voice.

"We're not! I didn't even know she was going to be at the pool house." Mira lingered by the back door and looked out at the patio. Her mom had uncovered the furniture already because it had been so warm. "When Zoe showed up, she was nice enough to ask about that art class I'm trying to get into, and then the next thing I knew, she was taking my picture."

Izzie bit her nails, and Mira tried not to look horrified. "Sorry for the inquisition." She hesitated. "I just feel weird seeing you two together. She was so awful to my family, and when I see you laughing with her..."

Now Mira felt bad. If she was taking sides, she was on Team Izzie. "I always have your back," she promised. "Zoe's probably just being nice to me because she knows it's a good way to get to you." Izzie frowned. "To get to know you, I mean," Mira quickly clarified. "That's why she's so into getting me a modeling contract."

Izzie finally smiled. "*You're* into you getting a modeling contract."

"True!" Mira sidestepped the sandbox. Connor had obviously been in it that day because the lid was off and sand was everywhere. "I'll travel the world and forget all about Kellen, but he'll be forced to think about me because my face will be everywhere."

"The ultimate revenge," Izzie agreed. "Have you talked to him?"

"A little." Mira was too exhausted to rehash the texting and the phone conversations. "At least we're talking—which is what you and Zoe should do." Izzie groaned. "Maybe she'll know what's in that safe-deposit box that you refuse to open."

"Maybe." Izzie seemed to think about that for a moment. "I'm not ready to know anyway. I'm just starting to feel like myself again."

Mira didn't want to push it. She knew what it was like to feel sad, and her sadness didn't compare to Izzie's in any way, shape, or form. When Izzie got quiet, Mira saw the opening she had been waiting for. "That's good because I have just the thing to cheer you up waiting in the kitchen."

Izzie looked suspicious. "What is it?"

Mira ignored her and opened the back door. "Mom? Is it time?"

"Yes! We're in the dining room!" Mira's mom yelled.

"Who's 'we'?" Izzie asked. Mira didn't say anything. They both took off at a run, trying to race each other through the house. Izzie beat Mira by a half a second. She looked pleased with herself till she realized the *we* was her aunt and a woman bearing lots of magazines, swatches, and a laptop presentation that said SWEET SIXTEEN. Mira swallowed hard.

"Oh good, you found Isabelle!" Mira's mom said. "Girls, I want you to meet Kimberly Mays." Ms. Mays was impeccably dressed in a gorgeous navy pantsuit.

"It's an honor to meet you," Mira said. She felt like she was meeting royalty.

"Why does her laptop screen say *sweet sixteen* on it?" Izzie asked. She did not sound pleased.

Ms. Mays smiled serenely. "Mira warned me about your

dislike of parties. That's just because you haven't had one planned by me yet." Izzie's head spun around so fast, Mira thought it might fly off.

"I begged my mom not to tell you," Mira squeaked. "Because you would say no! Just hear her out, okay? She's the best party planner on the East Coast."

"Great, then you use her," Izzie said with gritted teeth. "I don't want a party."

"You mean you don't want to *plan* a party." Ms. Mays misunderstood. "That's the beauty of me. I plan everything. All you have to do is sit back and enjoy."

Izzie looked at Mira's mom. "I appreciate what you're doing, but I am not in the mood to celebrate when..." She trailed off. "It feels wrong."

Mira's mom put an arm around her. "I know you feel strange, but Grams would want you to celebrate your life, and turning sixteen is a huge milestone."

"Quite the milestone!" Ms. Mays chimed in, and Mira winced. For a great party planner, she sure was clueless when it came to people's emotions.

Izzie still looked unsure. "I don't like being the center of attention. When those stories came out about me in the paper, I felt like I couldn't breathe. I don't want a showy party that will make everyone talk again."

Mira couldn't believe how opposite their views were on getting attention. She loved celebrating her birthday and wanted everyone to know it was her special day. When she was little, they used to celebrate her birthday at Disney World, and she'd wear a *happy birthday* pin all week long so that people would congratulate her.

"I thought you might feel this way," Mira's mom told Izzie. "That's why Ms. Mays has an alternative in mind. How would you two feel about a joint party in April?" Before Mira could protest, her mom went on. "Izzie's is just a month away, so that doesn't give us much time to plan, and yours is in May when school is getting out. You complain every year that people are usually on vacation when you have a party," her mom reminded her with a twinkle in her eye.

That was true. No one was ever around for her birthday.

"April would be right between your two birthdays, and then all the pressure wouldn't be on just Izzie," her mom added. "You could share the spotlight."

Mira and Izzie looked at each other with interest.

This wasn't what Mira had in mind when she got her mom to hire Ms. Mays. On one hand, she hated sharing attention, but Mira also couldn't help thinking how much bigger a joint party would be. Plus, Izzie hated party planning and had her hands full with Founders Day, so she'd let Mira make all the decisions. "I'm in!" she exclaimed.

They stared at Izzie. "This is like the cotillion ambush. You guys are not going to give up until I say yes, are you?" Mira and her mom nodded, and Izzie's mouth started to twitch. "I guess we could have a *small* party." Mira practically tackled her. "But here are my rules: I don't want to invite the whole town. Just family and our *real* friends," she stressed. "And no gifts." Mira froze. "Maybe people could donate to our favorite charities instead," Izzie said, looking at Mira's mom.

"I like it! That is quite the trend these days." Ms. Mays jotted something down in her journal, and Mira felt her presents vanish in front of her eyes. Izzie was right, though. They already had so much. And her family would probably still get her *something*.

"We want something tasteful," Mira's mom told Ms. Mays. "I promised their father we would not blow this party out of proportion. We're in the middle of a race, and it wouldn't look good to spend a fortune on some overblown spectacle."

"It won't be a spectacle, but it will be superb." Ms. Mays began a slide show on her laptop. Mira was dizzy with anticipation at the sight of it. "I had some ideas."

Izzie seemed to take that as her cue. "Okay, I'm done here. Let me know what you pick!"

Ms. Mays looked shocked. "Don't you want to be part of the planning?"

Izzie shook her head. "That's more Mira's thing. She can pick a theme."

Mira squealed. She was in charge! She sat down and happily looked at the laptop.

Two seconds later, as if sensing Mira's ideas taking form, Izzie was back. "Correction! You can pick anything—as long as we don't show up in a pumpkin-shaped coach or by camel."

Mira frowned. A Cinderella theme was her top choice. She must have let it slip at some point. Oh well. There were still plenty of ideas she could go with, and Izzie had given her free rein. It might have to be small, giftless, and sans camels, but if Mira had a say, their joint party was going to be one EC wouldn't soon forget.

Nine

"What do you mean, you don't want tiaras at our street-fair booth?" Savannah's indignant voice boomed over the phone. "Tiaras are perfect for any occasion!"

Izzie covered the phone with her hand and looked wearily at Mira, Kylie, Violet, and Nicole. "Remind me again why I called her?"

"Because it was better than inviting her here to yell at you in person," Violet said. "She would have taken one look at this dive and squirted the place down with Purell."

"Hey, you guys wanted a bargain." Kylie was grouchy. "This place serves up party supplies for cheap."

Both girls were right. Savannah would have taken one look at the hoarderlike aisles, fluorescent lighting, broken store sign, and dirty floors and have run screaming, but there was no place better than Harborside's Party Goods and More for deals.

Izzie put her ear back to the phone. "Savannah, we went over this the other day. Tiaras don't make sense for a booth about mining."

Savannah sighed loud enough to be heard through the phone. "They do if we want *cute* miners. The girls won't want to wear ugly plastic hard hats!"

Izzie banged the phone against her head. When they had met the other day to discuss the street fair, the booth seemed like the simplest part of their plans. Emerald Cove was a town built on mining emeralds. That's why founder Victor Strausburg named their town Emerald Cove. So Izzie argued that a booth that allowed children to pretend they were mining for emeralds was quintessential EC. All they had to do was make a mining station. Everyone agreed on the idea of building a large standing sandbox and filling it with water and sand for "mining." All they really needed for supplies were toy shovels, plastic jewels, sand, loot bags, and plastic mining hats. Unfortunately, the plastic mining hats were Savannah's sticking point.

"If I was a girl coming to our booth, I would be *devastated* if you asked me to wear a green plastic hat," Savannah went on. "Think of all those poor mothers! No one is going to want a photo of her daughter in a miner's hat."

The only person who thought like this was Savannah.

Izzie was ready to scream, but she knew that would be just the reaction Savannah wanted.

"Just hang up on her," Violet whispered.

"No! Don't be a coward!" Kylie said a little too loudly. "Hold your ground. It's a good thing she isn't here, because I would have decked her by now."

Izzie ignored her friends. "The hats are only forty-nine cents each," she said calmly. "I'll send you pictures of them. They're perfect! So are the jewels and all the other stuff we found. We don't need tiaras, too."

"If you had told me you were going, I would have saved you the trip," Savannah sniffed. "I'd rather order from Oriental Trading. My new boyfriend Pierce's dad practically owns that company. Their stuff is much more quality than what you've found somewhere in Harborside." Izzie was ready to throw the phone out the window.

Mira must have realized that because she gingerly pried the phone from Izzie's grasp. "Savannah?" Mira took over, surprising everyone. "It's Mira. Just listen," she said in a soothing tone. "These mining hats are perfect, and they don't look cheap. The kids can decorate them with stickers before they go mining so they look more fancy." She listened for a moment then she winked at Izzie. "Of course no one expects *you* to wear one, but if we buy these we'll have money left over for you to buy whatever you want for the Butterflies to wear the day of the fair." Mira bit her lip and side-eyed Izzie. "Butterfly wings? Um, sure. Those would look great."

"Butterfly wings?" Izzie cried, and lunged for the phone. "No way!"

Violet held her back. "Do it for the greater good!" She struggled against Izzie's strength. "If you have to wear butterfly wings or even glitter war paint to make Savannah happy, then just do it so you can buy what you want!"

"Yeah, who cares about your dignity, Iz?" Kylie deadpanned. "Ms. Priss wins again and you get a bargain. It's worth selling out for!"

Violet's face darkened. "I'm not telling her to sell out. She's doing what she has to in order to get the job done for our club. A club you know nothing about. And if she can do it all for a great bargain, isn't that worth kissing butt for?"

Izzie knew that look. Violet and Kylie were about to go at it.

"Yeah, because I'm sure you're all about bargains." Kylie rolled her eyes.

"How would you know what I'm about?" Violet snapped. "You don't know me."

"I can read you like a book." Kylie looked Violet up and down. "Rich girls like you just swipe your credit card and never look at the price of anything. Like you care about getting a bargain. I bet you've never set foot in Bargain Basement in your life."

Violet stepped forward. "Even if I had, I at least know the difference between buying cheap and *looking* cheap." Izzie felt her stomach tighten.

"You better shut your perky little mouth, rich girl, before it gets knocked right off." Kylie's face was inches from Violet's, and she had made a fist.

"Um, maybe you two should calm down." Nicole pulled Violet back. She actually looked frightened. "You're both overreacting."

Izzie grabbed Kylie. "Yeah, let's all just chill." Kylie always seemed like she was one second away from a meltdown lately. Why did her friend have to take things so far? "Violet was just trying to help me out. The situation with the Butterflies is complicated."

"Fine." Kylie glared at Violet. "I'm going to go outside and get some air. Hayden should be here soon anyway." She walked out of the shop without looking back.

Izzie tensed again. So they were still hanging out. And this is how Kylie decided to bring it up.

"Great idea, inviting her." Violet's dark eyes narrowed at Kylie's retreating back. "Not everything has to turn into a tirade on the rich versus the poor, you know. I'm on scholarship at EP. Does she even realize that?"

"She just gets bent out of shape." It was hard to defend Kylie when she acted out the way she did. "We've been burned before."

"We all have." Violet smoothed her long peasant top. "The difference is you and I don't start throwing punches to prove a point."

"Mira looks like she has good news," Nicole said to break up the awkwardness.

"Exactly!" Izzie heard Mira say. "Mrs. Fitz is going to think you two are geniuses for being so cost-effective." Mira gave Izzie a thumbs-up sign. Less than a minute later she hung up. "The tiaras have been officially nixed." Nicole cheered. "You have Her Highness's official permission to buy the miner's hats and assorted fake jewels."

"Nice work, power broker." Nicole twirled a plastic glitter wand like a real pro. She had been on the color guard before she'd ditched it for swim.

"Thanks, Mira," Izzie said gratefully. It killed her that she didn't know how to handle Savannah as well as her sister did. "Let's buy everything before she changes her mind." She glanced at the shopping carts behind them. They were full of burlap sacks, bags full of multicolored fake jewels and jewelry, and the plastic miner's hats.

"Or before Kylie threatens me again." Violet pushed one cart toward the front of the store, but it was hard to move because the aisles were so crowded with boxes.

The color crept up Izzie's face. Kylie meant well. The fact that she even wanted to help today proved that. Neither of them loved parties—probably because most Harborside parents could never afford to throw them for their kids when Izzie and Kylie were growing up. She hadn't even told Kylie about the joint sweet sixteen she and Mira were having. She wasn't sure how she would react.

"Where is Kylie now?" Mira asked, looking anxious.

"She went outside to wait for Hayden," Izzie said, and Mira's eyes widened. "Guys, can we talk about this later? Kylie's mom just started working here and I don't want her to hear us." Violet looked like she wanted to make a comment, but she thought better of it. "I'll talk to her about what happened, okay?" Violet wasn't exactly innocent in their exchange either, but her friendship with Violet still felt new, and sometimes Izzie hesitated to rock the boat.

Nicole nudged Violet. "Forget it. Let's just drop it."

"Are we going next door after this?" Mira was the best at changing the topic when needed. "Kylie said there's a costume shop. We can look for costumes for the Crystal Ball." She looked at Izzie. "You know you have to wear a period dress to that, right?"

Izzie imagined Mira in a petticoat and a big hat. Costumes were right up Mira's alley. They were not, however, up her own. "Please tell me we don't need corsets."

Mira looked indignant. "Of course we need corsets! You won't look right wearing an old-timey gown without one." Nicole and Violet nodded in agreement.

Izzie decided it was best not to argue about poufy pink gowns just yet. She began unloading the items on the counter and looked around for Kylie's mom, but she was nowhere to be found. After a few minutes, Violet tapped the bell on the counter that was next to a sign that said *Ring for service*. And then Violet kept tapping it.

"Hold your horses! We're coming!" Izzie heard Kylie's mom say. Two seconds later, she came out a back door carrying a toddler on her hip. Mrs. Brooks—still considered a Mrs. even though her husband ran off last year—saw Izzie and her scowl turned into a smile. "Hi, sugar! Kylie told me you were coming in. Where is that girl, anyway?"

"She's outside waiting for Hayden," Izzie said. She touched the chubby chin of the little boy in Mrs. Brooks's arms. "Hi, Ray-Ray. Do you work here, too?"

"Yep. He's my right-hand man." Mrs. Brooks pushed her hair out of her face. Her long blond locks had just enough of a wave that it looked like she had her hair professionally blown out every day. For as long as Izzie had known her, Patty Brooks had had bags under her eyes that couldn't be concealed and clothes that seemed a few years out of date. (She had on acid-washed denim jeans and a button-down denim shirt at the moment.) But she had hair that everyone in town envied.

"You met Mira at the wake," Izzie said, making introductions. "These are my friends Violet and Nicole." Everyone nodded. "This is Kylie's mom and her youngest brother, Rayland."

Mrs. Brooks shifted the squirmy little kid from one arm to the other and started to sort Izzie's party goods with her free hand. "She really likes that stepbrother of yours. Nice kid. Too nice, if you ask me," Mrs. Brooks added warily. "You have to watch out for that type. That's what I'm always telling Kylie's older sister. They promise you the world and then leave you with this." She motioned to the store.

"Hayden's a great catch," Nicole piped up.

Mrs. Brooks grunted. "Today they're picking out costumes for some fancy shindig he's taking her to in a few weeks." Mrs. Brooks didn't sound impressed. "She always said you hated doing that stuff in EC, so I have no clue why she's so desperate to fit in over there. Something about meeting your dad and aunt or something."

"So he's taking her to the Crystal Ball." Violet made a face. "Must be more serious than we thought. I didn't see that coming."

"Why don't we let you catch up with Mrs. Brooks and we'll head over to the costume shop?" Mira suggested.

Clothes shopping—especially for a period ensemble—was never high on Izzie's list, but getting Violet out of the store before she bad-mouthed Kylie was. It was as if Mira could read her mind. "Good idea. I'll meet you guys in a few minutes," Izzie said.

Dress shopping twice in one weekend. How had this become an important part of her life? She shook her head. At least there was no chance of photographers catching up with them in a place like Harborside. When they'd gone boutique shopping in EC last night, two photographers snapped them entering the store, and then Aunt Maureen worried that the shop they were in was too high end. This had become an ongoing topic the past week—*If the* Gazette's *cameras catch you, how is Grayson going to spin the story?* It felt like Grayson's name was uttered more than her own lately.

But right now, it wasn't Grayson she needed to be worried about. It was Kylie. She was coming to the Crystal Ball and hadn't told Izzie. Kylie would have a boatload of comments about spending the evening in Izzie's new world.

Nicole looked at the two carts. "Are you sure you can manage all these bags?"

"She can leave them here until you guys are done, hon," Mrs. Brooks said. "Now scoot! I have to talk to Iz-Whiz here." As the girls filed out, Mrs. Brooks kept ringing up items. "Nice girls—for rich folk." They both laughed. "So how you holding up, honey? Kylie said you were pretty low there after the funeral. She was real worried."

Izzie immediately felt bad. It seemed like Kylie was always worried about her and she was just worried about how Kylie fit into her new life. *What is wrong with me?* she wondered. *Since when do I care what other people think?* She had promised herself that EC wouldn't change her, but maybe it had already. "I'm doing better now." She leaned her elbows on the counter and her oversize hoodie's sleeves slid down her arms. "Having a project takes my mind off things."

"Good." Mrs. Brooks put the final bag on the counter and Izzie dropped it in the shopping cart. She could feel Mrs. Brooks watching her. "Zoe treating you okay? I saw her last week, and she said she was moving into your family's pool house for a stay." Mrs. Brooks cocked her head and grinned. "You really have a pool house?"

"Yeah." Izzie felt like a traitor. "Zoe couldn't afford to keep paying for a hotel, so she's staying with us for a bit. My dad and aunt thought it would be a good idea if we cleared the air before she leaves town in a month or so." Something Mrs. Brooks said made Izzie wonder. "I didn't know you're friends with Zoe."

"*Were* friends," she clarified. "This is the first time I've seen her since…" She stopped herself. "Well, it's been a long time." She stared at Izzie curiously. "She said she told you what happened when your grandmother's illness was diagnosed last year. That was awfully big of her."

Izzie played with the zipper on her hoodie. She didn't have much to say on that subject.

"She beat herself up about that." Mrs. Brooks picked at one of her chipped nails. "Of course, Zoe thinks about how her actions affect people after the fact."

"She says she's trying to make things up to me now," Izzie said, realizing it sounded like she was defending Zoe. *Am I?* she wondered.

"I'm sure she intends to," Mrs. Brooks said evenly. "But what Zoe says and what she actually does have always been two different things." Rayland had grabbed a squirt gun from the counter and Mrs. Brooks tried to wrestle it away from him with one hand. "You go meet your friends, sugar. If you need me, you know where to find me."

Izzie couldn't shake the feeling that there was something Mrs. Brooks wasn't telling her, but she didn't want to push it. Instead she said good-bye and walked to the costume shop next door. She could hear her friends laughing as soon as she walked in.

A guy looked up from behind the counter. "Are you with the group trying on the period costumes?" Izzie nodded. "They're in the back. You shouldn't have trouble finding them. They're pretty loud."

Izzie wondered what all the commotion was about, but when she rounded the corner she knew right away. Hayden looked like a giant penguin in a white shirt and a black top hat while Mira had on a starched red overcoat dress and bustle that made her butt look three times its normal size. Nicole and Violet were prancing around goofily beside her in silk gowns while Mira tried to get Kylie to wear a feather headpiece.

"Do not tie that thing on my head!" Kylie was dodging

119

and weaving like a street fighter, but Mira wouldn't give up. The bird hat appeared to be the crowning touch to a green velvet dress that had such a wide skirt Kylie looked like she had a two-inch waist. Izzie couldn't help bursting out laughing at the sight of them all. Kylie looked up. "Oh, you think this is funny?" She hiked up her dress, revealing her combat boots, and strolled over. "Wait till you see what we have planned for you, Iz-Whiz." She was calmer and more playful than she had been in the party-supply store. Violet was right next to her, and neither of them were barking at each other or rolling their eyes. Maybe the tension had passed and she didn't have to speak to Kylie after all.

Izzie touched one of the ribbons on Kylie's dress. "You look ridiculous."

"Yeah, but it's kind of fun," Kylie whispered. "Did you ever think two girls from Harborside would be going to some ridiculous charity costume party?"

"If you had told me last summer that I'd be going to any kind of charity gala, I would have said you had swallowed too much salt water," Izzie told her.

Kylie played with the velvet fabric on her skirt. Her smile faded. "Tell anyone you saw me dressed like this and you die." She stared Izzie down. "Seriously."

Izzie crossed her heart, but she was still laughing. Mira was busy fretting over which color petticoat to wear with her dress and Violet and Nicole were choosing accessories. Hayden, meanwhile, was deciding between top hats. Whatever concerns Izzie had about Kylie seemed to melt away when she was standing right in front of her. They were in a room full of people, but it seemed like just the two of them at the moment, which is how she and Kylie worked best. "You don't have to worry about me." Izzie flashed her a wicked grin. "Worry about the photographers who will be at Founders Day. If you're going with Hayden, they're going to have their eye on you, too."

Kylie sighed and looked back at Hayden, who was still trying on hats in a full-length mirror. "I will never live this down, will I?"

"Nope," she told Kylie, "but if you can let yourself go, sometimes playing dress-up can be fun. But don't tell Mira I said that."

"Playing dress-up can be fun?" Kylie questioned playfully. "What have you done with my best friend?" Izzie didn't notice her friend grab a can of Silly String from a shelf of extra costume props nearby. Kylie fired it before she had a chance to react.

"Oh no, you didn't!" Izzie wiped the string from her cheeks and laughed. She knew she shouldn't retaliate, but she couldn't resist. Kylie made her more fearless. She fired a long shot at Mira, who shrieked and ran away. Hayden held her in place, and Kylie shot a few more rounds in Mira's direction before taking aim at Violet. Violet was prepared with a can of her own, and she shot back while Nicole ran for more ammo.

Izzie remembered thinking at the time that it was all completely harmless and fun.

And it would have been—if they hadn't been secretly followed by a *North Carolina Gazette* photographer, who caught the whole thing on camera.

Ten

Their dad held up the lifestyle section of the *North Carolina Gazette*. Mira and Izzie cringed. Their picture was plastered across the front along with the headline **Bad Parenting! If Bill Monroe Can't Control His Daughters, How Will He Control the State?** "*This* is the kind of coverage I wanted you to avoid," their dad said.

Mira felt sick as she stared at a photo of them in the costume shop shooting Silly String all over one another and the shelves. The sun shining through the family room windows reminded her that a new season was starting, and Mira couldn't wait for it to arrive. Seeing her dad's grim face reminded her of the scandal-heavy winter. And she was *so* done with winter. "We're sorry, Dad. We had no idea there was a photographer trailing us all morning."

"Funny how he didn't take any pictures of us cleaning up the store." Izzie sounded bitter. "As soon as the fight was over, we apologized and cleaned up everything! Mira even took one of the costumes to the dry cleaners. It was hardly something that should have made the news."

"Anything less than perfect in the Monroe world is news to Grayson Reynolds." Their dad dropped the paper on the dining table with a thud. "I know you girls didn't set out to create a mess, but you need to pay extra attention to your behavior while we're in this race."

"I hate that we're being hunted when *you're* the one running," Izzie mumbled.

"I know." Their dad sighed. "But that is unfortunately Reynolds's MO. He's just waiting for one of us to screw up big-time so he can sink my campaign for good."

"That's not going to happen," said Mira's mom as she put a hand on her husband's shoulder, her favorite emerald ring flashing in the light. "Being on display is something this family knows how to handle, right, girls?"

"Shouldn't Hayden be here for this conversation?" Mira spun her silver bracelet around and around on her wrist absentmindedly. "He was there with Kylie and she's the one who started the whole thing." Mira shot Izzie a look.

Their dad removed his reading glasses and rubbed his eyes. "We already spoke to Hayden. He knows nothing like this can ever happen again. The reason we wanted to speak to you two separately is to discuss dating." He cleared his throat.

Mira and Izzie looked at each other quizzically as their dad took a seat on the edge of the table, much to her mom's chagrin. "Your mother, uh, aunt, and I like Kellen and Brayden very much."

Liked, Mira wanted to say because Kellen was gone. She had spoken to him the night before, and there had been a lot of awkward silences.

"But if you are going to date, we expect you to conduct yourselves appropriately." Their dad sounded more uncomfortable with each passing word. He looked even paler when he turned the page in the paper and there were several more photos of Mira and Izzie out with the boys. There was one of Mira and Kellen in a tight embrace on the trolley, and it looked like Kellen was trying to suck off her face. Another showed Izzie and Brayden kissing in a horse-drawn carriage. Someone had taken a series of pictures that included them cuddling under a blanket.

Mira felt queasy. Her dad had a picture of her kissing her boyfriend. The whole town could see a picture of her kissing her boyfriend. *Former* boyfriend, but still.

"I don't want to have to enforce stricter curfews on the two of you, but from now on we need to know exactly where you're going and with whom," their dad continued. "This way we can avoid any more, uh, coverage like this."

Izzie was flabbergasted. "You're lojacking us because we kissed our boyfriends in public?"

Mira knew it was best not to argue. After dating a guy who was school royalty because he was the team quarterback, she was well aware of her parents' dating protocol, but Izzie hadn't learned it yet. Even if Grayson Reynolds weren't out for Monroe blood, her parents wouldn't want to see pictures of either of them making out with a boy. They were all about decorum.

"We're not saying you can't kiss your boyfriend." Her mom tried to toe the line between sweet and stern, which was always tough for her. Mira knew how much her mom worried about Izzie, especially after all she'd been through. "We would just prefer you not do it in such a public setting, like a carriage ride, where you're on display for the whole town. People in this town talk." She clutched her pearls for strength.

"What could they have to talk about?" Izzie pushed. Mira admired Izzie's strong principles, but her approach was not working in this situation. "We were only kissing."

"I know." Their dad sounded funny. "We just don't want people to get the wrong idea about you girls." He loosened his shirt collar as if it were choking him. Mira felt like she was going to overheat. This conversation was getting embarrassing.

"You need to set an example for Connor. And for all the girls your age, really, who see you standing beside your father at rallies," her mom said hastily. "Show that you're good,

Southern girls who respect their parents' wishes. Your joint sweet sixteen is going to be a great example of that." She looked at the clock. "I think we've kept you long enough. Mira's art class starts in an hour, and she can't be late for her first day."

Selma Simmons's assistant had called just a few days ago to say Mira had been accepted. Charlotte had gotten in, too, which made Mira think things were looking up—with or without Kellen.

"Knock Selma dead, Pea," her dad said as Mira's mom hugged each of them, being careful not to wrinkle her tailored shirtdress. "You girls enjoy your Saturday afternoon. Just remember what we said, okay?"

Izzie only made it halfway down the block before she exploded. "Be careful *where* you kiss your boyfriend?" She startled a kid riding by on his bike. "Who says stuff like that?"

Mira stuffed her hands into her coat and shrugged. "Don't look so outraged. Most parents around here would say the same thing. One time Taylor kissed me at an Emerald Prep auction event, and my mother almost died. Parents in EC are not big on public shows of affection unless they are family ones."

"And that doesn't bother you?" Izzie reapplied lip balm. Mira couldn't get her to wear lip gloss yet, but at least Izzie had learned to moisturize.

"It's just the way it's always been," Mira explained. "I've had to watch what I said, who I talked to, and what I wore in public since I was five. I don't even notice anymore."

"Well, I hate it," Izzie said. "Grams always trusted my judgment. She let me figure things out with boys and friends on my own."

"Well, my mom and dad are way more involved than that." Mira self-consciously patted her bag to make sure her art supplies were tucked inside. She was a little nervous about meeting Selma Simmons for the first time. "That's just how they are."

Izzie stared straight ahead as if she had a specific destination in mind. "I haven't had parents in a long time." Mira couldn't help but think how sad that statement was. "And I've never had a media watchdog before. I didn't know the press was something I was going to have to deal with for the rest of my life." Before Mira could think of a good reply, she saw Brayden walking toward them, and Izzie's face brightened considerably.

"How'd you know where I was?" she asked as he leaned in for a kiss.

"I called your house and your aunt said you were headed into town by foot, so I thought I'd meet you." He slipped his hand easily into hers. "Hey, Mira."

"Hey." Mira loved the way Brayden was looking at Izzie. He was completely smitten. It dawned on her that as close as she and Kellen had grown, he had never looked at her like that.

"I thought we could go to the hardware store," Brayden said. "We'll get you everything you need for that Founders

Day float of yours. Savannah will be floored when you show up with your own toolbox. Every Southern belle should have one, isn't that right, Mira?" Mira couldn't help but smile.

"I love how your mind works," Izzie said with a laugh.

They were so cute together that Mira was starting to be jealous. "Have fun buying screwdrivers," she said as they headed in the other direction. She continued on toward Emerald Arts. She had a feeling this was going to be a good day. If Selma Simmons liked her piece, then her work had to be good! This was the woman who had painted every decorative bench on Main Street. She had designed the fountain at town hall. Her work was on display in the North Carolina Museum of Art. Studying with Selma Simmons was huge, and Mira was determined to show her she was serious about her craft.

"Hey, Mira!" Clarissa said when she walked in. "Ready for your first Selma encounter?"

"I'm so nervous I feel like I'm going to throw up," Mira admitted. She didn't notice that Clarissa had company. A cute guy was standing next to her. He was about Mira's age, and he had the longest eyelashes she'd ever seen on a boy and perfectly disheveled dark brown hair. Normally the guys she drooled over looked like they'd come out of a J. Crew catalog, but this one was different—his blue camo T alone showed he had a brooding thing going on. Still, it was kind of hot. "Is Selma here yet?" she asked to distract herself.

"No, she always comes a bit late so she can make a proper entrance," Clarissa said, sounding a hint sarcastic. "You can go on in and set up, though. Some people have been in there for an hour! And pick your seat wisely," she warned. "Selma will make you stick with the same one for the whole semester."

"What is this, the third grade?" the guy asked. "Does she make us write our spelling words three times each for homework, too?" Mira couldn't help but laugh. Who was this guy? She had never seen him around before.

"Mira, this clown is Landon," Clarissa said. "He's in Selma's class, too. More important, he's my number one volunteer for the Art Equals Love program."

"The art therapy class," Mira recalled, looking at Landon. "I hear it's pretty cool."

Landon gave her a warm smile then that was anything but brooding. "Cool, it is. You should check it out. We always need more hands on deck. Most of our kids are ten and under, and let's just say they haven't mastered the art of art yet. They're more into making a mess."

Mira laughed again. "Well, I am great at cleaning messes. Maybe I will come by."

He leaned on the counter, his eyes glued to hers. "I hope you do, Mira."

He remembered my name. "Well, I guess I should get ready. See you back there." She could feel Landon watching her as she walked to the classroom, but she was quickly distracted by the smell of acrylic paints. To an outsider, the classroom wasn't much to look at—cinder block walls did no room justice—but Mira loved the clotheslines that crisscrossed the room. Artwork by kids as young as four and people as old as eighty hung from them with clips. The counters lining the walls were filled with all of Mira's favorite things—paintbrushes of every size and width, chalks, colored pencils, and jar after jar of different-colored paints. They wouldn't be using those supplies for Selma's class, because everyone was required to bring their own, but just being surrounded by the artists' tools was comforting. The room was mostly full, and Mira realized that if she didn't grab one of the few remaining easels fast, she'd be stuck in the first row.

"Mira!" Charlotte waved frantically from the center of the room. "Thank the Lord you're here!" Mira hurried over. "This was one of the last empty rows, and I've been beating people back with my bag to keep this seat free." Her blue eyes were as bright as her sweater, which had a yellow flower pinned to the chest pocket. "Someone said the seat you pick today is the one you have for the whole semester."

"I heard." Mira placed her new art bag on the seat next to her easel. "Clarissa told me when I walked in." Clarissa made her think of Landon and those lashes of his. She blushed. "Hey, did you see the hot guy out front?" she whispered, afraid to be overheard. Charlotte immediately looked interested. "He—"

"Is this seat taken?"

Charlotte squeaked and Mira turned around. Landon was standing behind her, and he looked even cuter than he had a few minutes ago. His dark eyes locked on hers. *That smile could melt a Hershey's Bar.* "Do you have room for one more in this row?"

"You can have my seat," Charlotte flirted, not realizing she was giving up her own easel.

He grinned. "You might need it. How about this one?" he pointed to the seat next to Mira that Mira had just placed her bag on. The girls nodded so quickly they looked like bobbleheads. Mira took her bag off the chair for him.

"Is that him?" Charlotte mouthed when Landon turned to set up. Mira nodded and Charlotte's eyes grew wide. "You know, the seat you take now is the one you keep for the whole class," Charlotte reminded him.

Landon glanced at Mira. "Yeah, I think I heard that."

Did that mean he wanted to sit next to her? How was she supposed to impress Selma Simmons when Landon was oozing hotness next to her? Okay, she had to calm down. He was cute, but this was nothing to freak out about. She liked Kellen. *Kellen,* she thought as Landon continued to sneak glances her way while he unpacked. "Uh, Charlotte, this is Landon. Landon, this is Mira. I mean, Charlotte," she said, mixing up the introductions.

"Landon," Charlotte repeated as if in a trance. "Welcome

aboard row three! You're lucky that seat was open. Some guy tried to take it earlier and I sent him packing. He smelled like paint thinner." She laughed giddily, and Mira shot her a look.

"That could give you a nasty headache." Landon pinned an abstract painting to his easel. It was a swirl of blue and gold with flecks of red thrown in. Not Mira's style, but it was mesmerizing. "I'm better-smelling company," he said, looking at Mira. "I hope."

"You are!" Mira said out loud, then wished she hadn't.

Charlotte clicked her tongue and glanced from Mira to Landon. If Charlotte hadn't noticed it before, Mira sensed she was seeing it now. Mira thought Landon was cute, and Landon seemed to have a thing for her, too, if she did say so herself. It was altogether flattering, heart-pumping, and nerve-racking at the same time. She liked Landon—*no, Kellen!* It didn't matter that they were over and living in different states. It would be wrong to move on so quickly. Wouldn't it?

Charlotte smiled mischievously at Mira, then she glanced at Landon's easel. "Wow, Landon. That's so existential. Did you paint that at school? Where do you go, anyway?" She tried to sound casual, but Mira started to squirm.

"St. Barnard's Prep." That was an all-boys school on the other side of Emerald Cove. "What about you guys?" He seemed to direct the question at Mira.

Mira forced herself to break eye contact and stared at the

paintbrushes she'd just dropped into a cup on her easel tray. "Emerald Prep."

"Ah, the Fighting Cardinals," Landon said. "Your school needs a cooler mascot."

"What's wrong with cardinals?" Mira demanded.

Landon's dark eyes held hers. "Nothing, but they're not exactly known for being *fighters*. I never could have gone to a school with a bird on my basketball jersey. Now, the St. Barnard Bears. That sounds fierce, don't you think?"

He flashed her another charming smile, and Mira felt slightly overcome by all the paint fumes. Yeah, that's what it was. The paint fumes. She pulled out her own painting and pinned it to the easel. Kellen's face stared back at her.

Landon leaned over. He smelled like a mix of clean laundry and sawdust. Definitely better than paint thinner. "Was that your submission?" he asked. She managed a nod. "Who is that? You and your boyfriend or something?"

Or something. "Yes, I mean, no. It's complicated." She was growing flustered.

"They broke up because he just moved to Detroit," Charlotte offered, and Mira gave her a look.

Landon's mouth twitched slightly. "Oh, well, sorry about that. The painting is nice, though. I'm just surprised you chose a beach scene." Mira looked at him questioningly. "You know, because Selma hates them."

"Hates?" Mira began to feel ill.

Landon sat on his stool and leaned forward. "She said it in the *North Carolina Journal* last month. Didn't you read up on her?"

No. "But this was the piece that got me into this class," Mira told them. She had to sit down. "Her assistant called and told me she liked it."

"Her assistant?" Charlotte took a seat, too. "Selma didn't call you herself?"

"No. Why? Did she call you guys?" Landon and Charlotte both nodded. Mira felt the color drain from her face.

"Forget what I said," Landon backpedaled. "If you got in on this painting, then she must have changed her mind about beach scenes."

Or… "Do you think I got in because of my dad?" Mira asked Charlotte worriedly.

"No way!" Charlotte insisted. "Selma Simmons is above that sort of stuff."

"Who's your dad?" Landon looked amused.

"Mira is Senator Monroe's daughter," Charlotte explained and Mira blushed.

Landon didn't say anything. Most people didn't know what to say when she told them her last name. They either thought it was really cool or they made a comment about how much they hated her dad. Landon didn't appear to think either. She felt her phone vibrate, and she was happy to look down at the text for a distraction.

ZOE'S CELL: Sorry didn't answer UR txt. Lots of shoots. Promise 2 finish UR head shots soon. XO Z

Mira tried not to look disappointed. She had tried Zoe twice about seeing the pictures she'd taken that day in the pool house. She didn't want to let modeling be yet another project she let fall away. Still, Zoe was doing the head shots for free, and from what she'd heard, they normally cost a fortune.

"Psst. You might want to lose your cell phone for the next hour," Landon whispered.

Mira was so focused on responding to Zoe, though, that she ignored him. That's why she didn't notice that Selma Simmons had arrived until someone took the phone right out of her hand. Mira looked up, surprised.

"I see someone didn't read the course outline." Selma pursed her lips. She looked exactly like the picture Mira had found online. Short, white-blond bob, thick black glasses, and brown eyes that looked anything but happy at the moment. "If you had, you would know I don't allow cell phones. Your only focus should be on what I am teaching you."

Mira struggled to find her Southern charm. "I am so sorry, Ms. Simmons."

"Selma," the teacher corrected. "This isn't preschool. You're an adult, or close to it, and I expect to treat you as such." Her perfectly plucked eyebrows arched. "Unless you don't think you deserve to be treated as an adult. What is your name?"

Mira flashed a friendly smile. "Mirabelle Monroe."

"Mirabelle Monroe!" Selma gave a short laugh. "I forgot I let you in here. Why am I not surprised the esteemed senator's daughter thinks she is exempt from rules?"

Mira paled. "Oh, no, ma'am, I didn't..."

Selma walked over to Charlotte's easel. They had been told to bring their submission projects in for the first class, and Selma was wasting no time critiquing them. "Ah, Charlotte Richards. I would recognize your style anywhere," she said in a pleasing tone. She took one of Charlotte's elaborate charcoal drawings off the easel and held it up to the class. "See this? Some call it a sketch, but I call it art. Anyone can paint a beach." Mira knew that comment was meant for her. "Design is a different medium entirely. Look at the lines in this gown," Selma continued. "What is this dress designed for, Charlotte?"

"The Crystal Ball," Charlotte said. "I'm designing my own dress."

"Lovely." Selma stepped around Mira and took Landon's painting next. "This is incredibly unique work, too, wouldn't you agree, class?" People in every row murmured their praise. Anything to appeal to Selma. "See how—what is your name?"

"Landon Archer," he said, eyeing Mira.

"Landon. Yes, I remember because your work is exploring the very heart of post-modern art," Selma told him. The closer Mira looked at Landon's painting the more she noticed how many different mediums he'd used to get those colors.

Instead of on a canvas, he had painted on an old piece of wood planking and had used metallic paint, along with some sort of gritty, almost sandy material in places. She liked the way the light created different colors in the paint when Selma held it at various angles. "Art can be anything you make of it, and that's what I want to teach you in this class. Stop with the beach scenes you can find at Target for ten dollars framed." Mira winced. "Think outside the box and I will work with you in ways you've never imagined. But if you show me something like this—" She took Mira's painting off the easel and held it up. "You aren't giving me much to work with."

Mira had had enough. She didn't care who this woman was. She had no right to pick on her. "You must like something about my work, Selma. I got into this class with this submission." Charlotte's jaw dropped, but Mira held steady. Izzie would have done the same in this situation. "And the beach is just my background. I concentrated mostly on the portrait."

"You have talent—there is no denying that," Selma said, "but if the portrait is what you're proud of, then you have a ways to go. Your faces are flat and the colors muted. And why are they floating? It's as if you ripped off Jack Vettriano without any of the whimsy."

Mira tried not to cry. Twenty-two pairs of eyes were watching her.

Selma took off her glasses, as if the strain of staring at

Mira's painting was enough to give her a headache. She seemed to be waiting for a response.

"I..." Mira didn't know what to say. Selma Simmons, North Carolina's most famous painter and her new teacher, hated her. And this was their first class.

"Selma?" Landon raised his hand. "Wouldn't you say that beach scenes are some of the hardest to master because of their simplicity?"

"I guess it could be argued..." Selma started to say.

"You said so in your bio on your website," Landon reminded her. "In the part where you talk about how you started out painting beach scenes." Landon winked at Mira when Selma wasn't looking.

Charlotte dug her fingers into Mira's arm. Landon was defending her.

Selma gave him a weak smile. "I'm glad you did your homework, Landon." She pinned Mira's work back to her easel and walked away. "Now, who has something to show me that would be classified as an ode to the Renaissance?"

Mira looked shyly at Landon. "Thank you for going to bat for me," she whispered.

The smile that lit up his face made Mira weak in the knees. "Anytime."

Eleven

Izzie saw Savannah before she could hear her. Dressed head to toe in green, she looked like an oversize elf barking orders from atop a ladder in her backyard.

As Izzie neared, Savannah was yelling so loud she sounded like she had a megaphone. (She didn't.) "Lea! There is a *huge* hole on the left side of the float! You need more glitter. *What?* We're out of glitter? Millie, go to Emerald Arts and get more!"

Izzie stopped at the bottom of the ladder and folded her arms. "Hi, Savannah," she said calmly. Savannah was so startled she practically fell off.

"Izzie! Hey! I didn't know you were, uh, here." As Savannah quickly descended the ladder, Izzie noticed even her shoes were covered with glitter. "We were wondering where you were." She turned to the two dozen Butterflies scattered around her enormous backyard. "Hey, y'all! Look who finally showed up!"

The Butterflies looked like they had been working for a while. Half the girls were gluing green sparkles to the plywood covering the back of the Founders Day float, which was on a large flatbed truck. The other half were by the pool working on what would be the street-fair booth that looked like an old mine. Mira and some of the girls were painting signs that said *emeralds spotted in these here parts!* and *watch out for falling rocks!* Both would grace the tent covering their booth.

Izzie was thrilled to see their club working so hard—she just wished she had been invited to pitch in, too. "The e-mail I got from you last night said we were meeting at the *school* today," she told Savannah. "If I hadn't called Mira, I wouldn't have known you moved locations."

Savannah took an interest in her green nails. "Really? I could have *sworn* you were on that e-mail about the switch! My mother said it was silly for us to have to go all the way to school when she was willing to host and provide refreshments."

"School's only a ten-minute walk from your house." Both girls turned and looked at Brayden. He had been standing next to Izzie the entire time, but Savannah's latest approach to dealing with the fact that he had dumped her was to act like he didn't exist.

Savannah looked at Izzie, and only Izzie. "My backyard is the perfect staging area. We're going to be working around the clock the next few weeks and we can leave our supplies here. Besides, everyone loves my backyard." Izzie resisted making a comment. It was nice. The gardeners were working around them cleaning out flower beds and planting flowers. The patio furniture had been uncovered, throw pillows were on the chairs, and in the distance a covered canopy was being built by the pool. "I called Mrs. Fitz and she was fine with it. She's stopping by to see our progress and to meet Zoe."

"*Zoe.*" Izzie only knew one Zoe in EC. She and Brayden exchanged glances.

"Yes, we know she's your aunt," Savannah huffed. Izzie's ambivalence about Zoe was something she had managed to keep quiet. "My mother hired her to take some portraits, and she liked her work so much that she hired her to chronicle the Founders Day activities for the Junior League. That includes our behind-the-scenes work."

Izzie spotted Zoe circling the parade float. She snapped away as Nicole and Violet tried to get the DJ stand and speakers set up for the float's moving dance party. Izzie hadn't seen Zoe since the day she moved into the pool house. They'd texted a few times about meeting up, but at the last minute, the plans always fell through. Izzie wasn't sure how she felt about interacting with Zoe around her friends. Everyone in town was in love with Zoe Scott and her work. Izzie seemed to be the only holdout.

"It's fine if we work at your house, but don't leave me out of the loop again," Izzie warned Savannah quietly. Every time she and Savannah interacted, she knew everyone was expecting a showdown.

Savannah's smile was as fake as her oversize emerald earrings. "Oh, I see. It's only okay if you leave me out of the loop, like when you went shopping for the booth supplies and forgot to invite me." She waved to someone across the yard.

"That was after you tried to ruin my Valentine's Day," Izzie reminded her.

"Why would I do that when I had a date with Pierce?" Her voice was tight as she gave Brayden a look that could freeze water, which would be hard to do considering the temperature had reached the sixties. "You know, the guy I'm seeing from St. Barnard's."

"Vanna?" Lea had a look of panic on her face as she ran over and interrupted them. "We can't seem to get the papier-mâché to stick to the wire frame the art students made for Mr. Emerald's costume. Can you take a look?"

Mira was right behind her. "You're here!" she said, seeing Izzie. "Good. The mining station is done, but we're not sure if it will leak. Can you come see it?"

Violet and Nicole were next. "We have the green songs

loaded on the iPod, but one of Nic's friends who DJs said our speakers might not be loud enough for the parade."

Savannah and Izzie looked at each other. Without saying it, they both knew: It would take more than one person to run two projects for an event as big as Founders Day. It was time to divide and conquer. They had to be a team, no matter how much it killed them.

"I'll tackle the mining station if you look at the papier-mâché," Izzie suggested.

Savannah didn't argue. "When that's done, we'll look at the float," Savannah told Violet, sounding more decent than normal. "For now, we could use more help with the costumes." She modeled her own sparkly getup. "Isn't it great?" Every time Savannah moved, Izzie was momentarily blinded. "We are wearing these for the float and the butterfly wings for the street fair." Izzie opened her mouth. "Remember? You and Mira said I could get them since you picked out those miner's hats that are so dull I could die."

Izzie could not imagine anything more humiliating than wings and glittery tees. "I remember," she said weakly. Brayden looked like he was trying not to laugh.

"Speaking of statements," Savannah said as she began to walk away, "your friend who showed up today certainly knows how to make one." Lauren snorted.

"Ignore them," Mira said.

"What are they talking about?" Izzie asked.

"Kylie." Mira frowned. "Didn't you ask her to help today?"

No. Izzie glanced in Mira's direction. Hayden was threatening Kylie with a paintbrush, and she was squealing so loudly that everyone in their vicinity was looking. Izzie couldn't believe what Kylie was wearing to Savannah's. She had on her favorite short shorts and a midriff-exposing T that was not suited for March. It felt strange seeing her friend in EC. It felt even odder that she hadn't told Izzie she was coming.

"I can't believe Savannah let her in looking like that," Violet commented.

"Savannah would let the mailman pick up a hammer if he was willing to help," Mira said. "You guys said we should invite everyone we know today," Mira reminded Izzie. "Hayden offered to help and bring Kylie and thank God he did. They were the only two who would agree to pick up a hammer and nails." For the mining station, Izzie and Savannah had drawn plans for a giant sandbox in which kids could bury jewels. A second section looked like a water table. The kids would pour sand through sifters and the water would wash the sand away till only their jewels remained. From a distance, Izzie could see Kylie and Hayden had gotten it right.

"Kylie knew what she was doing," Violet admitted, "when she wasn't stopping to try to pull Hayden away for a make-out session."

"I think they're cute actually." Nicole looked over at them. "Hayden's so jokey around her."

"Hayden's always jokey," Mira and Izzie said at the same time.

Hayden did look happy, but did they have to make out in Savannah's backyard while Zoe was running around with a camera? *God, I sound like my dad*, Izzie thought and cringed. She just didn't understand why Kylie couldn't tone it down.

"Well, I guess we should see how the station came out," Izzie said. Brayden took her hand and they walked across Savannah's lawn. Mira, Nicole, and Violet started talking about the Crystal Ball again and walked a short distance behind them.

"So I heard from Dylan last night," Brayden changed the subject. He and his sister, Dylan, didn't have the best relationship, but they had been trying to make amends. "She wants me to visit her at the University of South Carolina."

Izzie had already made her peace with Dylan. She couldn't hate the girl after she had gotten Brayden and her back together at cotillion. "That sounds fun. You should go."

"I was hoping you'd say that, because I want you to go with me." Brayden gave her a sheepish grin. "I thought we could make it an early birthday celebration of sorts. You know I can't ignore your birthday," he stressed. Izzie had said a dozen times already that she didn't want to do anything special. Mira's party-planning for their joint bash was too much to handle as it was. "We can do something small while we're there." He paused. "Or go to a big frat party." Izzie laughed. "What do you say?"

Her actual birthday was only weeks away. Aunt Maureen kept saying they needed to do a big dinner, but she didn't feel up to it. Going with Brayden to USC sounded like the perfect alternative. "I'm in. Let me ask my dad."

Brayden squeezed her hand, which was a lot more appropriate than the lip-lock Kylie and Hayden were in the middle of when they approached. Izzie was embarrassed by the way they were acting at a Butterflies prep session, but she couldn't help being impressed with their work on the wooden structure they were now leaning against. The only problem she could see was in the thin pegs they had used to hold up the tables. They didn't look too secure. As Izzie approached, one leg started to buckle and Brayden reached out to grab it.

"Whoa!" Hayden pulled Kylie back before the whole table buckled. Brayden quickly pushed the peg back in place. "Guess I don't know my own strength," Hayden joked, making a muscle with his arm.

"Strength?" Kylie made a face. "Who pushed the Charger to the side of the road last Friday when it ran out of gas? Me!"

"Seriously? Who runs out of gas?" Violet interrupted, her voice disapproving.

Hayden winked at Kylie. "Two people too busy talking to look at the gauge. It won't happen again, that's for sure. We had to walk two miles to a pump and Miss Athletic over here was wheezing. Tell me again how I have no muscles?"

Izzie felt funny hearing Hayden talk about her best friend. Last Friday she had called Kylie twice and her phone had gone to voice mail. Now she knew why. Couldn't Kylie have just told her she was with Hayden?

"So what do you think, Iz?" Hayden asked, and knocked on the wood structure. "You're lucky the two of us showed up or you'd still be staring at a pile of two-by-fours. Kylie was the brains behind this operation. She knows her way around a toolbox."

"Hells yeah." Kylie gave everyone a wolfish grin. "Not everyone will risk breaking a nail to get the job done." Violet huffed, getting Kylie's attention. "What is your problem today, princess?" Her demeanor had gone from almost giddy to grim in less than a second. "Oh, I know. Maybe you're jealous that you have to live inside this shallow plastic bubble while I can do whatever I want."

Izzie winced. Is that what Kylie really thought of EC? If so, then why was she suddenly spending so much time here?

"Jealous of your life in Harborside?" Violet sputtered. "Don't flatter yourself. No one is jealous of anyone who lives there."

So that's how Violet really felt about Izzie's hometown. Izzie was getting more uncomfortable by the second. She didn't know whose side to be on.

148

Kylie stepped forward, her blue eyes full of anger. "Are you really going to let her talk about Harborside like that, Iz-Whiz?"

Violet didn't back down. "Hey, you're the one knocking EC, which is where Izzie lives now, if you've forgotten. And you're the one embarrassing her here." Violet looked her up and down. "Who dresses like that in public? You could benefit from this thing we have here called cotillion."

"I like what Kylie is wearing." Hayden tried to ease the tension, but it didn't work. His eyes willed Izzie to step in and stop what was happening, but she froze.

"You have a problem with my clothes, too?" Kylie snapped. "You're unbelievable! You know what I think your problem is? You're threatened by me."

Violet crossed her arms. "Is that right? Want to tell me why?"

"You're afraid Iz-Whiz won't become a cookie-cutter clone like the rest of you and she'll come running home to me instead!" Kylie's voice was growing louder.

Izzie felt ill. Why were they fighting like this? It was embarrassing. First off, Violet hadn't done cotillion, either. And Kylie, for all her knocks, was spending more time in EC than ever. At least Violet was keeping her voice down. Kylie was getting louder and louder as they argued, suddenly reaching forward to give Violet a light shove.

"Don't touch me!" Violet yelled.

Izzie noticed Savannah watching from across the yard with Mrs. Ingram and Zoe. Kylie and Violet bickering… Savannah laughing… her friends staring… Izzie couldn't take it anymore. "Kylie!" Izzie finally snapped. "Just shut up, okay? Shut up!"

Kylie looked as if she'd been slapped. "Iz, she just…"

"I don't care." Izzie was shaking she was so mad. "You can't just go around fighting people. You know what would happen if you decked someone at the Ingrams' house?" she hissed. "They'd drag you away in a cop car. Then what would we do?"

"Let's let them talk." Brayden steered Violet and the others away, but Hayden wouldn't budge. She could sense he was disappointed in her, but Izzie was beyond caring.

"What is your problem?" Kylie played with the bottom of her T-shirt. It had ice-cream stains on it, but Kylie never cared about that stuff. Izzie had always felt the same way, but even she showed up at Butterflies' events dressed a certain way. "Hayden and I had other plans, but I said, let's come help you. Not that you invited me. I was good enough to take you to the party-supply store so you could get my mom's discount, but an actual event with your friends? That you don't want me around for." Kylie sounded hurt.

"You mean the way you don't want me around when you have plans with Hayden?" Izzie asked. "We were supposed to hang out last Friday and instead you sent all my calls to voice mail. Who's the one leaving the other out?"

Kylie glared at her. "You wouldn't have wanted to hang out with us anyway. You won't even say Hayden's name around me. It's like we're not even happening."

"As much as I like being a hot topic of conversation…" Hayden tried to butt in, but both girls ignored him.

"That's not true and you know it." Izzie was starting to feel weird.

"It *is* true!" Kylie barked. "I know you're embarrassed of me. I'm not stupid, Iz. I see it all over your face any time I'm around your prissy new friends or Hayden."

"You're wrong," Izzie said, but she wasn't, and they both knew it.

"God, at least be honest!" Kylie said. "Did you forget how when you moved to millionaire land?"

Izzie hated it when Kylie bashed EC. "No, I learned how to have a little bit of class." Kylie looked stung. "You can't just say what's on your mind all the time! It's like you say and do these things just to get a rise out of my new friends! As long as I've known you, I've never seen you threaten someone unless it was for a legitimate reason. I'm trying to fit in here, Kylie," she whispered hotly. "And you're not making it easier by causing scenes or starting Silly String fights in a store that is being watched by the press."

"I didn't know that photographer was there and neither did you! Just admit it, already." Kylie pushed Izzie, which only made her angrier. "You're embarrassed of me!"

"Yes! Okay?" Izzie blurted out. "Is that what you want to hear? If you're going to make scenes, then yeah, I don't want you here!" Hayden's face fell. Izzie had actually shouted that last part, and now she was embarrassing herself, too.

Kylie's face paled. "Fine." She started to walk away and thought better of it. "You know, when you couldn't stand this place, you came to Harborside all the time." Kylie's voice dropped considerably and Izzie could hear how hurt she was. "I wasn't so bad to hang out with then, was I? I even introduced you to my new friends. Dylan was *my* friend, but I didn't try to keep you away from her. I included you! Now she's gone, you're gone because you've settled into your new digs, and you don't want me to hang out with a guy I really like. Guess I am not good enough to have anyone, huh, Iz?"

Izzie's stomach lurched. "Kylie."

Kylie grabbed her bag from the grass. "You swore you wouldn't let EC change you." Her face was more sad than angry. "Well, look at you now. I hope you're happy." Kylie headed toward the back gate, making sure to bump into Violet on her way out.

Izzie turned to Hayden to explain. "She always has to cause a scene. This is exactly why I didn't invite her today."

Hayden eyed her disapprovingly. "Kylie felt funny being at the Ingrams and around your new friends, but I told her,

'It's Izzie. She's not going to let you feel unwanted.'" He headed after Kylie. "Guess I was wrong."

Izzie could feel everyone watching her. She needed air. She put her head down and ran for the privacy of the Ingrams' gazebo, praying Brayden would keep the others away.

"Hey. You okay?" Zoe startled her. She ducked down to enter the gazebo. "I saw you head this way and wanted to check on you. You put on quite the show back there."

"I'm never going to live this down," Izzie mumbled, thinking of Savannah.

Zoe removed her camera strap. "What are you talking about? We heard you yelling, but I couldn't make out a word of what you said. Mrs. Ingram had me taking pictures of the patio furniture she wants to sell." Zoe rolled her eyes. "Glam work I have in this town. Family photos of the fabulously unfamous and photos for Craigslist."

For some reason, the idea of Mrs. Ingram selling her lawn furniture was highly amusing and Izzie started to laugh.

"It's not funny," Zoe lamented. "God, I am so bored."

Izzie bristled. "I hope you're not staying here on my account."

Zoe grabbed her hand. "That came out wrong. I would have been on the first plane back to California weeks ago, but I am here to make things right with you." Zoe sat down on the gazebo bench next to her. "I am the only Scott you have left in this world and I owe it to you to tell you about our family. As much heartache as there was, there are good memories, too."

Izzie felt a strange sensation in her stomach. This might have been the first time she'd ever heard Zoe talk about someone other than herself.

"One summer when your mom and I were little, your grandfather broke his leg and was out of work for six weeks," Zoe recalled with a smile. "So your grandmother got it in her head that it was the perfect time to travel down the coast. Your grandfather said we didn't have the money, but she produced this huge jar of change that had over a thousand dollars in it. We went to Florida and back, staying at all these motels and seeing every crazy tourist site you could imagine. I think it was the most fun we ever had together." She reached over for her camera bag. "The other night I was going through old photos your mom sent me and I came across this from that summer. I had brought them with me when I came to town, but haven't had the chance to give them to you yet." She pulled out a slightly bent Polaroid photo. The picture was of Zoe and her mom around the ages of six and ten. They had their arms wrapped around each other on the beach. Zoe was missing her two front teeth and her mom's legs were badly sunburned, as was her nose. Izzie didn't think she'd ever seen a picture of her mom at this age. "I thought you'd like to have it," Zoe told her. "There are others, but you can't have them

154

unless you promise to stop by some night and let me tell you the Scott stories behind each one."

Izzie held the picture in her hand wistfully. She had been longing to hear stories about her family. She looked at Zoe. "I'd really like that."

When Zoe grinned, Izzie thought of her mom. They had the same face. "Good. I have albums, too, you know. When they cleared out Grams's house, Kylie's mom mailed me a bunch of pictures and family things. Grams would want you to have them."

"I didn't know Grams had any pictures of Mom when she was little," Izzie said in surprise. "The past few years she had been forgetting a lot. She kept throwing things out. I was always rescuing pictures from the garbage." The words got caught in Izzie's throat. "I thought anything important like albums were long gone."

Zoe rubbed Izzie's shoulders. "You have been through a lot, kiddo. No one I know needs a vacation more than you do. Is your dad planning on taking you on one anytime soon?"

Izzie shook her head. "He's too busy, with the primaries coming up. Aunt Maureen says hopefully we'll go away when school ends."

"That's months away," Zoe said. "I never stay in one place for that long. I need to see new places and forget about the past." She looked longingly at the exit to the gazebo. Izzie realized she had never heard Zoe be this honest. "The longest

I've ever laid down roots is in California. There is such a chill vibe there. I never feel suffocated like I did growing up in a town where all people do is talk and gossip."

Izzie knew what Zoe was talking about. Emerald Cove was pretty big, but it felt small the way the community knew every move a person made. Harborside had been the same, in its own way.

Zoe stood up and put the camera strap around her neck. "I guess I should get back to work. I am sure Mrs. Ingram wouldn't approve of me playing psychologist when she's paying me to be a photographer."

Izzie thought of something as she followed Zoe out into the sunlight. "How was Kylie's mom able to send you Grams's things? I thought no one knew how to reach you."

"I checked in from time to time just to make sure your grandmother was okay." She shrugged. "I guess it was my way of keeping tabs. The last time I called was right after you moved here. Kylie's mom told me about the nursing home and by the time I got here, I was almost too late." Zoe pursed her lips. "But I made it in the end."

Something still wasn't adding up. "But if you spoke to Kylie's mom from time to time, wouldn't she have mentioned me years ago?" Izzie asked.

Zoe smiled sadly. "I initiated a 'no Chloe rule' for my calls. I told Patty Brooks that if she brought up Chloe, I'd stop calling. Stupid, I know. Anger does strange things to people.

Look, there's a lot more I want to say," she added, "but it's probably best to save it for a time when we're not standing in someone else's backyard."

Zoe was right. It was the same lesson Izzie had learned earlier that day with Kylie. There were some things better left unsaid—especially when you had an audience.

Twelve

Mira and Charlotte spun so fast that Mira thought she was going to throw up.

"Go faster!" yelled a small boy who was dancing in their circle.

"If we go any faster, you'll be airborne, darling." Charlotte's hair kept getting in her mouth as she spun. Mira had told her friend to put it in a ponytail, but Charlotte always preferred to leave her red locks loose, and the parade was moving so quickly there was no time for the girls to catch their breath.

The kickoff to Founders Day was starting with a bang. The parade would begin the two-week-long celebration that included a street fair the following Saturday and the Crystal Ball that Sunday. With so much happening, one could easily get party fatigue, but the Butterflies were starting things off right. The sight of their sparkly green float, loud DJ, and confetti guns that blasted every few minutes was working the crowd into a frenzy. It was a gorgeous day and Main Street was jammed as if it were the Fourth of July. People waved green flags, held up banners, and cheered when they weren't ushering their kids off the curb and into the street, of all places, to dance. There was a reason Victor Strausburg laid down roots here, Mira thought proudly, and Emerald Cove was nothing if not proud of its heritage.

"Okay, y'all!" Nicole's green getup shone bright as she yelled into a microphone from atop the Butterflies' float. "We have to move this party to our next stop or this parade will never end." The DJ lowered the music to background noise and the Butterflies began saying good-bye. "You can catch us again at the Founders Day Street Fair next Saturday. Kids can mine for emeralds at our mining station benefiting the Emerald Cove Children's Hospital. Hope to see y'all there!"

Mira had no clue how Izzie got Savannah to let Nicole be emcee, but she was glad she had. Nicole had the perfect voice for a DJ, while Savannah always did better playing the part of beauty queen. As the rest of the Butterflies jumped off at each stop to dance with people, Savannah stood high on her pedestal, looked pretty, and did a solo. Mira thought she looked ridiculous, but Savannah didn't seem to see it that way.

"My face is going to permanently freeze like this," Izzie

said with a fake smile as Mira ascended the sparkling green stairs at the back of the flatbed truck. Mr. Emerald continued to dance behind them, and was actually a *Miss*—Millie, whom Savannah had forced to wear a papier-mâché head and a green leotard as part of the thankless job. "Are we done yet?" Izzie groaned. "I'm already tired."

"Sorry, club leader, we still have two more stops." Violet spun by her, her long dark brown hair swaying in the breeze. Despite the insanity of being part of a moving dance party, most of the club had gotten into the idea, especially once the music started blasting.

Izzie sighed. "I could handle four stops if we didn't have to wear these costumes."

The green leggings and fitted tees Savannah had picked out made everyone look like the Jolly Green Giant. Charlotte had tried to fix the situation by BeDazzling the tops and adding glitter to the pants, but there was only so much she could do.

Izzie looked up at Savannah, who seemed to be auditioning for *Dancing with the Stars*. "Hey, Ingram!" she yelled. "Mrs. Fitz texted me. She says she's at the last parade stop with the mayor and the Junior League president. We need to pause the float for a picture and make a statement to the town paper."

"Already done! I did an interview with the *Emerald Cove Herald* on my own this morning." Savannah was too busy dancing to Elvis to look at Izzie. Float rule number one:

Never stop dancing. "They couldn't have been nicer. They loved the idea of using songs with the word *green* in the title. They couldn't believe how creative I am."

Izzie stopped dancing. "That's because you aren't. It was my idea."

"Really?" Savannah feigned innocence. "I could have *sworn* it was mine." Izzie looked like she wanted to hurl Savannah from the moving float, so Mira stepped in front of her. "Oh, look!" Savannah said. "There's Daddy! Hi!"

"Maybe she'd like to join him on the sidewalk," Izzie said under her breath. "I know a way we can get her there quick."

"That would be messy," Violet quipped. "Plus we don't want to stop the parade."

"I can't believe she took all the credit," Izzie complained as she started dancing again. "I was up late every night this week trying to find more green-themed songs."

Mira bopped by her. "Don't sweat it. Mrs. Fitz is never going to believe Savannah did all of this on her own. Or that she..." The sounds of the DJ and the parade-goers seemed to disappear when Mira saw Kellen standing in front of Corky's. She made sort of a strangled noise and froze. He had flown back to see the parade! She was two seconds from ditching the float, when Kellen turned to talk to someone next to him and Mira realized it wasn't Kellen after all. It was just a boy who looked a lot like him.

"Did you just 'see' Kellen again?" Charlotte was so intuitive it was scary. Mira nodded. "Oh, honey. We have to find you a new guy."

"I don't want a new guy." Mira turned her attention back to the crowd. *I want Kellen.*

"Have you talked to him?" Violet ran a hand through her hair, and Mira noticed the green streaks. Several of the girls had sprayed their hair with glitter, including Izzie. Mira had chosen accessories instead (earrings and a headband). She was not a fan of having paint in her hair.

"He's doing great," Mira said even though it killed her. "He really likes his new public school. Says we don't know what we're missing."

"Metal detectors?" Izzie spoke from experience.

"I bet he can't wait to come back and see you," Charlotte gushed. "He should come for the Crystal Ball and stay through your party." Mira avoided eye contact.

"She didn't tell you?" Izzie said, and Mira felt a sharp pain in her chest. "He swore he'd be back for Easter, but now he says he's not coming back to EC till summer, *if* at all." Mira was ready to fling her glittery green headband at Izzie's head.

"What?" Charlotte and Violet stopped dancing and crashed into each other.

"Sorry," Izzie said when she saw how upset Mira was. "I know you technically broke up, but I didn't think he'd get over you that fast." Mira winced. "I am just mad for you! It's not your fault he isn't coming."

"Why didn't you tell me?" Charlotte looked mournful.

"I didn't know what to say." Mira was reluctant to rehash the story. They hadn't planned it this way, but the week Kellen was supposed to come coincided with her birthday party. Then the visit fell through. "He wanted to be here, but his mom thinks it will be too hard for him to visit EC so soon." Mira played with one of her earrings. "He told me two nights ago." She had cried for an hour. She knew they were no longer together, but she still wished they were. She had thought that if he felt the same way, he would have pushed to come see her. Instead, he barely sounded bothered.

"Did you call him or did he call you?" Charlotte demanded.

"I called him." Mira wondered where the conversation was going.

"And the time before that?" Charlotte wanted to know.

"I called him." Nicole looked over from the DJ booth and waved. Mira could barely lift her hand halfway to wave back.

Violet frowned. "Does he *ever* call you?"

The weight of the situation was getting to her. "If I leave him a message. He's really busy!" The girls stared at her. "You guys are forgetting how amazing his Valentine's Day plans were." How could Kellen give her dolphins and now barely pick up the phone?

"No one is denying he cared about you, but he's clearly moving on," Violet said. "You should, too."

Mira clutched the float railing. She didn't want to move

on, but somehow she sensed that wasn't the thing to say. "Can we not talk about this?" Mira said weakly. Everywhere she looked, people were enjoying the kinetic energy of a parade. Everyone but her. Talking about Kellen made her feel like she had a big black cloud hanging over her head. "Please?"

"What about Landon!" Charlotte made his name sound like a battle cry. "He's this gorgeous guy in our art class who totally has a thing for Mira," she told the others.

"He does not," Mira said, but even she suspected otherwise.

Charlotte ignored her. "He's like her own personal knight in shining armor," she gushed. "Our teacher seems to have it in for Mira. Probably because she's the most talented one in our class." Mira rolled her eyes. "And every time she lays into Mira's work, Landon has some great defense about art that proves Selma wrong." The girls cooed, even Izzie, who wasn't normally the cooing type. "Last week he asked us if we wanted to go to Corky's, but this one said she had some press thing with your dad."

"I did!" Mira protested. That didn't mean she didn't regret it. She liked talking to Landon and there wasn't much time to do it in class. Then she'd remind herself that breakup or no breakup, she liked Kellen and she couldn't move on so soon. But was that what he was doing?

Charlotte kept going. "He's cute and has this smoldering thing going on."

164

"Enough yapping!" Savannah snapped, all the while moving her arms like a belly dancer. "Get back to dancing! Our next stop is coming up."

Mira and the others did as they were told. Mira promised herself that if she made it through their last stop with a smile, then she could go home, peel off her string-bean costume, and watch E! all afternoon. As their group danced their way off the float, Mira tried to muster the last of her enthusiasm.

"Girls!" Mira heard her mom and looked over. She and her dad were waving green flags while Connor held a sign that said *Go Butterflies* in kid handwriting.

Mira danced over, and her dad kissed her cheek. "What are you doing here?" she asked as Izzie did her best to dance up beside them.

"Aren't you supposed to be on a float right now?" Izzie asked.

"The police are escorting me back up to the start of the parade in a few minutes." He was wearing a suit and a green EC logo tie. "I couldn't go till I saw your dance party. I might have to hire you to do something like this at one of my rallies."

"It will cost you," Izzie said. Mira had a feeling she was serious. That girl was going to be a great philanthropist. Or a ruthless businesswoman. Mira wasn't sure which.

"Where's Hayden?" Mira asked.

Her mom glanced at Izzie. "He had plans. He said to wish you two luck."

Izzie and Hayden hadn't spoken since Izzie's fight with Kylie the week before. It seemed like neither girl was willing to apologize first. Instead, they avoided each other.

Zoe walked over wearing an EC press badge. "Girls, can I get a quick picture of your club and the mayor? Mrs. Ingram wanted me to take pictures along the parade route, but I was on the phone with Sarah Jessica Parker and she just kept yapping." Mira's dad coughed.

"Sure." Izzie called the group over. After a few seconds of figuring out who would go where—Savannah wanted to be front and center—Zoe fired off a few shots, then brought in the mayor and Mira's dad for a few more.

"That wasn't so bad." Zoe looked at her watch and frowned. "Now I just have to get back to the start of the route to get ahead of the rest of the floats."

"You can catch a ride with Bill," Mira's mom suggested. "The police are escorting him there in a few minutes."

Zoe and Bill looked at each other warily. "Oh, well, if you don't mind."

"Nope," her dad said. "It's the perfect time for us to catch up." There was something in his tone that worried Mira. What could they have to talk about other than Izzie?

Zoe looked around. "You know, if I leave now I could probably make it on foot."

"Don't be silly!" Mira's mom insisted. "Ride with Bill. You don't want to be out of breath when you get there."

"How is the pool house?" her dad asked. "I thought we'd see you with Izzie now that you were staying there, but it seems like you're around less than ever."

"I know, right?" Zoe missed the dig. "Izzie and I are planning on having a good girl talk soon, though." She smiled at her niece. "I've just had so much work in New York. The timing on this visit couldn't have worked out better."

Mira winced. *Timing meaning Grams's death?* If Izzie caught the reference, she didn't say anything. Mira knew Izzie was happy about the talk she and Zoe'd had at the Ingrams', but it was clear she was hoping to hear more about their family. Zoe kept swearing they would meet up, but something always got in the way.

"We're glad to hear your visit has been so successful," Mira's mom said graciously. "We're so happy you're here to spend time with Izzie."

"And with Mira," Zoe said it as if she were willing it to be true. "I am moving forward with *Justine*." She winked. "Any day this one is going to be a huge star."

"You called *Justine*?" Mira couldn't believe it.

Zoe pushed her hair behind her ear. "Well, I lost their number, but my friend is getting it for me."

Mira felt foolish. Was Zoe ever going to put in a call for her?

"I did remember to have someone send me a box of pictures of your mom and me from L.A.," she told Izzie.

"I'm sure Izzie would love to see them," Mira's mom said.

"We will figure out a good time to go through them. They are great," Zoe said. "You can really get a sense of your mom's personality in these. She was such a free spirit."

"You think so?" Her dad looked pensive. "Chloe seemed so grounded and responsible to me. Like Izzie. She always put other people's needs first."

"Maybe that was her problem." Mira detected an edge to Zoe's voice. "Everyone needs to shed their responsibilities once in a while. Take Izzie, for example." She looked at her. "After all that's gone on, I'm sure she would love to get away for a day or two."

"Like to New York with you?" Mira's mom pressed, and Zoe pursed her lips. Clearly that was not what she had in mind.

"Actually, I did have an offer," Izzie said apprehensively, and they looked at her. "Brayden asked me to visit Dylan with him at USC after everything with Founders Day is over." The color drained from Mira's mom's face. "I know what you're going to say." Mira had a feeling she didn't. "Dylan can be trouble, but she's been better, and Zoe is right. I could use some time away." She snuck a glance at a photographer hovering nearby. Another shot of Brayden and Izzie kissing had been in a Grayson article last week. The caption said *Does Bill Monroe know what his daughter is up to?* Mira seemed off the hook now that she had no one to kiss, but Izzie was an easy

Thirteen

Mira had been pacing in Izzie's room for the last fifteen minutes. If she kept this up, she was going to leave a permanent indent in the carpet. "Let's go over this again," Mira said as much to herself as to Izzie. "If Mom and Dad ask where you are, I'm going to say, 'I don't know.'"

"Yes," Izzie repeated slowly and for the thousandth time. "You're not lying if you technically don't know where I am."

"But I do know!" Mira freaked. She reached for the first thing she saw, which was Izzie's Lambie blanket. She gave it a squeeze. "You're going to USC with Brayden!"

Izzie pried Lambie out of Mira's hands while simultaneously shaking her sister. "They're not going to ask you! And if they do ask, say anything—I'm at the community center, Corky's—just stall. I'll be on my way home before the big birthday dinner your mom planned." She frowned. "I still wish we weren't having one. Brayden will put me on a three PM bus and I should be home by seven. They will never even know I'm gone." By the time she got there, she'd only have a few hours before she had to turn around and go home, but it was worth it to spend her birthday with Brayden.

Mira was still skeptical. "You shouldn't be going at all. It's supposed to rain all day!" she ranted, looking almost comical in her pink striped pajamas. "And Ms. Mays is bringing by sample party favors. Don't you want to see them?"

"You pick one." Izzie tried to sound soothing. "You're better at that stuff. Remember when you asked me what kind of flowers we should have for the arrangements? I said daisies, and you said white anemones were better. I don't even know what an anemone is!"

"I do have good taste when it comes to flowers," Mira admitted.

Izzie stuffed her iPod and wallet in her messenger bag. "Okay. I think I have everything, so I'm going to go, and I'll be back before anyone even knows I'm gone."

Mira bit her lip. "Let's hope so."

Izzie hated when Mira got wound up like this. Did she really think Izzie liked lying to the family? She'd been so good about keeping her nose clean. Why couldn't her dad and aunt see that visiting Dylan was just what she needed? Zoe said it was okay, and she was technically an authority figure, so Izzie figured that was permission enough. "Stop worrying. I'll see you tonight." Mira remained stiff when Izzie hugged her. Then she snuck down the stairs and closed the front door behind her. Everyone was still sleeping, which is what she normally would be doing, too. She hadn't seen five AM on a Saturday in forever, but her and Brayden's bus left in a half hour and she did not want to be late.

Brayden was early. When she arrived, he was waiting by the buses with a bag from the bagel store. "Happy birthday! I brought you breakfast, but I forgot a birthday candle for your bagel." Izzie could smell the cinnamon-raisin-swirl bagel (her favorite) from where she was standing. "I figured you were so busy sneaking out that you'd forget to eat." Brayden kissed her before handing her a bus ticket and the bag. Inside was her bagel, her favorite orange juice (no pulp), and, because it was getting closer to Easter, a Cadbury egg (her favorite chocolate of all time). "Happy birthday," he said again.

"Thanks," she said shyly. "You thought of everything, didn't you?"

"Everything but the weather." Brayden looked up at the gray early morning sky.

The weather had been perfectly March-like all week. One day it was sunny, beautiful, and sixty-two degrees. The next, a cold wind blew so hard that you'd think it was December. That weekend called for all rain, which is why the street fair and Crystal Ball (which was held in a tent in town square)

173

had been moved to the rain dates the following weekend. That changed everyone's plans, including Brayden's trip to visit Dylan. With Izzie's permission, he moved his trip to her actual birthday weekend, thinking she was allowed to go. Izzie figured with all the changes, no one would remember where she was supposed to be. But that didn't mean she still didn't feel guilty about letting her aunt and dad down.

"Someone said it's supposed to rain all day." Brayden linked his arm through hers. His blue-green eyes looked all blue in the dull light of the sky. "But I don't care, as long as I'm celebrating your sixteenth with you."

Izzie had been so busy with Founders Day that she was looking forward to four hours of cuddling with Brayden herself. "Maybe we should schedule bus rides more often. It's guaranteed alone time," she teased as they boarded the Greyhound. The bus was only half full, so they had their pick of seats. They settled into ones near the front.

"We could be the couple who has all our dates on a bus." Brayden grinned. "We could pick routes blindly—that way every trip would be a surprise."

She laughed. "I had a hard enough time getting away for one bus trip. I'm not sure I could pull them off weekly." She slid into the seat next to him.

Brayden frowned. "I know. Are you sure this is a good idea? I can see Dylan anytime. I'd rather do something you want to do on your birthday."

"No. I'm glad we're going there today," she insisted. "I need to get out of EC."

"I know, and I want you to come, but your dad and aunt like me," Brayden said. "If they find out where we went, I'll be lucky if they ever let us hang out again." Brayden slumped down in his seat and pulled his sweatshirt hood over his head as if they were being watched. Izzie assumed it was possible. The press was everywhere, but even photographers didn't stalk on Saturdays before breakfast. At least she hoped not. He quickly texted Dylan to let her know they were on their way. "I hate that I'm going to miss your birthday dinner," he added.

"I told you." Izzie nudged him. "We're going to be together all day. I don't need you to be at a dinner with my family, too. You should spend time with your own family." Brayden didn't look convinced. "If they find out where we went, I'll deal with them," she added, putting her knees up on the back of the seat in front of her. "Zoe thought our road trip was a great idea."

Brayden put his arm around her. "Ah, Zoe is playing the good cop, bad cop routine. Clever. Is that why she and your dad were bickering at the parade last weekend?" Izzie nodded. "What's that about?"

"I don't know. They knew each other when my parents were dating, but my dad never even mentioned Zoe till she showed up." Izzie gave Brayden a skeptical look as the bus began to pull out of the station. "He says it was so long ago, he forgot about her."

"Weird," Brayden said. "I thought you said Zoe told all these stories at your dinner about things they had done together."

"She did." Izzie couldn't put her finger on it, but she wasn't stupid. One of them was holding out on her. The question was, who?

"Well, at least you two seem to be getting along now." Brayden's fingers tickled her hand. "That's good, right?"

"Yeah, but I really want to talk to her about my mom and she is always so busy. I thought her living in our backyard would make things easier, but it doesn't." Izzie watched the scenery whiz by. Tiny raindrops pelted the window, and it made her sad. She was tired of discussing her life. "Let's talk about something else," she suggested.

"You mean there's other stuff to talk about?" Brayden joked, but he got the hint.

They spent the next few hours talking about school and music and even took a nap as the rain fell hard outside their window. Before she knew it, they were in South Carolina, and Dylan was standing under an umbrella at the bus station waiting for them. Her hair was in a ponytail, revealing the nautical star tattoo by the nape of her neck.

"You couldn't have left the rain home?" Dylan asked. She looked relaxed and happy, a sharp contrast to how she had seemed at cotillion. "I'm excited you two made it. I have so much planned your head is going to spin," she told them as they trudged across the water-logged campus. The place made Emerald Prep look like a preschool. USC's theater and dance building looked like a Roman temple. "I'm just mad it's raining. I wanted you guys to see the Horseshoe. It's part of the original campus and the buildings are gorgeous. Some are on the National Register of Historic Places."

"Did you just name-drop the National Register of Historic Places? That move seems a little 'Junior League' for you," Brayden teased. "Emerald Cove has lots of places on that register—including our house—and I don't think you've mentioned it once."

Dylan laughed. "What can I say? I like my school." Dylan filled them in on her classes, her professors, and how much she liked going to a college she could get lost in. There were almost thirty thousand students, so Izzie could see how that was possible. Even in the rain, students were everywhere. When they finally made it to Dylan's room, they looked like drowned rats. Dylan gave Izzie something to change into and threw their clothes in the dryer down the hall. Her dorm room was smaller than Izzie had expected it to be, but the decor was classic Dylan with punk rock band posters above her bed, Uglydolls for pillows, and a huge corkboard that had pictures of her friends, favorite tattoos, fortune-cookie sayings, and a school bumper sticker. "My roommate, Missy, is in California this weekend for a wedding, so we have the place to ourselves," Dylan explained when she came back with their warm clothes. "So now that you're dry again, what do you feel like doing? Are you hungry? It's raining, but we can make it to my car and be at Chick-fil-A or 2 Fat 2 Fly in minutes."

Brayden had crashed on Dylan's bed. He rolled over and looked at Izzie. "We have been on a bus since five thirty this morning. I'm thinking food."

Dylan grabbed her keys and her umbrella again. "Great. We'll eat, hopefully the rain will stop, and then we can walk around campus. Then we'll come back, change, and get ready to celebrate." Dylan's eyes glimmered. "B tells me it's your birthday. I can think of several great parties we can hit tonight where they will definitely serenade you."

"Actually, Iz can't stay. She has to take a bus back at three," Brayden said.

"Seriously? That's crazy," Dylan said. "You have to stay over."

"I can't. My dad doesn't even know I'm here." Izzie didn't make eye contact. She felt like a little kid.

Dylan cheered. She reminded Izzie so much of Kylie sometimes. "You are such a rebel! I love it. Sucks that you can't stay, but okay, don't worry, we'll get you back to your bus before it turns into a pumpkin. We'll just do a birthday lunch instead."

The hours seemed to fly by even if the rain didn't stop. Dylan wound up taking them on a tour of campus in the rain first and they got so wet they had to take a detour to the campus bookstore to buy sweatshirts. It was only after Izzie had plunked down money on a garnet-and-black zip-up that she realized she had no way of sneaking the jacket home. Maybe she could tell her dad that Dylan sent one with Brayden as a birthday gift. *That would work*, she thought as she put it on. But she still felt lousy.

The wind had picked up and so had the storm. Izzie even heard thunder. So instead of leaving campus to eat, they decided to go to the student union. Dylan apologized that Izzie was going to miss out on the Columbia, South Carolina, birthday dining experience, but Izzie was just happy to be out of the rain. The cafeteria had food stations just like Emerald Prep, and Izzie had never met a hamburger she didn't like. Brayden even joked he'd find a candle to stick in her burger. She had only an hour before she had to catch her bus back.

"So how is Kylie?" Dylan asked when they were finally seated and eating. Izzie was so surprised she almost choked on a fry. "Did I say something wrong?"

"She didn't tell you?" Izzie asked.

"Tell me what?" Dylan looked from Izzie to Brayden for answers. "I haven't talked to her in weeks. She's been ignoring my texts."

"That could be because she's busy now that she's dating Hayden, Izzie's brother," Brayden said. Izzie was thankful he didn't add that she and Kylie were fighting.

Dylan smacked the table. "How come no one tells me these things? That's great! You must hang out all the time. I always wished my girlfriends had boyfriends when I did." She picked up a fry. "But that never happens. Girls don't like me around their boyfriends."

"I wonder why," Brayden said under his breath, and Izzie nudged him.

"I am texting her right now to tell her we're together," Dylan declared, and Izzie reached out to stop her. "Oh right! She'd tell Hayden. God, you'd think I'd be better at lying after all the practice I had growing up in EC." Dylan put the phone away, to Izzie's relief. "I miss Kylie. That girl is as real as they come. Next time drag her down here, too."

Suddenly Izzie wasn't hungry. This was the longest she had gone without talking to Kylie since the third grade. That time, they'd had a stupid fight over who had the best pizza in town—Harborside Pizza (Izzie) or Roma (Kylie). Roma went out of business, but what good was being right if her best friend wasn't there to share that pizza with? She quickly changed the subject. "You really seem to like USC."

"I love that I can be part of the crowd here." Dylan looked around the cafeteria. "I know a ton of people already, and yet I don't think I know anyone in here at the moment. I don't have to be on all the time. I needed that after a few months in suffocating EC."

Izzie understood what Dylan meant. In Emerald Cove,

everybody seemed to know everyone's business. Some days Izzie wished she could blend into the wallpaper and disappear, but that wasn't going to happen when she was living under the microscope of a senatorial campaign.

A crack of thunder rattled the student union, and everyone looked out the windows. "Wow, it is really coming down." Dylan frowned. "I hope the frat parties aren't canceled. Last time it stormed like this, some of the roads flooded. There was no bus service for days." Her eyes widened. "Oh shoot. You better check on your ride."

Izzie felt her throat tighten. Brayden was one step ahead of her. He fumbled for the return ticket in his pocket and dialed the number on it for times and route information. When she saw his brow crease, she knew she was in trouble. "They've suspended bus service indefinitely due to flooding," he said, sounding worried.

"Bummer." Dylan took another bite of her burger. "At least now you get to stay!" Dylan obviously didn't realize the severity of the situation, but Izzie did. Her dad was going to flip. Dylan's phone buzzed. "And good news on the party front—my friend Mack says his frat is ready to go, rain or shine." She laughed at something on her phone. "They're calling it a hurricane party and are asking everyone to come in raincoats."

Izzie was no longer listening. She had to hear the bus-company message to believe it, but the calm voice on the recording didn't lie. All bus service in Columbia had been suspended because of flash flooding on major highways. Service would be restored as soon as possible and they apologized for any inconvenience.

Any inconvenience? It was a huge inconvenience!

"What am I going to do?" Izzie asked Brayden. He looked green himself.

"Say you're staying at a friend's house," Dylan suggested. "They'll never know."

Kylie was out. If she said she was with Violet or Nicole, her dad or Aunt Maureen would come get her. Her aunt was probably cooking a birthday dinner right now, and she was going to miss it! This lie was getting too complicated to keep up with. "I'm going to call Mira," Izzie told Brayden. She walked to the quietest corner of the cafeteria. Rain and wind were pelting the windows. She knew without even calling what her dad was going to say. First he was going to be disappointed; then he was going to be mad. She hated the disappointed part more. But she had no choice. If she didn't show up tonight, they would call the police.

Unless...

Izzie quickly scrolled through the contact list on her phone and thought for half a second before calling. "Hello?" a voice answered on the second ring.

"Zoe!" Izzie felt relief at the sound of her voice. "Thank God you picked up!"

Music was playing in the background. "Izzie!" She sounded giddy. "What's up?"

Izzie clutched the phone tightly. "I have a problem. I went to USC today with Brayden and…" She heard someone laughing in the background. "Are you having a party?"

"Don't tell your dad. Some friends of mine couldn't get out on JetBlue because of the weather so they're crashing." Her voice was muffled for a second. "I'll be right there!" she told someone. "Are you having fun?" Her voice sounded crackly and far away, and Izzie wondered if they were going to lose their connection because of the storm.

"Yeah, but listen, Aunt Zoe, I can't get home." Her aunt was laughing at something and Izzie wasn't sure she heard her. "The buses aren't running because of all the rain, and they don't know when they will start up again."

"What?" Zoe was laughing so hard she could barely understand her. "I'm sorry, Izzie. My friends are toddlers. Go away so I can talk to my niece! Yes, I have a niece!"

Izzie was startled. Zoe's friends didn't even know about her?

"Sorry, sweetie. Did you say you can't get home?" Zoe asked. "I'm not surprised. You should see the trees in your backyard. They are practically blowing sideways."

"I know." Izzie looked out the window. "They're doing that here, too. Now I can't get home, and Dad doesn't know I'm here." She could see Brayden watching her. "If I don't get home for my birthday dinner, I'll be grounded for eternity."

"That's right, it's your birthday! I totally forgot! *Happy birthday to you*," she started to sing. "Guys, it's my niece's birthday. Sing!" Izzie held the phone away from her ear as Zoe sang off-key. She was starting to get annoyed, and not just because Zoe didn't remember what day it was. "Izzie? Listen, it's going to be fine. Your dad will be a little mad, but he'll get over it. You'll be home tomorrow."

Izzie leaned against the window. It was cold and, if possible, the rain was falling even harder than it had been a few minutes before. She could hear it pounding on the roof. Her aunt wasn't getting it, so she was just going to have to come out and ask. "Will you come get me?" She'd never heard her voice so small and she hated it. "If you leave now, I can tell them that I am at the Harborside Community Center and need to stay a little later because of the storm, but I'll still get back for dinner and they'll never know I was gone. Please?"

"Hon, I have company." Zoe didn't sound the least bit remorseful. "I wish I could help, but I can't just ditch everybody. Besides, even if I could leave, I do not drive well in the rain. We try not to go out in this stuff in Malibu!" She laughed again. "Remember that time I got stuck on Pacific Coast Highway? Shut up! I did not!"

She was talking to her friend again. Didn't Zoe realize how upset she was?

"You be safe, okay?" Zoe was back. "And call me when you

184

get home tomorrow. I'll give you some pictures as a birthday gift. What? No, that's not lame!" she said to someone else. "Have a great birthday!" Then she hung up without saying good-bye.

Izzie stared at the phone in disbelief. Zoe wasn't coming, and she didn't seem at all concerned that Izzie was in a jam. How could Zoe leave her like this? Izzie dialed the bus line one more time to see if anything had changed, but of course it hadn't. The storm was at full force. It was time to call Mira.

Her sister picked up on the first ring. "Where are you?" she whispered. "The weather is bad and I don't like you being on a bus. Those things tip over all the time."

"Well, you don't have to worry, because I'm not on one," Izzie said quietly. "The buses are canceled because of the storm and I can't get home."

"Oh, Lord, Izzie." The enormity of what she had done hit them both.

Izzie felt her voice waver. "I won't say you knew. I promise."

"I'm just glad you're okay." Izzie could hear Connor running around in the background. Mira sighed. "My mom might go easier on you, so I'll put her on first."

Izzie could hear Mira's muffled voice and then the sound of heels. She psyched herself up for what she knew would follow.

"Isabelle?" Her aunt's voice sounded like a warm blanket.

"Wait till you taste my homemade ravioli and sauce! Hayden just tried to swipe one! Are you headed home? I was getting worried about you being out in this storm. Where are you, again? The community center?"

"No." Izzie was barely audible.

"Violet's?" Her aunt sounded confused. "I'll come get you. I want all of you home. The weatherman said it could rain all night, and they're worried about twisters with this storm system. This is not a day to be out."

That's for sure. Izzie traced the condensation on the window. "I wish you could come get me, but I don't think that will be possible. I'm at USC with Brayden."

"Oh, Isabelle." Aunt Maureen sounded really disappointed.

Flash floods, a strange campus, lying, and making Mira cover for her. What had she been thinking? "Now the buses aren't running and I can't get back." Might as well lay it all on the line. "I was planning to be back for dinner, I swear. I just really wanted to go and…I know what a mess I've caused."

"Just breathe. We'll sort this out." Aunt Maureen didn't sound so sure, though. "Let me get your dad." It only took a second before her dad was on the line.

"Isabelle?" His voice was tense. "Are you okay?"

"I'm fine. I just can't get home." Her voice wavered. "I'm so sorry I lied."

"I-95 is flooded out in several sections, and there are tons of accidents. As much as I don't like it, the safest thing for you to do is to stay put. You hear me?"

"Yes, sir." Izzie's hand was shaking. *That was it?*

Aunt Maureen had picked up the other receiver. "Is Brayden with you?"

"Yes." He was going to blame himself, but she had done this on her own.

"Stay put." Her dad's voice cut in and out. "We'll check on you every few hours."

"Or call us," her aunt added. "I'm charging my cell in case we lose power."

Lose power? She hadn't even thought about that.

"If the buses haven't started running by morning, your father will come get you both. Just be safe," Aunt Maureen said. "Promise?"

They were being so nice. She knew there would be hell to pay later, but for now, they weren't blasting her the way she thought they would. They genuinely sounded concerned. Maybe this was how parents acted. "I promise. And again, I'm really sorry."

"We'll talk tomorrow. Oh, and Isabelle? Happy birthday," he said sadly.

Izzie felt a lump in her throat. She could picture the cozy family room and kitchen adorned with birthday decorations and her aunt's famous sauce cooking on the stove. She'd probably baked a birthday cake, too. This was her first birthday with the family, and thanks to her selfishness, she was missing it.

"Thanks," Izzie choked out. She saw a crack of lightning and stepped away from the window. She wouldn't have believed it earlier, but now she wished she had never left Emerald Cove.

Fourteen

Kellen picked up on the first ring. "Hello?"

"Hey! It's Mira." She was so relieved he had actually answered. The past two days her calls had gone straight to voice mail. "How are you?"

"How are *you*?" Kellen's voice sounded so low on the phone. "My aunt said you guys had some wicked weather down there. She lost power for two days and we saw on the news that a tornado touched down in Raleigh. Scary. Did you guys manage okay?"

She was walking along Main Street after school on the way to her second Selma Simmons class, which was rescheduled for a weekday because of the weather over the weekend. There was still a lot of debris from the storm, but the flowering dogwood trees along the sidewalk were unscathed. "A tree came down in our backyard, but we only lost power for a few hours, so it wasn't so bad."

If you forgot about the fact that Izzie was more than a hundred miles away on her birthday and her parents were worried sick. Or that Dylan had posted pictures of what they had been up to during the storm on her public Facebook page and had tagged Izzie, which meant that everyone could see them, including Grayson Reynolds, who republished them in this morning's paper along with an op-ed piece on her dad's parenting. The pictures weren't scandalous—shots of Izzie and Brayden hugging some people she'd never seen before—but the setting was: a college party with alcohol. Even Brayden got in trouble for that one. Both of them were grounded and could only go to school activities.

But now that Mira's conversations with Kellen were limited to the phone, there didn't seem to be time to tell him all this. So instead she said, "We're fine."

"Good," Kellen said. "I was so worried."

If you were worried, then why haven't you called? she wanted to say. Hayden said guys hated the phone, but if it's the only way you can talk to your girlfriend—correction: *former* girlfriend whom you supposedly still care about—then wouldn't he do it?

"So…is there a reason you called?" he asked.

Mira stopped short on the sidewalk and a mother with a stroller had to maneuver around her. "No." Now she needed a reason to say hi? "I guess I'll let you go, then."

Kellen fumbled for an explanation. "Sorry, I'm just on my way out. They're having a dance at school tonight, and I have to go early to set up."

"I thought you hated school stuff." Mira tried not to sound accusatory, but it was true. She practically had to beg him to go to the Falling into You Fest, and when she'd originally brought up cotillion, he'd thought it sounded lame.

"New school, new attitude, I guess. My parents think it's a good way to fit in, and I don't mind. I like it here already. Especially not having to wear a uniform," Kellen added. "I'm thinking of hosting a bonfire to burn mine."

He didn't seem to miss EP at all. Did that mean he didn't miss her, either? "Send me a picture when you do," she said.

"I will. What are you up to?"

"I'm on my way to that art class I told you about."

"Cool." He sounded like he was on the move, too. "How's that going?"

The teacher hates me, so I pretty much have to fight my way through class, but I'm no quitter. "Great!"

"Take a picture of your latest painting so I can see it." He sounded lighter. "I should go, but I'll talk to you soon, okay?"

When is soon? There seemed to be more she didn't say than things she did these days. "Okay." She hung up. No *I miss you.* No *I wish you were here.* Nothing.

Annoyed, she tossed the phone in her bag and vowed to leave it there the rest of the day. Last week she had missed his call, so now she kept her phone glued to her side in case he checked in. She hated being *that* girl. She had come so far from her phase of total boyfriend adoration (with Taylor) to having a seminormal relationship (Kellen), and now it felt like she was back to square one. She did not want to sit by the phone and wait for his calls, but somehow she couldn't stop herself.

"Oh, mercy, what happened now?" Charlotte cried when she saw Mira's face. She was already at her easel putting the finishing touches on this week's assignment, and Landon was two easels away working on his. The room smelled overwhelmingly of turpentine and paints. He looked up and smiled when he saw her, but she just scowled and threw her art bag down in disgust.

"Aren't you a ray of sunshine," Landon said. "Rough day?"

"Rough *week*." Mira pulled her painting out to look it over one last time. Selma had asked them to paint a vase. It had sounded so simple that Mira and Charlotte figured there was a secret to it that she wasn't telling. Mira had decided that instead of painting her vase a solid color, she would painstakingly draw a square pattern all over it and paint every square a different color. She had used paint that had a glasslike sheen so that every square was iridescent. She dared Selma Simmons to hate this project. She had given it her best effort. Charlotte had, too. Every detail of her Tiffany blue vase was perfect, down to the single yellow rose. "Char, that's stunning."

"Really?" Charlotte looked at it from an angle. "Does the shadow work?"

Landon offered up his own critique. "I like how you mixed up the mediums and used chalk for that element."

Charlotte grinned and looked at Mira conspiratorially. "Well, if you like mine, then you will love Mira's." Mira gave her a look. "Why don't you two discuss it?" Charlotte got up and walked away.

Mira's scowl returned only briefly because seconds later she could feel Landon standing behind her. Their arms touched when he leaned forward to get even closer to her painting. "That is some pattern you have going on. That must have taken forever."

"It did." She'd been working on it every night for a week. "Can I see yours?"

Landon stepped aside, and Mira saw his work. It was a painting of a clear vase full of marbles. His art blew hers and Charlotte's out of the water. "That looks so real! How did you do that?"

"I took a class in photo-realism once." The way he looked directly at her while he talked made her stomach flip-flop. "The teacher said to paint what you see, not what you *want* to see." His fingers swept across his paper to prove a point. "See how distorted some of the marbles are? I did it like that so they would look like a different shape through the glass. My teacher said to focus on the colors. They need to pop." His did. The marbles were a mix of bright yellows and greens that melted together in the jar.

"Sounds like you had a great teacher." Mira couldn't help but sound envious.

Landon pursed his lips. "If she starts with you again, try not to take it to heart."

Mira sort of laughed. "How? I work so hard and she crushes me."

Landon made a face. "Don't take this the wrong way, but did you ever think Selma just might not like you personally?" When Mira gaped, Landon laughed deeply. "I have a hard time imagining anyone not liking you, either, but maybe this has got nothing to do with your work. She just doesn't like you for some reason, so she takes it out on your paintings." He shrugged. "Some people get a rise out of making others uncomfortable."

Mira thought about it for a moment, then cried, "How could anyone not like me?"

"Who doesn't like you?" Charlotte, who'd returned, gave Landon a suspicious glance.

Landon held up his hands in surrender. "I can see I said the wrong thing. Let me explain." He looked around, then pulled both girls toward him. Mira was so close to him that their bodies were touching. "You know your dad nixed funding for a new wing of the North Carolina Museum of Art, right? Well, Selma was a huge supporter of the project, which means you were probably right on that first day," he translated. "She might be holding something against you because of your last name."

Mira blinked. Could that really be true? "How do you know that?"

"The newspaper," Landon said. "Don't you have to read it for your journalism classes?"

She didn't take journalism.

"I wonder why your dad said no to it," Charlotte said.

"He turns down proposals every day," Mira said. "There just isn't enough money in the state budget to do everything everyone wants. People forget that. They think when he says no, he's being an ogre." Mira looked at Landon. Suddenly she felt so much lighter. "Why didn't you just tell me that earlier?"

Landon shrugged. "I didn't know how you'd react."

So it wasn't her. It was her dad. Sure, her work wasn't perfect, but at least now she knew why Selma's critiques were so vicious. She couldn't help but smile.

"Why are you smiling?" Charlotte seemed surprised. "I'm happy if you're happy, but I still think he owes you an apology." She pointed to Landon, who seemed surprised. "For, you know, upsetting you before class." Mira could practically see the matchmaking wheels turning in her friend's head. "I'm thinking dinner would suffice."

Mira's cheeks began to redden. "That's not necessary. He was trying to help."

Charlotte was undeterred. "It would have helped if you knew weeks ago! No, dinner is the least he can do after keeping something like this from you."

Was it her imagination, or did Landon look amused? "I have my Art Equals Love class after this, but if you want to help out, we could grab something after. Least I could do is buy you a soda after causing you so much anguish." Charlotte nodded in agreement.

The sound of Selma Simmons's heels echoing on the wooden floors was enough to end all conversations. The three quickly took their seats and faced forward, waiting for the teacher to start her critiques. For the first time, Mira felt calm about the impending criticism. After a short exercise—paint a pair of eyes in great detail—Selma started her interrogations. The first few students' works were so dreadful Selma skipped the next two rows and went straight to theirs. As she had the past two weeks, she loved Charlotte's work, praising the shadow and the coloring on the vase. Landon, too, got a pat on the back, and the class got a lecture on photo-realism paintings. Finally she turned to Mira.

Mira sat calmly as Selma quietly unclipped her painting and held it up to the class. "Can anyone tell me what is wrong with this vase?" Selma turned in a circle so that everyone in the front and the back could see the painting. No one raised their hand.

"I actually like how distinct it is," Landon said, coming to Mira's defense already. "She really knows how to pair colors. The vase practically shines."

Selma took off her glasses and let them hang from the eyeglass holders, as if the strain of Mira's awful work was too much for her. "I know I told you your work needed more definition, but you've taken that instruction too far," she said to Mira. "Your vase is so busy it outshines the daffodils you put inside it."

Usually this would be about the time when Mira argued with her, but instead she kept quiet. Selma didn't seem quite sure what to make of that.

"This vase is one-dimensional, the colors are dizzying, and the shadow is completely overpowering the rest of the background," Selma continued. "I think you should repeat this assignment." Mira still was quiet. "Don't you have any comments?"

"Not right now, ma'am." Mira was a lady, unlike Selma Simmons, apparently, and she didn't need an audience to tell her teacher how she felt. "We can talk after class."

Selma glared at her. "Whatever you have to say to me, Ms. Monroe, you can say in front of the whole class. We have no secrets in here."

Landon gave Mira a wicked grin that seemed to say "go for it!"

Mira took a deep breath. "While I appreciate your criticism, and I know I have a lot to learn, I no longer respect your opinion of my work."

Selma glared at her. "Excuse me?"

"You are a talented artist, but a good teacher judges a student based on her work, not what her last name is." Selma's eyes fluttered with recognition. "I hope you can remember that when I redo this assignment." Mira gave Selma a bright smile. A true belle always ended a conversation pleasantly.

Selma mumbled something Mira couldn't understand, then skipped the rest of the critiques and told the students to "free paint" for the remainder of their time because she suddenly had a migraine. Mira could barely contain herself. She happily took out her colored pencils and sketched a drawing of their backyard after the storm. Every once in a while she would look up and catch Selma staring, her cheeks tinged a pink hue.

When class finally let out and Selma had left the building, Landon surprised Mira by lifting her into the air and spinning her around. Mira didn't mind one bit.

"That was incredible!" Mira gushed as Charlotte quietly moved away to avoid ruining the moment. "Did you see Selma's face?"

"You schooled her!" Landon said. "And in such a smooth way even I felt guilty. And I did nothing wrong." Mira laughed. "Classy move."

Mira jokingly curtsied, but she was serious when she looked into his dark eyes. "Thank you for telling me that. I don't know how you remembered a newspaper story about my dad, but that tip couldn't have come at a better time." She thought of her crappy conversation with Kellen and her worries on the way to Selma's class.

Landon looked like he had something to say, but they both realized they weren't alone. Emerald Arts was already resetting the room for the next class. The easels were being moved aside to create space for large, paint-splattered tables. A girl was putting plastic cups of paint and jars full of water on the tables. Others started to trickle in, too, getting right to work. Everyone seemed excited to see Landon. The other volunteers chatted as they brought out buckets of used brushes alongside paint smocks and lampshades. Mira wasn't sure what those were for. All she knew was that kids were waiting eagerly in the hallway, some younger than Connor. When one of the girls beckoned them to come in, everyone seemed to know exactly where to go.

"Are you sure it's okay I'm here?" Mira felt a little uncomfortable.

Landon put a hand on her back, and Mira stiffened slightly. "We could use the help. Let me introduce you to everyone." He pointed out various volunteers before finally introducing her to the nine-year-old girl he worked with in class. "Don't be surprised if Jillian is a little shy at first,"

Landon warned as he led her over to a peanut of a girl with shoulder-length straight hair. She was wearing a Taylor Swift T.

"Jilly Bean, this is Mira. Mira, meet Jilly Bean." Landon made the introductions.

"Hi, Jillian," Mira said brightly.

"Hey." Jillian didn't make eye contact. "Landon, do you have to call me Jilly Bean around other people?" she whispered. "It's embarrassing."

Landon ruffled her shoulders. "If Taylor Swift was calling you that, I bet you wouldn't mind." He sang a few lines from one of Taylor's songs.

"*You* listen to Taylor Swift?" Mira asked incredulously.

Landon's cheeks colored slightly. "Maybe."

At the mention of Taylor, Jillian opened up. "Not *maybe*. He knows all her songs."

"Now you're embarrassing *me*." Landon wouldn't look at Mira as he rearranged Jillian's art supplies. There were small containers of what looked like crushed eggshells, each container holding a different color shell.

"Do you like Taylor Swift?" Jillian looked tentatively at Mira.

"Who doesn't like the goddess of pop country music?" Mira said. "Right, Landon?" He pretended to be hard of hearing while he took out construction paper and glue and placed them in front of Jillian.

Jillian clearly was catching on to the shaming. "He likes Justin Bieber, too. He sang one of his songs to me for my birthday." Mira started to laugh uncontrollably.

Landon let some crushed pink eggshells fall through his fingers back into the container. "Stop giving away my secrets! I'm starting to regret inviting you here," he grumbled jokingly to Mira.

"Why do you care what she thinks?" Jillian asked. "Is she your *girlfriend*?"

Mira stopped laughing, and she and Landon looked at each other. His cheeks grew more pink, and she was sure hers were the same color. "We're just friends." His eyes never left Mira's face. "Mira has a boyfriend."

Jillian's face fell. "You do?"

Mira felt an overwhelming urge to correct that statement. "*Had* a boyfriend. He moved away a few weeks ago." She looked at Jillian even though she knew Landon was watching her. It was a relief to say that out loud. It felt like Kellen had understood things were over the minute he stepped on that plane, but she'd needed time to wrap her head around the change. She and Kellen would always have a connection, but she needed to keep reminding herself that they weren't a couple anymore. She couldn't continue to act like they were one, because doing that only hurt one person: herself.

"Taylor Swift has had a lot of famous breakups, and she writes songs about them." Jillian was playing with the dyed eggshells as she gave Mira the rundown of Taylor's love life. "It probably has to do with all the touring she does."

Landon shook his head. "Darn touring."

"If I do well on my next math test, Landon promised he'd try to get tickets to a Taylor Swift concert. She's coming to the Greensboro Coliseum this summer." Jillian stared at the paint-splattered table. "But he said he'll only take me if I get a B."

"There have to be rules if you want me to take you to hear Taylor whine about her love life." Landon handed her a lamp-shade. Some of the other groups had already started working. "So, Bean, today we're gluing eggshells on this shade. You can make whatever design you like." Jillian stared at her construc-tion paper for inspiration. "Why don't you sketch a design on the shade first?" She nodded.

Mira followed Landon over to the counter to get more glue. Jillian had put her iPod earbuds in and was singing along to a Taylor song. "She's a really sweet kid," Mira said, and hesi-tated. "What qualified her for a class like this?"

"Everyone's story is different," Landon explained. "Some kids are on the autism spectrum or have other special needs. Some come from bad homes. Jillian's parents were going through a really bad divorce, and she wasn't coping well at school. She needed a shot of self-esteem. She's been with me for about a year now, and she's come a long way. I can't believe how easily she opened up to you." He looked over at her. "She never would have done that a few months ago."

target because she had given the press so much to work with from the beginning.

"Just ignore them," her dad had said as if it were the easiest thing in the world.

"I think getting away is nice, but USC is a few hours away," Mira's mom said.

"I thought I could stay at Dylan's dorm overnight and come back in the morning," Izzie explained. "Brayden wants to celebrate my birthday while we are there. It could be fun."

Warning! Warning! Mira wanted to scream. She knew her parents were going to flip, but there was no way to warn Izzie.

"With Brayden's parents?" Mira's mom looked tense.

Izzie shook her head. "Mrs. Townsend and Dylan haven't spoken since she left. Brayden and I were going to take the bus since his mom doesn't want him driving so far."

Mira's mom looked like she was going to pass out. "I... Bill?"

"Senator Monroe?" A police officer approached them. "We need to get you to the start of the parade, sir."

"Yes, one second," he told him pleasantly, and turned to Izzie. "We can talk more about this later, but I think the answer will be the same. I am sorry, Isabelle, but it's just not appropriate for you to be visiting a college campus overnight."

"Why?" Izzie sounded flustered. "Grams used to let me stay overnight at my friends' houses all the time."

"Bill, you're making too big of a deal out of this," Zoe agreed.

"This does not concern you," Mira's dad said tightly. A photographer kept taking pictures. Mira suspected he was from the *Gazette*.

For some reason, her dad's comment seemed to tick Zoe off. "She's almost sixteen, Bill. You can't monitor every move she makes. She's not a caged bird."

Izzie turned to Mira's mom while they argued. "I really can't go?"

Mira's mom glanced at her husband. The cop was pulling him away and Zoe followed unhappily. "Let's discuss this tonight, okay?" she said. "You just enjoy the parade." She smiled as the photographer took a picture from a distance.

Mira didn't say anything, but she knew what her parents' response would be tonight, and the next day and the day after that. Tenth-grade girls did not get to go away with their boyfriends overnight. Ever.

It was nice to see a guy so invested in a kid like that. "You really care about her."

Landon didn't hesitate. "Of course." He leaned over and whispered in her ear. "And I already got the Taylor Swift tickets. She's going whether she gets a B or not." He grinned proudly. "The only problem is I got stuck with four seats even though I only need two. This guy on eBay wouldn't split his four, so I bought all of them. I already had been outbid on another set, so I didn't want to let these go. I used all my birthday money, but Jilly Bean deserves it."

That might have been the cutest thing she'd ever heard a guy say.

"So now I have two extra tickets." Landon leaned on the sink and tried to look cool even though the topic was totally adorkable. "Know anyone who might want to see Taylor Swift with me?"

"Charlotte is obsessed with her," Mira teased, and he looked slightly disappointed. "I don't think she's so bad, either. If you're asking."

The corners of his mouth turned up. "I'm asking. So it's a date," he said, and she felt her stomach lurch. "But not until July." They both laughed. "I'm not sure that will fly in Charlotte's book. After all, she did say I owe you dinner for withholding valuable intel on Selma Simmons."

Mira tried hard not to smile. "That is true. So how do we fix this?"

"I take you out," he said simply. "Tonight, though, is just the dress rehearsal. You guys didn't really give me time to come up with a plan." He looked at her searchingly. "Maybe next time you'll let me take you out for real."

Her whole body tingled. Her voice was small but clear. "It's a deal."

Fifteen

Zoe had the music cranked up so loud that Izzie had no choice but to enter the pool house without knocking. She found her aunt huddled over her laptop in the kitchen while Adele played at full blast. Zoe didn't notice Izzie till she was standing in front of her.

"You almost gave me a heart attack!" Zoe said, clutching her yoga-toned stomach.

"You're going to have a heart attack if you don't lower that music." Izzie walked over to Zoe's iPod dock, which was on the kitchen counter next to a pile of unwashed dishes and a half-empty Chinese food container, and lowered the music from deafening to normal. The ringing in her ears stopped. "I could hear Adele from inside the house."

"Sorry!" Zoe barely looked at her as she clicked away on

her laptop, her mouse swirling in circles. "I work best when the music is loud, and right now I have a monster assignment that is way overdue—two actually. I can't do anything else till I'm finished."

I can see that, Izzie thought. She could only imagine how Aunt Maureen would react if she saw the pool house like this. In addition to the dishes piled in the sink, there were takeout boxes stacked like magazines, dirty laundry on the floor, a mound of unfolded clothes on a living room chair, and camera equipment and backdrops everywhere. Zoe was in yoga pants and an oversize sweatshirt with her hair piled on top of her head with what looked like chopsticks. "I didn't know you were working," Izzie said. "I'll come back."

"Stay. I'm...done!" Zoe clicked Send and looked up triumphantly. "Gwen and Gavin's cute family pictures are in their in-box, and crusty Vivian Ingram has her photos of her precious Founders Day parade." She slammed the laptop closed and flung herself from the kitchen chair to the couch. "Talk to me. I feel like I haven't seen you in ages."

"It's been almost a week," Izzie said. A whole week since she had asked Zoe to help her out of that bind at USC and Zoe had flat out said no. Zoe hadn't called or stopped by once to check on her. Didn't she wonder how things worked out?

"Has it been that long?" Zoe pulled out one of her chopsticks and scratched her head. "I guess I did fly to New York

Tuesday for Gwen and Gavin, then back here Thursday, and Vivian has been calling every day for those pictures." Zoe rolled her eyes. She pushed the pile of clothes Izzie thought were clean onto the floor and motioned for Izzie to sit. "But enough about me. Did you have fun at USC?"

Izzie blinked. Zoe had to be joking. "I got grounded for going without permission and missed my birthday dinner, so I guess you could say no, I didn't have too much fun."

Zoe slapped her forehead. "I totally forgot. So Bill was really mad? Even on your birthday? God, he's such a stickler for rules. I'm sorry I couldn't come get you."

It still bothered Izzie that Zoe had blown her off. Her aunt had said she was hanging around EC to get to know her better. Instead, they'd barely bonded and Zoe had totally forgotten her birthday. She wasn't sure what Zoe wanted her to say.

"How long are you grounded for?" Zoe jumped up and started opening cabinets.

"Two weeks." Izzie watched Zoe open all the cabinets till she found a cup. Then she went to the fridge and poured herself a glass of sweet tea. She didn't offer Izzie one. "I can go to swim team practice and work on the booth for the Founders Day Street Fair, which is tomorrow, and the gala on Sunday, but other than that I am under house arrest." Not hanging out with Brayden was the worst part about being grounded. Thank God she got to see him at school.

Zoe grinned. "They didn't say anything about not visiting the pool house, though. You can chill out here as long as you like. You can even say you're here and then really go meet up with Brayden. I'm cool covering for you."

Izzie didn't need any more problems than she already had. "That's okay. I'm going to see him tomorrow and Sunday anyway." Plus he had given her a sweet "grounding survival kit" at school that had her favorite Ice Breakers gum, a Butter Me Up cookie from town, and a note saying he had DVR'd her favorite shows and a Dara Torres swim competition, since she was banned from the TV. In the boyfriend category, Brayden couldn't be beat.

"Did Grams ever ground you?" Zoe wanted to know. "She never punished me or your mom. She was a total pushover."

"Grams was more of a talker," Izzie said. "She never took away TV or gave me curfews. My dad might not have, either, if those pictures hadn't turned up on Facebook."

Zoe's arched eyebrows raised. "Facebook?"

Izzie grimaced. "Brayden's sister has a public Facebook profile, and she posted photos of us hanging out at this party we went to for my birthday." Izzie sorted through the mound of newspapers on the coffee table. She pulled out the Monday edition of the *North Carolina Gazette* and showed her the headline: **Senator Monroe Lets His Teenage Daughter Run Wild, A report by Grayson Reynolds.** It showed one of Dylan's grainy Facebook photos of Izzie standing in a frat house next to a girl wearing a USC sweatshirt. Her dad was unhappy about the party, but what was she supposed to do on a college campus on a Saturday night? Lock herself in Dylan's room? Izzie had figured that if she was stuck there, she might as well find a way to have fun.

"Lord, talk about getting caught in the act!" Zoe curled her legs under her and tugged at her fuzzy socks. She could have passed for one of Izzie's friends even though she was in her thirties. "You had no way home. What were you supposed to do, stay in? God, he overreacts." There was that edge to her voice again. It was the same one she had heard Zoe use on her dad at the parade. "One time he was furious at your mom and me because we went to see this band in a dicey Queens neighborhood. He said he should have been there to play bodyguard. He likes being in control, I think."

"He says he's trying to protect me, but sometimes I feel like he doesn't trust me." It felt weird to talk about her dad to Zoe. "I told him I've been on my own for years, with Grams so sick, and I've managed fine. I could handle a trip to USC."

"Of course you could," Zoe agreed. "I was the same way you are. That's why I wasn't worried about you in the storm. I knew you could take care of yourself."

Izzie played with a loose strand on one of the throw pillows. "The voters don't see it that way. Dad says that to them it looks like I don't listen." She yanked the loose thread from the pillow, causing another string to unravel. "I don't want to make him look bad in the middle of a campaign, but I hate being under a microscope. As long as he's in the news, I am stuck in the public eye, too."

Zoe took the other chopstick out of her hair as if the conversation was giving her a headache. "One thing I will say about your dad is that he is magnetic. People are drawn to him, and that can be both good and bad. It was the same way when he was dating your mom," she said softly. "He was only a rookie ballplayer back then, so he was always worried about how it would look if he was seen at this bar or doing something with your mom. It drove us crazy."

"Us?" Izzie made herself comfortable on the couch. This was the kind of conversation she'd been hoping to have with Zoe for a long time.

"Your mom," Zoe corrected. "She didn't like being micromanaged. She never worried about image, and it drove her crazy that Bill did."

Izzie had avoided this question ever since Zoe showed up on the Monroes' doorstep. "So is that why my parents broke up?"

Zoe hesitated. "I don't know. I wasn't in the relationship; they were."

"Dad won't talk about it. He just says they grew apart." Izzie wrapped the pillow's loose thread around her finger, making it tight, and then loosening it again. "But they weren't together that long. How could they grow apart? Did they have a fight?" Izzie pushed. "I'm old enough to know."

Zoe exhaled slowly. "You're right." She played with the chopsticks in her hand. "It wasn't a dramatic fight or anything. In the end, your mom just knew their relationship could never work long-term. Your dad was a rising baseball star and your mom was always going to come second to his career. She deserved to be more than just a ballplayer's wife," Zoe said determinedly. "The other guys on his team always had, like, three girlfriends and at least two more groupies on the side. Bill *seemed* faithful to your mom, but how long could that really last?"

Her dad didn't seem like the cheating type, but Zoe looked so annoyed Izzie didn't want to argue.

"We heard the rumors all summer long that he could be traded, and your mom didn't want to do the long-distance thing. That never works. So when he got the official word he was moving on, she stopped taking his calls. She wouldn't see him when he dropped by. I tried to talk to her, but she was determined not to be a lovesick idiot and she wasn't willing to follow him around the country. She said it was better to break up before she got hurt. She didn't know she was pregnant." Zoe wouldn't look at her. "I thought with him leaving, she'd stay, but she said the memories were too much. She left New York, and me, before I could talk some sense into her."

Izzie couldn't decide how to feel. Was her mom so wrong

to take control of her life? "I get why Mom wouldn't have wanted to be number two, but when she realized she was pregnant, why didn't she tell Dad about me?"

"I don't know." Zoe stared intently at her. She looked so much like Izzie's mom. It was an eerie feeling. "I know this is hard for you to understand, but things worked out for the best. Your parents never would have lasted, and Maureen is a doll."

The words stung. She loved her aunt, too, but how could Zoe be so blunt about her own sister? "Why do you hate my dad so much?"

"I don't hate your dad. I just hate how concerned he is with public image. Your free spirit is one of your greatest gifts, and I don't like how he's tried to stifle yours." Zoe sounded angry. "If you were with me, I'd let you run your own life. Swim with sharks, shave your head, take a year off before college, you can do it all, as long as you tell me *why* you want to do it." Zoe's face lit up from the sunlight streaming through the windows. "Your grandmother gave me freedom, but she wasn't supportive. You need both and if you don't have those things, then you have to go out and find them for yourself. That's why I left and never looked back."

The room was so quiet Izzie could hear the air-conditioning kick on. Maybe she and Zoe were more alike than she'd thought. Izzie hadn't let her upbringing hold her back in life so far, and she wasn't about to let it start now.

"You're sixteen," Zoe said quietly. "I don't know if your

dad told you that you have a choice, but you do." Izzie didn't understand what she was talking about. "If you're unhappy here, you can come back with me to California."

"Wh-what?" Izzie stammered.

"California," Zoe repeated, shifting slightly. "Oh, Izzie, you'd love it there. It's so laid-back and I'm so much more chill when I'm home. Just being on the East Coast is giving me hives. I have to get out of here and soon, and you could come. I wouldn't give you big rules. Just brush your teeth and leave a note if you're going out. We'd be like sisters," she said with a smile. "We'd have so much fun. You'd love my friends and…"

Come back with me to California. Was Zoe serious? Izzie could see her mouth moving, but she couldn't believe what Zoe was saying. Could she really just pick up and move to California with an aunt she barely knew? Was that even allowed? And if it was, what about her and Brayden? And her and Mira, Connor, Hayden, Kylie (even though they weren't speaking), her friends, her swim team… Izzie's mind was reeling.

"So you'll think about it?" Zoe was asking. "Don't worry about what your dad will say. Just decide what *you* want and try to decide soon, because I give it another two weeks before I lose it completely." She laughed. "It was fun to be back for a split second, but now I am itching for a change again. We could go to Cali first, but then I'm thinking we head down to Mexico for a bit. I go there in April anyway, but we could stay on and I could do some work, too."

"I have school," Izzie reminded her.

"That's right. You're still in school." Zoe's smile seemed to deflate slightly. "We will work it out. Maybe we'll do home-schooling!" she said with renewed energy. "So many of my friends' kids—well, the ones who have kids—do that and they say it's great."

Homeschooling? Mexico? With someone who barely gave her the time of day as it was? Izzie jumped up, afraid to hear another word. She felt guilty for even entertaining Zoe's suggestion. "I should go before Aunt Maureen looks for me." Izzie eyed the mess again. On top of the pile was a purple paper mask. It was her sweet-sixteen invite.

Zoe noticed her looking at the invitation and picked it up. "Oh! Your party is in April, isn't it? I guess we could go to Mexico a little later than planned." She bit her lip. "I'll figure it out. The most important thing is whether you want to come home with me."

"About that," Izzie started to say.

"Don't worry," Zoe interrupted. "This stays between us till you say otherwise."

Izzie was relieved to have an out. She stepped over a tripod on its side and walked to the door. "Will I see you tomorrow at the street fair? Our booth looks amazing. Mira and some guy from her art class are doing a huge mural." She waited for Zoe to say no.

Zoe flung the invite onto the pile on the table and hopped

off the couch. "Um, I think so. Vivian needs me to take pictures. I know I wrote the time down somewhere."

"The fair starts at ten AM," Izzie told her. "I'm sure she wants you there earlier."

Zoe walked over and tugged on Izzie's chin. "See what I mean? We'd make a great team." Izzie didn't answer her. She just let herself out and Zoe followed. "Wow, it must be seventy degrees. I could use some air after being cooped up for twenty-four hours. Want to take a walk and get pizza?"

"I'm grounded," Izzie reminded her. It was a shame, too, because it was a beautiful afternoon. It was supposed to be even nicer tomorrow for the street fair.

"Oh please." Zoe stripped off her socks and threw them inside. Then she slipped on a pair of flip-flops near the front-door mat. "They won't even know you're gone." Zoe hooked her arm through hers. Izzie couldn't believe Zoe was leaving the house in yoga pants with no makeup, and her hair so disheveled. *Oh, geez, I am starting to think like Mira,* she thought ruefully.

They'd barely made it past the pool when they heard talking. Zoe stopped short when she saw Hayden, Kylie, and Kylie's mom walking toward them.

"Well, isn't this a picture!" Mrs. Brooks said when she saw Zoe and Izzie. "I never thought I'd see the day when you two were together." Izzie felt Zoe stiffen.

Izzie eyed Hayden and Kylie. Neither of them looked at her. "Hi, Mrs. Brooks."

Kylie's mom pulled Izzie out of Zoe's grasp and in for a tighter hug than usual. "Hey, darlin'. Just getting a tour of your fancy house here. Good thing your parents aren't home. They won't notice anything missing." She started to laugh. "Just kidding!"

"Mom," Kylie said through gritted teeth. Izzie felt bad for her. Kylie's mom could be embarrassing, kind of like Kylie, but both had good hearts.

"It's okay. My mom loves any excuse to shop." Hayden lightened the mood. "Just don't touch the sports equipment. That's mine."

"See, Kylie girl?" Mrs. Brooks nudged her daughter. "Hayden knows I'm joking. I don't have sticky fingers like this one here." She looked at Zoe. "She once stole the last bagel in the cafeteria right out from under me."

Zoe laughed. "That is not stealing, Patty. I just moved faster than you in the cafeteria line. You had another twenty pounds on you then." Kylie and Izzie quickly glanced at each other. It looked like this was going to turn ugly.

Mrs. Brooks pursed her lip-glossed lips. "True. I never did move like you did. You're always on the go. When are you picking up and leaving town? Tomorrow?"

"In a few weeks." Zoe's tone changed. "Throwing me a going-away party? I hear that friends do that sort of thing."

Mrs. Brooks's eyes narrowed. "It's hard to throw something like that when you never know when a person is coming or going."

"If you want a going-away party, talk to Mira," Hayden jumped in. Izzie noticed him take Kylie's hand. "She can plan one in her sleep. Right, Iz?" Hayden was acknowledging her for the first time in days. Both of them knew how uncomfortable this conversation was getting for everyone.

"Right!" Izzie spoke up. "She could sic our party planner on you in under an hour if you are interested." Zoe and Kylie's mom just continued to stare at each other.

"Your aunt should have been a magician," Mrs. Brooks said to Izzie. "She loves to make a mess and then disappear."

"Oh, please, Patty!" Zoe threw up her arms. "Here we go again."

"Chloe needed you," Mrs. Brooks said, and Izzie froze. "But you were too selfish to come back and make things right with her. You never got to know your niece or talk things out with your mama. I would have told you that years ago, but every time I brought up your sister's name, you threatened to hang up on me! You called so infrequently as it was. You couldn't bother to turn up until Chloe was buried!"

Izzie felt momentarily stunned. "What did you say?" Mrs. Brooks paled, and Izzie knew she was telling the truth. She looked at Zoe. "You knew my mom died?" Zoe looked away.

Mrs. Brooks spoke up. "She was at the funeral for about thirty seconds."

"What?" Izzie felt like her legs were going to give out. "But

I didn't see you there. I would have remembered someone who looked like my mom."

"I was hiding a bit so no one would recognize me," Zoe admitted shamefully, and Izzie's face twisted angrily. Zoe reached for her and almost tripped. "It's not that I didn't want to meet you. Your grandmother wouldn't let me! She was so mad that I said no about the friggin' guardianship that she made me leave before I even got to go up and say good-bye to Chloe." Zoe's voice was shaky. "I wanted to tell you the truth now that I know you, I swear, but I didn't want to hurt you any more than I had!" Izzie stared at the ground. "I was young. I didn't know how to deal with a kid of my own."

All the pieces were starting to click together. "So Grams didn't just ask you to be my guardian last year; she also asked when my mom died," Izzie realized. "You turned her down twice." Her voice cracked, and Kylie put her hand on her back to steady her.

Zoe could barely look at Izzie. "I was upset about losing my sister who I hadn't seen in years. I couldn't take care of her kid! Try to understand what I was feeling."

"What *you* were feeling?" Izzie focused on breathing. "I lost my mom."

Zoe reached out again, and Kylie blocked her. "I was self-ish." Zoe's voice wavered. "But I'm here now and I want to take care of you. Does it really matter when I decided I wanted to be in your life?"

"Yes!" Izzie said incredulously. She couldn't look at Zoe one second longer. She took off for the side gate and heard yelling—it could have been Mrs. Brooks and Zoe for all she knew—but she didn't stop till she got tackled to the ground. "Let go, Kylie!"

"No!" Kylie struggled against Izzie's strength. "You can't run away again!"

"I am not running away! I just don't want to deal with this right now!" Izzie yelled, and even as she said the words, she felt her will to fight slip away.

This was what Kylie did. She pushed problems out into the open, and she forced her friends to do the same. Kylie's arms unlocked. She helped Izzie up and they looked at each other. "Sorry. I thought you were going to run, and that would be a dumb move since Zoe is the one who was a total jerk."

"She *is* a jerk." Izzie smoothed her hair, plucking a twig out of it. "I can't believe she lied to me like that. She abandoned me," she said quietly. "Twice."

It was the first time they'd talked since their fight. Were they still fighting? Izzie wasn't sure, because Kylie was here now when she needed her most.

"But she's back. That must mean something," Kylie said. "She knows she made a mistake and she's trying to make up for it."

Kylie had a point. Izzie had gone through every stage of anger when she found out Zoe didn't want her—anger at her, anger at Grams, anger at herself for not being good enough to be wanted—she didn't think she had enough fuel left to go through the cycle again. Abandoning her niece once was the same thing as doing it twice. Right?

"My mom said Zoe has always been selfish," Kylie added. "When Grams said she was going to ask Zoe to be your guardian last summer, my mom thought it was a bad idea. She knew there was no way Zoe was going to be able to take care of a teenager."

Izzie's face darkened. "You knew about Zoe all this time?"

"N-no," Kylie stammered. "I mean, not last year. My mom only told me the story a few weeks ago." She sounded ashamed when she saw Izzie's crushed expression. "But we weren't talking. How was I supposed to tell you something like that? You were already so mad at me as it was!"

How could Kylie hold back information like that? Fight or no fight, Izzie wouldn't have done the same to Kylie. "And now I'm even more angry. You and I? We're done," she said shakily, and Kylie's face fell. Then Izzie turned toward the house and took off at a run. She half expected Kylie to tackle her again, but she made it to the front door without so much as a single scratch.

Sixteen

When the bells in the clock tower rang 10 AM, the Butterflies let out a loud cheer. This famous piece of EC history only rang on ceremonial occasions, and the Founders Day Street Fair was one of them. As the clock continued to chime, the Butterflies stood with Mrs. Fitz in front of their booth and listened to final instructions.

"Ladies, the crowds will be here any minute," Savannah told the group as Izzie looked like she was resisting the urge to roll her eyes. "I know—*we* know," she said, glancing quickly at her cochair, "how hard you've worked on this project. So let's give all we've got and wow EC with our amazing booth that speaks to our town's history!"

Another cheer went up, and Mira tried not to laugh. It was funny how on board Savannah was with the mining station now that it was the booth everyone was talking about. Ever since they had started setting up right around dawn, street-fair vendors had been stopping by to see what they were doing. While the other stands were the same ones that were there every year—old-timey photo booth, candle making, Founders Day souvenirs, traditional Emerald Cove food favorites like green bagels and green spaghetti, assorted old-school carnival games and other crafts—Savannah and Izzie had created a booth that was one of a kind. Mira thought Izzie would be celebrating, but she seemed subdued.

"Let's go over your jobs one more time." Izzie read from her planner. "Mira and Lea, you give out the jewel bags. Lauren and Millie, you make sure each child decorates their own mining hat at the prep station outside the tent. Charlotte, you can—"

Savannah interrupted sweetly. "I thought we agreed Millie would wave people over to the booth. She's so personable." She leaned over to look at Izzie's notes, as if Izzie were reading them wrong, and her butterfly wings almost hit Izzie in the face.

Mira never thought she'd see the day when Izzie would wear pink fairy wings in public. Everyone looked so cute that Mira wanted to snap a picture of the club in them, but she didn't want to face Izzie's wrath. She seemed grouchy, which was a shame because the booth looked amazing.

"Mira, are the inside murals done?" Izzie asked.

"Pretty much," she replied pleasantly, and Izzie gave her a stern look.

"Well, you better make sure everything is dry." Izzie glanced down the street at the approaching crowd. "We're about to get our first customers."

Most street fairs had a start time and an end time, but the Founders Day Street Fair had an actual starting *gate*. Main Street was blocked off at one end by a green ribbon. When the official bells tolled, the mayor would have someone ceremonially help her cut the ribbon to signify the beginning of the fair. It was the same tradition they'd followed since the first street fair in 1949. (EC was not one to break with tradition.) Mira's dad was doing the ribbon cutting today, and the only reason the girls had gotten out of it was because of their duties at the booth. Izzie seemed relieved. She would kill someone if she had to appear at a photo op in a pink shirt and glittery wings.

Mira headed into the booth, which was clearly marked by a huge banner that said *Emerald Cove Mining Company*. The first thing people would see when they walked under that banner was a table stacked with mining hats and tons of stickers and glitter pens for decorating. Once the kids finished their hats, they would be sent to the second table to gather mining tools—a shovel for digging, a tray for sifting for jewels, and a bag for carrying loot. While there, one of the club members would talk to the parents about the Butterflies' charity mission. Izzie had printed a picture of the kids at the

Emerald Cove Children's Hospital on poster board along with a statement about the Butterflies' plan to donate all proceeds. One of the girls' jobs was to collect the donation (as little as a dollar), but no child would be turned away if they didn't have the money. After that, it was time to dig for treasure. Kids would enter the tent, which was painted to look like a mining tunnel. That's where Mira and Landon came in. She was headed back there when her phone rang. It was Kellen. Mira ducked out of their booth area again and tried to find a quiet spot, which was tough to do with all the people around. A kid walking by Mira saw the mining sign and started to shriek. It felt like he was doing it right in her ear. "Hey!" she yelled to be heard.

Kellen started to laugh. "Where are you? Was that Connor?"

"No." She watched as the boy and his mom got in line. Mira couldn't believe how quickly the line was growing and she still had to finish up inside. She'd have to make this a quick call. "I'm at the Founders Day Street Fair."

"Ah, I forgot that was coming up," Kellen said, even though she was sure she'd mentioned it at least half a dozen times when they'd talked. "What are the Butterflies handing out at their booth this year? Green Rice Krispies treats?"

"No." Mira couldn't help but grin. "I won't say it wasn't suggested, though. This year we're doing a mining booth where kids can mine for fake jewels."

"Nice," he said. "Savannah does realize real jewels are not buried in there, right?"

Mira laughed. "I hope so." She saw Izzie come out of the booth and look around with a scowl. "Listen, I hate to cut you off, but I haven't finished painting one of the murals, and if Izzie finds out, she's going to kill me."

"Oh. Okay." He actually sounded disappointed. "I just called to catch up. I haven't heard from you in a while."

It had been a week, actually. Mira had finally realized that talking to Kellen almost every day wasn't helping. It was hurting. So she made Charlotte promise to monitor her calls and she gave Izzie her phone when they were home—all so she would stop calling Kellen. "I'm sorry," Mira said. "With Founders Day going on, it's been crazy."

"So nothing's wrong?" Kellen pried.

Mira thought about laying it out for him. How much she'd missed him those first few weeks. How much it'd hurt when he didn't call or when he acted uninterested about what was going on in EC, but what would be the point? Getting mad at him wasn't going to make any of this easier. So instead, she said, "No. I knew you were busy with your new school and I've had a lot going on with the Butterflies." But that wasn't totally the truth, either. "And I thought it might be better if we didn't check in every day anymore," she admitted. "It's too hard." *For me*, she didn't add.

"I know." Kellen's voice was quiet.

"So where do we go from here?" Mira asked. "Do we just stop talking?" She didn't want that, either.

"I'd hate to think that just because we're no longer in the same state, we're not going to be friends," he said. "Isn't this why Facebook was invented?"

Mira smiled. *Friends.* Maybe that was what they were always meant to be. Even though she was still getting to know Landon, being around him felt more natural than it ever had with Kellen. Kellen felt like a term paper she had no clue how to finish. She would always remember him, but her friends were right; it was probably time to let him go. "I expect to see a post on my wall when I get home tonight," Mira teased.

"Will do," Kellen said. "Now go finish that mural before Izzie hunts you down."

Mira actually felt lighter when she hung up. She snuck around the back of the booth and slipped inside the tent without Izzie noticing. Landon was putting the finishing touches on one of the mine walls. She was about to say something about wrapping things up when she heard him humming. "Are you singing a Taylor Swift song?"

Landon looked guilty when he turned around. He had paint on his right cheek and a dab of black glitter paint over his eyes. She decided not to tell him. He looked even cuter when he was an art-house mess. "Who? Me? Nope."

Mira laughed. "Any chance Jillian's mom is bringing her today? You can duet."

Landon gave her a wry look, then went back to his mural. He couldn't stop messing with it, even though you could hear the people already in line outside the tent. "I think around lunchtime. There!" He dropped his brush in a cup of water. "What do you think?"

The cave he'd painted on the tent walls looked lifelike. On one wall he'd painted a cave entrance that appeared blocked off by a boarded-up sign. The dreary brown cave walls were jazzed up with rocks and specks of green and gold glitter that hinted at emeralds and gold. Landon had even added a few shovels and mining tools lying around.

"My brother Connor is going to flip," Mira said in awe. "This looks so real."

Landon wiped his paint-covered hands on his jeans and looked at the tent surrounding them. "You didn't do such a bad job yourself. If Selma were grading you on this project, I bet you'd get your second 'exceptional work' remark of the semester."

Mira grinned. "I'm not sure my fruit bowl was exceptional, but at least she seems to be overlooking my last name now." The fruit bowl she'd painted the other day got huge points for the realism of her peach and grapes, while her banana left something to be desired. But that was okay. At least she was getting a real critique for a change.

Landon started to pull off his long-sleeved navy T, and Mira felt dizzy. *Is he taking off his shirt? Why is he taking off his shirt? Maybe I'll see his abs!* Then she realized he had a St. Barnard's logo T-shirt underneath. It *was* kind of warm for March. Mira tried not to look disappointed that Landon wasn't going shirtless after all.

"I'd still give you an A for excellent effort," Landon said. "I can't believe you thought you could finish this up yourself this morning."

"I didn't have a choice." Mira leaned on one of the two large sandboxes Kylie and Hayden had built. One was filled with water for cleaning and finding the gems. The other was full of sand for mining. "Izzie is such a stress ball about cochairing. If I had told her I hadn't finished, she would have wigged out."

Landon began cleaning up all their paint supplies. "Yeah, your sister seems a little rough around the edges, but I would be, too, if I'd been through what she has."

Mira looked up from the sand table, where she was letting the sand fall through her fingers. "I told you about Izzie?"

Landon pushed the paints under one of the tent corners so none of the kids would knock them over. "You didn't have to. Her story has been in every paper in town."

"She doesn't trust people easily, but I can't blame her," Mira felt the need to say. "This God-awful reporter from the *North Carolina Gazette*, Grayson Reynolds, seems to have made it his personal mission to destroy my family and is using Izzie more than the rest of us." Mira knew she sounded bitter. "It was bad enough when he was just focusing on my dad, but he wrote the most awful things about her when she got stuck at USC in that storm." Mira's hands clenched into fists without her even realizing it. "If I ever meet that guy, I am going to give him a piece of my mind."

Landon's mouth twitched. "I shiver just thinking about your wrath." Mira threw her apron at him and he caught it. "Are you sure this guy is out to get you guys? Maybe he's just doing his job."

"Some job. He gets paid to spread lies about my family!" Mira shook her head. "Nothing bothers me more than being judged by my name alone."

"I know the feeling," he said. She tried to remember what Landon's parents did for a living. They were lawyers, maybe? Landon didn't talk about them much.

He came up beside her and adjusted her butterfly wings. "Try not to worry about this guy. Your wings will droop." His face was so close they could bump noses.

"I can't have that." She wondered if they were about to kiss.

That was, until Savannah ruined the moment. "We're about to let the first group in!" Savannah said, startling them. "Act natural! Smile! Be friendly!"

"Savannah, chill." Izzie pushed Savannah into the tent ahead of her. Neither of them seemed to notice how uncomfortable Mira and Landon were. "We've got the Junior League grand-prize fair award in the bag. Look at this booth. It's like Disney World."

Savannah touched the diamond pendant around her neck as she stared at the booth in awe. "I did do a good job, didn't I?"

"*We* did a great job," Izzie said, but Savannah had already headed to the front of the booth to greet the first guest, her wings bouncing as she walked. "I'm going to wrap those wings around her neck by the end of the day," Izzie warned Mira.

Mira laughed nervously. She didn't want Landon to think Izzie was a total psychopath. "Iz, meet Landon. Landon, Iz."

"Hey," she said, sounding normal. "Art class guy, right?" She glanced briefly at Mira. "I've heard a lot about you."

"Have you?" Landon gave Mira a look, and she wanted to die of embarrassment.

"Where's Brayden?" Mira asked.

"He's working the Emerald Prep information center." Izzie noticed Landon's shirt. "You go to St. Barnard's?"

"Izzie! Let's go!" Savannah stuck her head back in, interrupting them. "A dozen kids are already making hats, and there is a line of at least ten more waiting. I can't be expected to take care of everything on my own while you sit back here chatting with—" She noticed Landon. "Who are you, anyway?"

"This is Mira's *friend*," Izzie emphasized. "Landon goes to St. Barnard's. Isn't that where that guy you're seeing goes?"

"Did I say St. Barnard's?" Savannah thought for a moment. "I meant St. Benedict's." The first kids made their way inside the tent wearing mining hats decorated with foam stickers and glitter pens. Several of the Butterflies and parents followed them in and the tent suddenly felt crowded. "I'll meet you up front. Mrs. Fitz said your father should be here any minute to see the booth. And he has a press entourage with him."

"I do not want to be paraded in front of the press," Izzie groaned when Savannah was out of earshot. "Can you deal with them?" she begged Mira. "You know Dad is gung ho about making us look like good Southern girls after my USC disaster, and I don't think I have it in me to turn on the charm. Especially when I am wearing wings. I'd rather save my cheer for the kids." A little kid tripped in front of her and Izzie caught him. "Please?"

"Okay, but you know Dad is going to want to know where you are." Mira almost forgot Landon was listening to her family drama. "I'm sorry," she apologized to him. "I have to go deal with this. You can hang back here if you want or you can come meet my dad." A second later, she felt stupid for even suggesting it.

"I'm all for making a good impression on the parental units, but I'm not sure covered in paint and with a camera crew on the scene is the way to go." He shuffled to the side to allow kids to get to the sandbox. "Maybe I should meet him another time."

"Smart move," Izzie mumbled.

Mira was actually relieved. "Sounds good."

"I'll bring Jillian back later, but if it's too crazy, I'll just see you tomorrow," Landon said as he made his way out of the crowded area.

"Tomorrow?" Mira questioned.

"At the Crystal Ball." Landon raised one of his eyebrows. "You are going, aren't you? That's the whole reason I agreed to go. I didn't think you'd miss a party that big."

Izzie started to laugh and Mira glared at her. Landon was going to the Crystal Ball! "Nope, I'm going, too."

Landon leaned against the sandbox, being careful to avoid a mini miner who seemed to think the booth was his own personal water park. "Great. That top hat I rented won't go to waste. Want to meet there?"

It sort of sounded like Landon thought this was their first real date. Mira liked the sound of that. "Sounds good to me."

A new group of kids entered the tent, and Izzie began escorting those who had full bags of jewels back out. Mira and Landon got separated in the commotion, so she made her way out front. It was even more of a mob scene than inside the tent. The fair was well under way by that point, and the street was packed with people, strollers, dogs, and shoppers. It didn't hurt that the weather was beautiful. As far as Mira could see, the rest of the stands had visitors, too, but the line at the Butterflies' booth seemed to be the longest. Nicole had a group of parents waiting to check in, and the tables out front were packed with kids decorating mining hats.

"Can you believe all the donations we've gotten already?" Mrs. Fitz sounded happy as she walked by with a jar stuffed with money. Mira and Izzie did a double take when they saw her. Their club adviser was wearing a pink T and wings, too. "I'm going to put these donations in a safe place and get another jar to fill."

"I hope Zoe is getting pictures of this," Mira said as Millie ran by with another stack of jewel bags and hats for kids waiting to start. "Has she come by yet?"

Izzie looked uncomfortable. "No. We sort of had a thing. I haven't talked to her since."

"What kind of thing?" Mira was immediately worried.

Izzie looked around to make sure no one was listening. "I found out that Grams asked Zoe to be my guardian twice—once when my mom died *and* again last year." Her face hardened. "Which means she knew about me for years and wanted nothing to do with me."

Mira inhaled sharply. She knew Zoe was selfish, but she hadn't realized how much. Mira braced herself for Izzie's anger, but it didn't come. "Why are you so calm?"

Izzie watched the kids happily waiting in line to go into the tent. "I'm not happy, but what point is there in getting mad again? She apologized. Does it matter when it happened?"

Um, yes. "I guess not," Mira said because it seemed to be the answer Izzie was looking for. Not only had Zoe lied to her—twice—but she also had completely abandoned her after her mom's funeral, which she'd said she never attended! Zoe might not have been a bad person, but she was someone who thought only about herself. She hadn't finished Mira's head shots, she never called *Justine*, and she hadn't sat down with Izzie to talk about her mom till recently even though Izzie had asked for weeks. She'd also left Izzie stranded at USC because she was having a party. Zoe was never going to be someone Izzie could rely on. Mira was about to say that when Izzie dropped another bombshell.

"She asked me to go live with her in California."

"What?" Mira exclaimed.

Izzie pulled her into a corner. "Don't freak out. I didn't say yes."

"Did you say no?" Mira asked. "You're not considering it, are you?" Izzie didn't answer, and that made Mira nervous. Zoe couldn't be serious. She would never follow through on her promise, and Izzie would be crushed. "But you love North Carolina. You can't move!"

Izzie looked uncomfortable. "California is North Carolina with a different beach."

Mira had to think fast. "No, it's not. They have earthquakes."

"I'm not moving, okay?" Izzie snapped, but it worried

Mira that she was so fidgety. "I was just tempted because who wouldn't want the chance to start over?"

"But you did start over—here!" Mira reminded her.

"Yes, but here people knew my life story before I even opened my mouth." Izzie's normally bright hazel eyes seemed cloudy. "Sometimes I wonder if I would be better off going someplace where my Valentine's Day dinner and my weekend activities didn't make Grayson Reynolds's news feed."

"It's not always going to be like this," Mira promised, but she wasn't sure she believed that. Her life had been under scrutiny as long as she could remember.

Izzie seemed to sense this. "It's only going to get worse if Dad gets elected."

Mira knew Izzie was going to make this decision on her own, just like she had made almost every other decision about her life, and that frightened her. She did not want her sister to leave. Not when they were finally becoming a family.

"Hi, girls!" They heard their dad and turned around. Five or six reporters and a camera crew surrounded him near the front of the booth. Her dad had on his Founders Day tie with the town insignia, while her mom had on a simple navy dress and a scarf that said *Emerald Cove* in tiny print all over it. They had their public-appearance smiles on. Izzie's shoulders sagged. There was no escaping now.

"These are my daughters I was telling you about," their dad said when the girls were within reach. He put one arm around each of them and turned them toward the cameras. "They're members of our town's most charitable school club, the Social Butterflies." He turned to Izzie. "Would you mind telling everyone what your club's mission is? Isabelle is one of the club's cochairs."

"I'd be happy to tell them, Mr. Monroe!" Savannah appeared from out of nowhere and quickly recited the club's mission statement before anyone could stop her.

Their dad looked on in confusion. "Why, thank you, Savannah."

"My pleasure. And I'd be happy to gather the club if your friends would like a picture of all of us." Savannah was so busy smiling she didn't notice Izzie's piercing glare at first, but once she did, she quickly faded into the background.

Mira's dad turned his attention back to the pack of reporters. "I know many of you came here today hoping to hear my views on state policy and the recent tax bill, but I wanted you to see my wonderful family doing things they love. My daughters are role models for others their age, and I deplore the way Grayson Reynolds and his associates at the *Gazette* have focused on their occasional missteps rather than the points of this election. My children are not running for office and they should be left out of such affairs."

Mira smiled warily. Her dad was trying to do right by them. Unfortunately, his comment opened up a can of worms.

"Bill, what do you have to say about Grayson's accusations that you can't control your own children?" one reporter asked.

"I would say that Grayson should worry about his own family," Bill said. "He has two sons of his own and I would question if he knew their every move. If there is something that worries me, I take it up with my kids directly. I don't need a photo in the paper to remind me that kids are kids and sometimes they mess up."

"Do your children have curfews?"

"Did Mirabelle get special treatment from the North Carolina Aquarium when she visited them after hours?"

"Did you know Isabelle was visiting the University of South Carolina?"

Things were out of control and even some of the parents waiting in line for the mining station were starting to notice. Mira's dad tried to rein in the questions, but it wasn't working. Finally her dad's campaign advisers hurried the press away, but it was too late.

Mira couldn't read minds, but she feared she knew what Izzie was thinking. The press were never going to stop hounding them, and if that's the way it was going to be, maybe she didn't want to be a part of this family after all.

Seventeen

To: ISABELLE SCOTT

From: ZOE SCOTT

Subject: Hey

I know how upset you were the other afternoon after our run-in with Patty Brooks, so I thought I would give you some space. I've gone to Miami for a few days to squeeze in another couple of shoots before I go back to California. I know you've tried to call me, but I think it might be good if we both clear our heads first.

I meant what I said about you coming to live with me. What happened in the past is the past. The important thing is I'm here now and I think I'm ready to grow up and be the parent you need in your life—one who gives you freedom and shows you how to have fun! I know the two of us would be a great team.

Sorry I skipped out on the street fair, but my return flight should get me back in time for the Crystal Ball. Hopefully you will be ready to talk by then so we can discuss our future. I want to get back to California as soon as possible.

Sending you love and peace,
Z

Izzie dove into the pool and swam underwater as long as she could. It was so freeing. There was no commotion, no distractions, and, today, there were no times to beat. Coach Greff had made arrangements with the school so that the girls could swim laps over the weekends, but since it was the morning of the Crystal Ball, Izzie seemed to have the pool to herself. It was the perfect time to think, which was good because there was a lot to think about.

Like Zoe's e-mail. She had reread it three times. Part of her wanted to reply, but she wasn't sure Zoe would even read it. She'd once said her in-box had over a hundred new messages she hadn't gotten to yet.

California.

Emerald Cove.

California.

Brayden.

Her mind went to him whenever she had this push-and-pull debate. How could she pack her life up and leave him and Mira? She didn't know if she had it in her to walk away from a place she was finally beginning to know like the back of her hand for the unknown with Zoe. When she was with her mom's sister, she always felt like there were more questions than answers. Why didn't her mom tell Zoe she was pregnant? Why wasn't Zoe talking to her mom when she died? Why did it take till now for Zoe to reach out to her? But the biggest question of all was the one she would never have an answer to: Why did Grams keep all this from her?

As Izzie rose to the surface to take a breath, she thought of Grams's safe-deposit box again. The key to it still sat untouched in her desk drawer. She wasn't sure why she was so afraid to see what was in there. She knew Grams wasn't hiding a small fortune. Maybe the box held the diamond necklace she always claimed she'd hocked or something of her mother's she'd kept. Whatever it was, Izzie still wasn't ready to open herself up to the emotions that came with seeing it.

She reached the end of the lap lane and stopped for a moment, resting her chin on the edge of the pool. She had turned on the pool's stereo system when she arrived, and instrumental jazz music floated through the high-ceilinged room. Coach Greff always had it playing during practice. She said it helped them concentrate on their strokes. Today, it was making Izzie sleepy. She was going to need a nap before the Crystal Ball, and Mira would be furious. She'd already planned on them getting ready with Charlotte, Nicole, and Violet back home. Knowing Mira, that meant starting at two. She pulled herself out of the pool and headed to the locker room. If that was the case, it was time to go home and face the grooming squad. She headed to the locker room and ran into Savannah. "Guess we both had the same idea this morning," Izzie said.

Savannah placed her goggles on her head, a stony expression on her face. "You and I never have the same idea."

Savannah was always less friendly without an audience, but Izzie wasn't sure why she was being so hostile now. Their booth at the street fair had been a smash, just like their parade float before it. Like each other or not, they were rocking it as club cochairs. Instead, Savannah was glaring at her as if Izzie had stolen the last Oreo in the box. "What's gotten into you?" Izzie asked. "I thought you'd be taking interviews with the local news by now about how you single-handedly reinvented the street fair."

"You think you're so funny." Savannah's voice wavered, and Izzie looked at her strangely. "You've won, okay? I give up. The only person anyone was talking about yesterday was *you*! 'Look how much the Monroe girl knows about the children's hospital. Isn't it lovely how well Isabelle holds herself in front of reporters.'" Savannah crumpled onto the locker-room bench, and Izzie could swear she was about to cry real tears. "The Junior League couldn't stop talking about what a turn-around you've made since you arrived in EC. Everyone thought your work on the Falling into You Fest was a fluke, but after the fair, people think you're the second coming of Victor Strausburg!" Her forehead creased. "No one thanked me for my work yesterday. It's as if I didn't even exist. Even my mom commented on how lovely your wings looked, and the wings were my idea!" Her brown eyes were hollow as she looked up at Izzie. "So gloat all you want. I know when I've been beaten."

Izzie wasn't sure how to react. Here Savannah was waving the white flag and Izzie still didn't feel satisfied. What fun was winning when the other team forfeited? Savannah tamed was not a pretty sight. She almost felt bad for her. "You're not beaten. If you're worried about losing your crown, don't be," Izzie told her. "I do not want to be queen. Just go swim." She started to walk away. "And try not to drown."

"I know you know there is no Pierce." Savannah's cool voice echoed in the empty locker room. "I guess you'll be using that as leverage now, too."

Izzie turned around. She'd had a hunch. "If you want to create a fake boyfriend, that's your issue, not mine. I just assumed you made him up to make Brayden jealous."

Savannah's brown eyes turned steely. "I've been over Brayden since the minute I found out he liked *you*. It was bad enough he dumped me, then left me hanging at cotillion, but to not

have someone else waiting in the wings? I looked like a loser."
Izzie wasn't sure why Savannah was telling her all this. "I couldn't
bear another question about who I was taking to the next
charity-league auction, so instead I made someone up till I
could find a guy who was everything I wanted." She shrugged.
"It's not the worst thing I've ever done."

That was for sure. Izzie was happy being with Brayden,
but if she didn't have a boyfriend, she wouldn't mind going it
alone. Savannah obviously thought differently. It was kind
of sad.

"The worst thing I've done in a while," Savannah said,
trancelike, "was humiliating Mira at my sweet sixteen." She
looked down. "Which is why I don't blame you guys for not
inviting me to yours."

Izzie blushed slightly. Sending Savannah an invitation
had been a hot topic between her and her sister. Some days
they felt they should invite her just to keep the peace; other
days Mira got upset all over again about what had happened
at Savannah's party. In the end, they decided not to send her
an invitation.

"It feels funny not being invited to something that everyone is talking about," Savannah admitted. "That's never happened to me before."

Izzie thought Savannah looked tiny without a posse
around her. Izzie still didn't like Savannah, but maybe there was
a part of her that was starting to understand EP's queen bee.

No one liked being left out, she realized, thinking of Kylie. Maybe she could extend an olive branch to Savannah just this one time. "Do you think you could find a dress to wear by next weekend?"

Savannah eyed her with suspicion. "I always have a dress on standby. Why?"

Izzie headed to the showers before she could second-guess what she was about to say. "Your party invite will be in the mail today. Just don't make me regret sending it." And just saying that made Izzie smile. It was nice to have the upper hand for a change.

~

"I'm home!" Izzie yelled as she came through the front door. She didn't expect anyone to actually answer. Her aunt and Mira were probably getting their hair done before Mira's and Izzie's friends arrived to prep together. (Izzie was just going to let the girls do her hair later.) Her dad had probably taken Connor to his friend's for the night, and Hayden was most likely helping Kylie get ready for her EC debut.

But Aunt Maureen surprised her by yelling back. "We're in the kitchen!" Izzie walked in and found her aunt sitting at the island with her dad, who was reading the paper.

"Shouldn't you guys be getting ready?" Izzie asked, and

then realized that Aunt Maureen's hair had already been fashioned in an updo.

Her dad looked at her over his reading glasses. "You don't look like you're getting ready yet, either." He smirked. "Have a good swim?"

She felt her wet head. Of course he would know where she'd been. "Yep. I was clearing my head."

Her dad frowned. "I'm sorry about the assault at the street fair. I was told the press wanted to talk about the Emerald Cove Children's Hospital, but obviously Grayson's coverage has everyone looking for a sleazier angle."

"It's okay," Izzie said, even though it wasn't. "I just wish they had shown up *after* the street fair. We could have bragged about how our booth made seven hundred dollars for the Emerald Cove Children's Hospital and that you matched the donation."

"Sadly, that is not the kind of story they want to cover these days." Her dad grimaced. "I just got off the phone with my staff. I told them from now on they are not to comment on anything regarding my children, and if they get any calls from Grayson, they are to turn them over to me immediately." His hazel eyes blazed. "Grayson is getting a warning call from my lawyers as we speak. If he wants to come after me and my record, let him try. But he cannot continue to gun for my children."

Aunt Maureen poured him another cup of coffee. "I wonder

how Grayson Reynolds would like it if someone went after his sons." She touched her pearls. "How can his wife allow him to pick on innocent children?"

"Whether I win this election or not, Grayson is not going to get off easily," he vowed. "I'm not going to be happy till I see him gone from his job at the *Gazette.*"

Izzie had never seen him out for blood before. "You'd really try to get him fired?"

"He's been trying to do the same to me forever," her dad said. "Maybe it is time for his life to be under the same scrutiny that mine is."

Izzie thought of Zoe. She was so good at spinning lies that she could have been a tabloid reporter herself. She talked a big game, but there was always another celebrity to charm, a shoot to do, or friends to see. Would life in California be more of the same? "My mom would have loathed a guy like Grayson, don't you think?" she asked suddenly, wondering how similar the sisters could be.

"Yes," he said without hesitating. "She wouldn't have liked Grayson's dirty work one bit. It was always Zoe who was a bit more theatrical."

That was the opportunity Izzie had been waiting for. "If you know Zoe so well, why did you never tell me about her before she showed up?" Izzie asked, somewhat hesitantly. She noticed her aunt and dad look at each other.

"Maybe I should give you two some time alone," her aunt

suggested. "I should start getting ready anyway. Once the girls descend on this house, there won't be a mirror free."

Izzie didn't want Aunt Maureen to feel like she was being pushed out, but she understood if the conversation made her feel uncomfortable. Even though no one said it, if things had been different, Aunt Maureen wouldn't be the one standing in this kitchen. Her mom would. But that's not the way life worked out, and who was she to say which way would have been better? She adored Aunt Maureen. That didn't mean she missed her mom any less. "Please stay," Izzie begged.

Her aunt shook her head. "This is a conversation for you and your dad to have." She squeezed Izzie's arm on the way out. "But if you need me, you know where to find me."

Her dad slid over a plate of cookies, but Izzie wasn't hungry. "So you want to know about me and Zoe," he said, sounding tired at just the thought of the conversation. "All right. But all I can tell you is what I remember from years ago. Until she showed up around Christmas, I hadn't seen her since Chloe and I were together." He stared at her sadly. "When your social worker told me your grandmother reached out to her first to be your guardian and she had said no, I thought, *She must be the same selfish girl I knew back then.* It made me think you were better off not having your heart broken by her after all you'd been through. That's why I didn't tell you about her."

We'd be like sisters, Zoe had said. Zoe had gone from

disowning her to wanting to be her sister. It was hard to wrap her head around. "So you two never got along?" Izzie asked.

Her dad gave her a politician's answer. "We didn't see eye to eye on many things."

"Like?" Izzie pressed.

He took off his reading glasses. "Zoe and I were always competing for Chloe's attention. It was comical at first, how we each wanted her for ourselves, but after a while, Zoe got bent out of shape about how much time Chloe and I spent together. She was the only thing your mom and I fought about. Your mom felt guilty and wanted Zoe to tag along, but I felt like Zoe was a third wheel always trying to stir up problems. Sometimes I think she's the reason we broke up." He looked pained. "Zoe was always inside your mom's head, telling her it would never work out between us because my job came first. And it did, sort of. I was just starting out, but that didn't mean I didn't love your mom." He moved the cookies around on the plate. "The day my trade came through for the Braves was the day your mom left me. She said she didn't want to do the long-distance thing. I tried to talk to her, but she wouldn't listen. By the time I got to her apartment, she was gone."

Izzie felt overwhelmingly sad. It was weird hearing about her parents' breakup. Their lives didn't seem so different from her own.

"Zoe told me then that your mom was tired of playing second fiddle in my life. I tried calling Chloe for weeks to say that wasn't true, but she changed her number and then Zoe stopped taking my calls, too. I finally gave up." It had been decades, but her dad still seemed torn up about it. "I told myself I was better off, but the truth was I was devastated."

He really loved her, Izzie realized. Did her mom know that? It must have been horrible carrying a baby thinking the dad was someone who'd chosen his career over the two of you. If anything, their breakup sounded like a huge misunderstanding. A misunderstanding that Zoe had made even worse. She wondered if their whole lives could have been different if her parents had just had one more conversation.

Her dad looked at her sadly. "Are you okay with all this? If Maureen finds out I made you want to skip the Crystal Ball because of this conversation, she will never forgive me."

"I'm okay," Izzie realized. "It feels good to know the truth. I should probably shower before Mira gets home." She slid off her stool and headed to the door, then hesitated. "Thanks for finally telling me all that."

Her dad put his reading glasses back on and looked at her. "You are welcome. I hope you know that I'm always here for you."

Izzie gave him a small smile. Knowing he was made all the difference.

Eighteen

Usually the restaurants along Main Street were crowded on a Sunday night. But tonight, horses clip-clopping down the empty street replaced the sound of the trolley bell, and most stores were going dark by seven. The Crystal Ball was worth shutting down Emerald Cove for.

Carriages were lined up as far as the eye could see. Mira watched as men in top hats and long black overcoats, carrying canes or wearing fake mustaches, descended from buggies to lend a hand to women in stunning ball gowns. Some of their dresses had long trains, while others had wide hoopskirts made of silk and lace. She could have watched people arrive and leave all night. In fact, that's what she had always done when the Butterflies were working the party. But this year, she got to attend and she was in her own carriage with her friends, waiting to be dropped off. She fanned herself in anticipation as the horses trudged forward toward the town square. Gloves and a fan were a must for every lady in 1888 Emerald Cove, and all of Mira's friends had them.

Sadly, not everyone enjoyed going back in time as much as Mira did.

"There is no way anyone wore their hair like this," Izzie grumbled. "I look ridiculous." Izzie's bob had been parted in the middle and was held in place by two thin headbands just like a picture they had found of a partygoer in EC in 1888. Izzie's dress was just as beautiful. The golden gown had a fitted bodice and puffy sleeves. Mira was just happy to see her wear a dress. Izzie hadn't found one for their sweet sixteen yet.

"I think you look like an old-fashioned Southern belle," said Charlotte, who looked amazing herself in a pink silk gown. "Girls didn't usually have short hair, but they did wear headbands like that, so your look is perfect." According to the historical society librarian, Mrs. Roberts, long hair was all the rage as were low décolletage that showed almost everything and big long skirts that revealed almost nothing. The girls had done a lot of research before picking their costumes. They made three trips back to the Harborside costume shop before each settling on one.

Mira still wasn't sure she was happy with hers, even if it was pretty. She kept pulling at the dress's bustline to keep it from dipping too low. The dress's bottom half was gorgeous, though. Several ivory layers were held up by pretty rosettes that allowed the blue fabric underneath to peek out. Nicole and Violet had similar dresses in lavender and rose. "Stop worrying so much," Mira told Izzie, and snapped a picture before Izzie could stop her. "Keep your smiles handy. I plan on getting lots of photos of us tonight." Hopefully some of those shots would also include Landon. Just knowing he was going to be there, and he wanted to hang out with her, had her excited.

"Good. I need a picture of all of us together." Nicole touched her hair to make sure her updo hadn't come undone. The bun made her look even taller than usual. "I have this lonely sparkly purple frame just waiting for a shot of all my friends."

Charlotte hugged Nicole. "Aww…You called us all your friends. We're like our own little posse!"

It was true. As spring had sprung, so had their friendships. Mira liked how it felt to be part of a group again. Everyone seemed to be happy to be together, but Izzie was also noticeably sad. "Does anyone know if Kylie is coming tonight?" Mira asked, hoping the answer would put Izzie at ease.

"She said she was when I saw her at the costume shop the other day," Nicole said quietly. "She asked me how you're doing, Izzie."

Izzie turned toward her, trying to find a comfortable position in the fitted dress. "Did she mention our fight?"

Nicole shook her head. "Nope. She was totally normal. I think she just gets flustered easily in a group, you know?" she told the others. "One-on-one, she's really nice. She helped me pick out these earrings and the bracelet."

Izzie played with one of her long gloves. "I wouldn't blame her if she never talked to me again. I said some pretty awful things."

"You're not the only one." Violet sighed. "I feel like your fight is partially my fault." She looked down at her gloved hands in her lap. "She reminded me a lot of Dylan, and I didn't think you needed another Dylan in your life. I guess that is why I was making things hard on her," Violet said sheepishly. "I'm sorry, Izzie."

"This isn't your fault. It's mine," Izzie said as the carriage lurched forward again. "Kylie has always liked to tease me about EC, but she had my back when I moved. Some of my other friends heard my new zip code and wanted nothing to do with me anymore. So how do I repay her for being a good friend? By freaking out that she's dating Hayden and by being embarrassed of her." She shook her head. "I can't believe I was worried about Kylie fitting in. Kylie is not Dylan. Kylie's my friend no matter what. Sure, she shoots her mouth off, but for the longest time, Kylie was the only real friend I had." She looked at Violet. "It would be great if you could give her the same shot you gave me when I was a social leper. I love you both, Vi, and I don't want to have to choose between you, but that's what I feel like I've been doing."

Mira was proud of Izzie for standing up for Kylie. She watched as the two hugged.

"Okay." Violet smiled. "I will give her another shot. But it's only because I love you, too, and if you love her, I'm sure I'll learn to."

Mira was happy the heavy discussion was out of the way before they exited their carriage. She barely had enough time to gather her bag and her fan before a gentleman in an old-fashioned tuxedo was holding out his hand to help them out. "Ladies." He tipped his hat. "Welcome to the Crystal Ball."

Mira wondered if the Crystal Ball had always been this gorgeous, or if she had just been so busy working the party that she had never really noticed. Because when she got to the entrance to the tent, she was awestruck. Her eyes were drawn to the ceiling, where thousands of twinkling lights had been strung over the dance floor. There was a traditional band, like there was for all EC events of this size, and an elaborate seating chart that she would have to navigate later, but what she couldn't stop staring at were the period touches—the china, the linens, and the oversize black-and-white photos of Founders Days past. Seeing everyone playing dress-up felt like stepping back in time into one of those photos. A woman in a stunning pale green V-neck gown with a wide skirt and the most elaborate feather headpiece Mira had ever seen walked past her with a man in a top hat. "Hi, Mom," Mira said.

Mira's mother turned. "Hi, sweetheart! Isn't this ball magnificent? It is the perfect mix of town history and glamour."

Izzie touched the headbands to make sure they were still in place. "I'd have to agree. You guys are the spitting image of the Whitabakers." Mira's parents blinked. "You know, that couple who used to hold that lavish party at their rice plantation?" Izzie gave them a wry smile as Mira's mom's jaw dropped along with Mira's. Her dad looked mildly amused.

"I know who they are," Mira's mom said. "But how do you know?"

"They're in almost every book the Emerald Cove Historical Society has at the museum," Izzie said proudly. "They're one of the founding families who helped shape the South's Junior League." Everyone was still gaping, but Izzie just shrugged. "Savannah was right. I should know more about the place I call home. But don't tell her I have been to the museum."

"You've been to the museum?" Mira and Aunt Maureen asked at the same time.

"Brayden took me on Valentine's Day after our carriage ride." Izzie adjusted one of her headbands. "Somehow that part of my evening got lost in Grayson Reynolds's coverage." She smirked. "I guess he finds actual facts boring."

Their dad smiled. "Grayson is underestimating you. In my book, you are officially an Emerald Cove lady."

She grinned. "Thanks. The EC history lesson was kind of

fun. I might even do my midterm English paper on Audrey Strausburg. That woman had guts." Izzie's smile suddenly froze, and Mira looked around to see why. Zoe was walking toward them.

"Hello," she said tentatively. Zoe looked out of place in a black shift dress, but maybe she didn't have to dress up to be the official photographer. Guests had to abide by the gala rules, which said to come in costume or not to come at all.

Mira glanced at her dad. His smile reminded her of the ones he gave to politicians with opposing viewpoints. "Hello, Zoe," her dad said. "We didn't expect to see you here. I thought you said you were leaving for California tonight."

"I am." Zoe eyed Izzie, who looked perturbed. "Just here to tie up some loose ends before I go."

Mira wondered if those loose ends included persuading Izzie to go with her. She had the sudden urge to yank Izzie by the arm and get her out of there so she couldn't consider the offer again. But she looked calm, and that gave Mira hope that the conversation they'd had yesterday was just that—a talk between two sisters griping about things they didn't like about their family.

"Vivian Ingram wasn't too forgiving when I said I couldn't stay for the whole party," Zoe explained, "so I promised I'd take some pictures before I go. Plus, I couldn't leave without saying good-bye and thank you. I really appreciate you letting me stay with you so I could get to know Izzie better."

"It was our pleasure." Mira's mom placed her hand on Izzie's back. "We hope you'll come back to visit her often."

"Yes," her dad echoed. "Now that you're a part of Isabelle's life, I hope you'll stay a part of it."

"Of course!" Zoe said, but Mira wasn't sure she was actually listening. She had just taken her phone out of her bag and was staring at a text message.

Mira looked at her sadly. Not long ago, she thought Zoe had it all together. She even sort of wished she could be like her, traveling the world and doing exactly what she wanted, but looking at the woman standing in front of them, Mira saw Zoe for who she really was: a big talker full of empty promises. Mira didn't want to be like that. She vowed right then that if she was serious about modeling, she'd have her head shots taken with her own money. They wouldn't be shot by the famous Zoe Scott, but they might still be good enough to impress *Justine* and *Teen Vogue*.

"Can we talk outside before you go?" Izzie asked Zoe. "It's kind of loud in here."

"Do you want me to come with you?" her dad asked.

Izzie shook her head. "I'll be fine." She looked at Mira. "Tell Brayden I'll be right back."

As Izzie walked away, Mira spotted Landon walking through the crowded room looking for her. "I'll see you guys later," she told her parents, and headed off to meet him. He looked cute in a top hat and tails, but she was beginning to think she liked his quirky concert Ts and worn jeans better. "You're really here," she said, then cursed herself for letting those be the words that served as their introduction.

Landon looked at her strangely. "Why wouldn't I be?"

Mira didn't want to say what she was really thinking. She'd had to strong-arm every other boy in her life into going to events like this, and she always hated herself later for begging. But Landon was already so different from Kellen and Taylor. While it felt weird jumping from the end of one relationship headfirst into another, there was something about him that she couldn't pull herself away from. "I just meant, I'm glad you're here."

"Me, too." He smiled. "I've been thinking about our first official date all day."

The tiny hairs on her arms stood up. *Our date.* The band started playing this sweet melody that sounded vaguely familiar and the twinkling lights that were strung from every rafter in the tent seemed to dim. She couldn't imagine a better location for their first date. "So...what do you want to do first?" she asked, suddenly nervous. "Do you want to get something to eat? Dance? I can ask the band to play Taylor Swift."

He pulled his top hat down so that it sat at a slight angle. "If I knew you were going to bring up Taylor every time I saw you, I never would have let Jillian tell you that," Landon said, and she laughed. "Just you wait. When I dig up some dirt on you, I'm never going to let you live it down, either."

He was joking, but the term *dig up some dirt* immediately made her think of Grayson Reynolds. She was glad there was no press allowed at the Crystal Ball. There was an arrivals area for local politicians and the committee members, but once you were inside, the only photographer who might stalk you was the official one for the gala. Maybe that was why her dad had seemed so at ease before the Zoe debacle. She glanced over at them. Her parents had obviously recovered. They were talking animatedly while they danced near the edge of the dance floor.

"Why don't we start with a dance?" Landon strained to be heard over a trumpet solo. "After four years of fox-trot lessons, I am practically a certified instructor."

"You took dance lessons, too?" Mira couldn't believe it.

"Every Saturday." He grinned. "Isn't it mandatory in these parts?"

"Pretty much." She looked at her parents again. They were still alone, which was rare. If there was ever a good time to introduce them to Landon, this was probably it. "As much as I want to see your fox-trot, do you mind if we say hi to my parents first? I promised I'd introduce you." Landon's face paled, and Mira instantly worried she'd said the wrong thing. "My dad is not going to swear you into office or anything. I just thought it might be easier if I introduced you before they stormed us on the dance floor." She rolled her eyes. "If that happens, they may never leave us alone. My parents think they are much cooler than they are."

Landon still looked uncomfortable. He took her hand, and she felt her body temperature go up another few degrees. "I want to meet them, but there is something I have to tell you first, and I'm not sure you're going to like it." His voice took on a serious tone and it scared her. For a moment, she felt like she was standing with Kellen again.

"Let me guess." Mira looked at him searchingly. "You're moving to Tahiti next week. You have six weeks to live. You already have a girlfriend."

Landon gave her a small smile. "It's nothing that dire, but it's still something I should have told you weeks ago."

He was starting to freak her out. What was so earth-shattering that she needed to know right now in the middle of the Crystal Ball? She felt a tap on her shoulder and turned around. Her mom and dad were looking from her to Landon curiously.

"We saw you with your friend and wanted to say hi," her mom chirped.

Mira blushed. "Mom, Dad, I want you to meet Landon Archer."

Her dad shook Landon's hand. "Archer. Nice to meet you. Have we met before? You look a little familiar."

"I don't think so, sir." Landon sounded slightly nervous. "Although I do remember my parents taking me to see you play when I was a kid. You were incredible. I had a shirt with your number on it and everything."

Her dad loved baseball talk, so Landon was on the right track. Mira wondered what he had been so worried about.

"Braves fan, huh?" her dad said with apparent satisfaction. "Do you play ball?"

"No, sir," he said. "I play basketball, but our season at St. Barnard's ended in February."

"St. Barnard? Your school has an excellent basketball team from what I've heard," her dad said approvingly. "Didn't you just finish in first?"

"Wow, how did you know that?" Landon looked amused.

"He follows the high school teams as if he has a stake in them," Mira's mom said, taking her husband's arm. "You'd think he was coaching."

"What's wrong with having a hobby?" her dad asked. "I'm so busy these days, I rarely even get in a round of golf anymore. I am envious of you kids." He stared at the twinkle lights. "The smell of the grass on a spring day, being part of a team and having that camaraderie. Those were great times."

Mira's mom winked at Mira. "Maybe I should get your father back on the dance floor before he starts boring Landon with old ball stories."

"I'd like to hear a few of those," Landon said, and Mira smiled. This was going better than she could have imagined.

"I'd be happy to share," her dad said. "Maybe we should have Landon over for dinner one night, Maureen, so he can—"

"Landon?"

At his name, the group turned and stared at a man in a dark brown suit and bowler hat. The corners of his mouth were turned down in a deep frown.

"*Grayson.*" Mira's dad's voice was like steel. "What are you doing here? This is a private party and there is no press allowed this evening."

Mira couldn't believe she was staring at *the* Grayson Reynolds. She always pictured a short, pudgy weasel of a guy with greasy hair, but the only thing that matched her description to this distinguished man in front of her was the hair. His gray hair was slicked back with an oily sheen.

"I am not reporting tonight, Bill," he said coolly, his eyes never leaving her dad's face. "I am a guest just like you. In fact, I thought we were both taking the night off from business, but somehow I find you conveniently talking to my son."

Son? Mira's legs suddenly felt like jelly. It couldn't be. Landon's name was Archer, not Reynolds. But when she looked at Landon, she knew Grayson was telling the truth. Landon was an ashy shade of gray.

"Your son?" Her dad's voice was thunderous, and he looked from Mira to Landon incredulously. Gone was the warm smile of a few minutes ago. "Mira, did you know?"

"No! Dad, I…" Mira wasn't sure what to say.

"You used your son to get to my daughter?" her dad accused

Grayson. His voice was more irritable than it should be for a public conversation. Mira's mom tried to calm him down.

"Watch your tone, Bill." Grayson was equally icy. "You never know what might work its way into tomorrow's paper."

Mira felt dizzy. Landon had used her? She was so confused. The band's trumpet player sounded like he was playing in her right ear, and her dad and Grayson's argument was in her left. She couldn't listen anymore. Before anyone could stop her, she broke for the door on the other side of the dance floor. Landon caught up with her before she got too far.

"Mira, wait!" He grabbed her hand and pulled her outside. The air was much cooler, and Mira inhaled deeply as if she had been gasping for air.

Landon looked as upset as she felt, which only made Mira madder. She shoved him as hard as she could, but the move didn't make much impact. "How could you use me?"

"I didn't! I like you, Mira." His dark eyes bore into hers. "That's why I made up a different last name." His voice was firm. "If I'd told you who I really was that first day in class, would you have talked to me?" She was quiet. "You probably would have been so mad, you would have dropped the class. I couldn't let you do that."

"Why?" Mira's lower lip was quivering. "Because you had to dig up dirt for your dad?" The words didn't sound right coming out of her mouth.

"Do you really think I would do something like that?"

As weird as this whole situation was, she knew deep down Landon wouldn't do that. How could a guy be in a group like Art Equals Love and also be a spy? It didn't make sense. Her head was pounding. The music had been so loud inside the tent, but it was so much softer now that they were outside. No one was out there but the horses from the carriage rides.

"I liked talking to you," he said. "You're funny. And sort of brazen around people like Selma Simmons." He smiled softly. "I liked that." She stared at the grass. "My dad being a total sleazebag isn't my fault, you know. I knew I had to tell you, but every time I tried, I couldn't do it. I really like you, Mira."

Mira's hands were shaking, but she wasn't cold. She was unnerved. This was wrong. All wrong. She couldn't like a boy whose dad was trying to destroy her dad's career and ruin all their lives. She couldn't. Her parents wouldn't let her. Once they caught up with her, she knew she was going to get a lecture about how she could never see Landon again. She suspected he was going to get the same one. But when she looked at Landon, she didn't see how shutting him out of her life was going to work either. "I like you, too," she whispered.

Then before she knew what was happening, Landon's lips somehow found hers and they were kissing. It felt more right than anything she'd done in forever. Afterward, she leaned

her head into his chest and held on for dear life, as if any minute their dads were going to appear and tear them apart. "So
what do we do now?" she asked. Landon's answer didn't make
her feel any better.

"I don't know." He stroked her hair. "I really don't know."

Nineteen

Izzie stood quietly by the Crystal Ball catering tent and watched harried waiters rush past her with the evening's first course (crab cakes, which smelled darn good). She could still hear the music inside the party playing over the shouts of "table sixteen is missing two apps!" Everyone inside was having a great time while she prepared to say good-bye to an aunt she barely knew. And if that was anyone's fault, it was Zoe's.

"You have expressions a lot like your mom, you know that?" Zoe took a seat on a stack of boxes marked *linens*. "And based on your expression right now, I would guess you're not coming with me to California."

Izzie lifted her dress so that it didn't drag in the grass (it was a rental!), and sat down beside her. "Starting over someplace where no one knows me is tempting, but if I went with you, I think I'd feel like I was running away from Emerald Cove." She thought of her mom fleeing to North Carolina when things didn't work out in New York. "I'm not a quitter. This place hasn't broken me yet, and I'm not going to let it now, even if this election is driving me mad. I like it here," she admitted as much to herself as to Zoe. "And I love the Monroes. They're my family. I wouldn't feel right abandoning them when they've been there for me when I needed them the most."

Zoe's green eyes looked sad. "I'm your family, too, you know."

Izzie hadn't forgotten that. "I still want you to be a part of my life. I just think I'm better off living here."

Zoe nodded. "And this has nothing to do with what happened between me and your grandmother?"

Izzie played with her skirt. "Maybe a little. It still bothers me that you lied, but if you had told me right away, I know it would have hurt too much." She searched Zoe's face. "I hope that's why you didn't." When Zoe smiled she looked so much like her mother. How could she not want her mom's sister to be part of her life?

"Have you always been this mature?" Zoe asked.

Izzie grinned. "Pretty much. Not that I always wanted to be. I took care of Grams the last few years. Here, I get to be a teenager and I like that." Maybe she'd have more freedom with Zoe than she did with the Monroes, but there was a small part of her that was beginning to realize she liked knowing she had parents who worried about her enough to set rules.

"I didn't intend for things to work out this way, you know," Zoe told her. "When I came back to see your grandmother, I wanted to set things right. I had such great plans for us." She smiled sadly. "You and I were going to do all the things your mom and I never got a chance to do. When she moved to New York, I thought the two of us were going to live together till we were in our nineties. Two old biddies fighting over a game of bingo at the local Y." She laughed for a moment. "I didn't realize she'd meet Bill and fall so hard. Bill changed everything."

Something in the catering tent came crashing to the floor and they heard shouting. Zoe leaned forward to see what happened, but Izzie didn't want her to get distracted. She had a feeling Zoe was finally going to tell her what went down that summer her parents and aunt had been together. "Why did Bill change your relationship so much?"

"I waited forever to have Chloe to myself, and then she came to New York and spent all her time with Bill. Your dad is too much of a gentleman to say it, but I think he suspects I played a part in his breakup, and he's right." Her face crumbled. "I just wanted them to take a breather. They got so serious so fast, and she had no time for me!" Zoe looked angry. "So I admit it—I got jealous—and that's why I started talking about how if Bill got traded they'd never last. Then miraculously, it happened. Chloe panicked. She didn't want to lose him, but I drilled it into her head how he was a young, hot ballplayer and there was no way he could stay faithful. I told Chloe about other guys on the team who had groupies. I didn't say Bill did, too, but when she pressed me, I didn't deny it. I guess I sounded convincing because after the trade, she broke it off. She didn't even say good-bye to him."

"Did you ever tell her the truth?" Izzie asked. Zoe's answer was written all over her face. Her cheeks were flushed in the low evening light.

"I couldn't. She would've been so mad." Zoe's voice was shaky. "I knew she was upset, but I thought she'd get over him. Your dad didn't go easily, though. He wouldn't stop calling, so finally I changed our number. We didn't have cells back then, so she didn't know he was trying to reach her. She thought he was being a jerk, and I was happy to have my sister to myself." Zoe looked away guiltily. "Neither of us knew she was pregnant. By then, it was too late. She had gone home to your grandmother."

Izzie's heart was beating out of her chest in time to the up-tempo tune the band was playing inside. How could Zoe have been so cruel?

"I know I was wrong, okay?" Zoe threw up her hands. "Selfishly, I liked having Chloe to myself for a while. And then, when she left and I didn't know why, I was mad at her. I felt

269

like I wasn't enough, you know? I felt like she had abandoned her kid sister." Zoe looked mournful. "I begged her to come back, but she wouldn't get on the phone with me half the time. I thought she was just depressed. Once I knew about you…" Izzie tried to block out the sounds of the frantic waitstaff trying to get out more plates.

Zoe grabbed Izzie's hand. "I never would have tried to split them up if I had known she was pregnant. Nor did I know Bill would move on so quickly. By the time I came to my senses, he had moved, and his number was changed, and a few months later, I read he was engaged. That's when your mom called me to tell me I was right about him," she recalled, her voice hoarse. "But instead of agreeing with her, I was vindictive. I was mad at her and feeling bad for myself. Here I was living paycheck to paycheck, alone, and she was back home with Grams. So when she called, before she could get a word in, I blurted out that I was the reason they broke up."

Izzie's eyes widened. "And you still didn't know about me?"

Zoe shook her head. "Nope. I probably should have figured it out by then. As soon as I told her that I caused her breakup, your mom started yelling at me and crying. She was furious, and she had every right to be. I ruined her life." Zoe's lower lip quivered. "I can't blame her for never speaking to me again after that." Her eyes welled with tears. "I called dozens of times to apologize, but your grandmother wouldn't put me through. Eventually I gave up." She looked at Izzie sadly. "The next time I saw your mom was at her funeral, and that's when I learned about you. When I realized how old you were, it didn't take me long to figure out who your father was, but it was way too late to fix things. Not only had I destroyed your mom's life, but I had ruined yours as well." She audibly sobbed.

Izzie wanted to be furious with Zoe, but, sadly, what did that change? If her parents had lasted the summer, who knows if they would have survived her dad's trade. Her mom still could have swallowed her pride and found him to tell him she was expecting, but she didn't, and Izzie would never really know why. If her mom had told him, would they have gotten married? But then she wouldn't have had Hayden, Mira, or Connor in her life. There was no use wondering "what if" if the answers changed everything she loved. Zoe was crying and Izzie put her hand on her aunt's shoulder, thinking how ironic it was that she was the one doing the consoling. "It's okay. This happened such a long time ago."

"It's not okay! I know what I did was awful." Zoe wiped her eyes. "But at least now I've come clean to the person who matters most. I just hope you don't hate me."

Izzie actually felt bad for her. "I don't hate you," she said honestly. "You're the only Scott I have left. How could I hate you?"

Zoe reached over to hug her. She didn't let go right away.

"You see what this state does to me? I have to get out of North Carolina before it swallows me whole." She attempted to laugh, but it sounded hollow. "Thank you for letting me get that off my chest," she said, stroking Izzie's hair. "I have something for you. I had a feeling you might say no about California, so I brought your sweet-sixteen present with me tonight." She pulled away and rummaged around in her bag. "I wanted to have one blown up and framed, but I never got around to doing it. Here." She handed her a Ziploc bag of photos.

The one on top caught Izzie's eye. It was a picture of her parents sitting on a blanket in what had to be Central Park. Her dad's hair was dark brown instead of gray, and (not that she would tell him this) he looked more muscular. She hadn't watched her mom age, so she looked the same as Izzie remembered her, maybe just a tad younger. But what stuck out the most about the picture was how happy they looked. Zoe had followed through with the one thing that mattered to her most. She had given her a chance to see her parents as a couple. "This is a great gift." Izzie tried not to get emotional. "Thanks."

Zoe hugged her again. "You're welcome. Well, as much as I hate to leave you after our cathartic conversation, I have a plane to catch. Now that you aren't coming, maybe I'll change my ticket and fly straight to Mexico to start my birthday celebration a few weeks early." She stood up and touched Izzie's cheek. "And when I get there, I'll say a toast for my niece. I know this year will be a great one for you."

272

Izzie watched Zoe walk away. Then she looked at the photos. In one, her dad was holding her mom. In another, her mom was sitting on her dad's shoulders. As she flipped back and forth between them, she had an overwhelming urge to see Grams. She wondered what Grams would have said about these pictures and what her take would have been on their short relationship.

Suddenly she wanted to see what was in Grams's safe-deposit box, and she wanted to see it now. She slipped the photos back inside the Ziploc bag and headed inside to find Brayden. The dance floor was more crowded than it had been when she left, but she spotted Savannah dancing with Millie, Lea, and Lauren. Savannah's royal-blue dress blew everyone else's out of the water. She noticed Izzie staring and gave a small wave. Maybe that sweet-sixteen invitation meant more to Savannah than she'd let on.

"Hey." Brayden found her first. He looked worried. "Mira told me what happened. Are you okay? Where is Zoe?"

Izzie couldn't help but smile. Few guys could pull off a black bowler hat, but Brayden was one of them. "She just left for Mexico." Brayden looked at her quizzically. "It's okay. That's where she should be and I belong here. I'll explain, but first there is something I have to do, and unfortunately that means I can't stay for the ball."

Brayden didn't flinch. Instead, he took her hand. "Let's go, then."

Izzie laughed. "Don't you want to know where I'm going?"

His mouth curled into a smile. "Nope. If you've got somewhere to go, then I'm going with you, no questions asked. We can do the ball next year." He touched the brim of his bowler. "I might hold on to this hat. It suits me, don't ya think?"

"That it does. Remind me to text Mira that we're going. If I don't, she'll think I'm on a plane with Zoe." Suddenly Izzie stopped. She could see Kylie standing with Hayden, and she couldn't help but notice how beautiful Kylie looked in a peach gown with her hair swept up into a bun. When Kylie looked over, she smiled tentatively, and Izzie basically threw herself at her.

"I suck," she blurted out, grabbing Kylie fiercely.

"A little bit," Kylie agreed and Izzie laughed.

Izzie pulled away and looked at her while the boys stared on. "You were right, you know. I let Emerald Cove start to change me and I hate that. I can't believe I let this place make me question our friendship."

Kylie grunted, but she was still smiling.

And that's how Izzie knew Kylie was going to let her off the hook. They both seemed to just want their stupid fight over with, but that didn't mean Izzie still didn't want to apologize. "You're the best friend I ever had and I am not going to let anyone come between us again, but you've got to dial some things back," Izzie said. "Go easy on these girls. They're not as used to your mouth or your attitude as I am."

"You're right." Kylie surprised her by agreeing. "Violet was just all up in my business and I hated it. I figured if you had her, you didn't need me. I got mad and took it out on her." She seemed contrite. "That's why I started coming around at first and that's how the whole thing started with Hayden. But I really like him, Iz."

"I'm happy for you." Izzie squeezed her hand. "Just promise me that no one—Hayden included—will ever come between us again. If you two start hating each other, you still have to be a part of my life." She thought of her mother and Zoe.

"Okay, don't get sappy," Kylie sniffed. "It took my mom an hour to do my makeup."

"She did great." Izzie hugged her again. "Have fun, okay? I want all the details tomorrow." Kylie gave her a look. "I can't stay. There is something I've got to do."

Kylie grabbed her purse off the table. "Then I'm coming, too. H!" He was standing with Brayden. "We're leaving! Or at least I am. Iz-Whiz needs me."

Hayden and Izzie looked at each other searchingly. "I know I owe you an apology, too. I'm sorry if I got between you guys."

Hayden smiled. "Next time you two duke it out on your own. I'll just be the ref."

"Deal." Izzie looked at her watch. It was past six. If there was any chance TD Bank would still be open, she had to go now. "We should go, then. We just need a car. Too bad everyone arrives at this thing in horse and carriage."

"Not me and Kylie." Hayden winked. "We bucked tradition." He pulled his keys out of his pocket. "Where do you need a lift to?"

Izzie grinned. "Where do I go whenever I need something? Harborside, of course."

~

Hayden got there quickly, even after swinging by the house to pick up Izzie's key, but it didn't matter. When they pulled up to the bank, the lights were dimmed and the sign clearly said the branch closed at six.

"We could come back tomorrow," Brayden suggested.

Monday seemed so far away. Kylie sensed that. The girls looked at each other. "Did you see that one light on in the lobby?" Izzie asked Kylie.

Kylie nodded. "Around the side there is a light on, too. Think it's Carl?"

"Maybe," Izzie said. "He had the job last summer. It's either him or Boyd."

"You guys aren't thinking of breaking and entering a bank, are you?" Hayden said, worried. "Because if anyone in Dad's campaign gets wind of this…"

"It's not breaking and entering if someone lets you in. Follow me," Kylie said. The four of them hopped out and walked down the side alley of the bank. Kylie banged hard on a steel door. "Carl? Boyd? Either of you in there?"

A guy with long, dark hair popped up in the window of the door. Carl looked at them like they were crazy. "Is this an old-fashioned heist?" he asked, but didn't look concerned.

"No, you fool! Iz needs to get into her grandma's safe-deposit box!" Kylie yelled.

"The bank's closed," Carl said. "Didn't you see the sign?"

"That's why we're here bothering you," Kylie said. "Can you let us in?"

"No!" Carl laughed. "You're crazy for even asking."

It wasn't a matter of life or death, but now that Izzie was finally ready to see what Grams wanted her to have, she didn't want to wait. "What if you brought the box to us?" she suggested. "I have the key. The number of the box is on it." Izzie held it up.

"Still stealing," Carl said. "You have to fill out a form. Just come back tomorrow!"

"Carl, what do you think Izzie's grandmother has in that thing?" Kylie lamented. "That woman didn't have two nickels to rub together. You've known Izzie her whole life. Do you really think she's here to steal something? She just wants what her grandmother left her. We won't tell anyone you helped us. Can't you break the rules this once?"

Carl disappeared, and Izzie thought maybe he had called the cops, which would be a problem, since Grayson Reynolds would know what she'd done. But Izzie didn't care. Let him try to find fault with her for opening a safe-deposit box that belonged to her. Before she could even start to worry, Carl was opening the door. "Give me the key fast before I regret this." Izzie smiled and handed it over.

He was gone for what felt like hours, but it was probably only ten minutes. When he returned, he handed her a small envelope. It was barely big enough for a card. Her name was written on the front in Grams's handwriting.

"You rock, Carl!" Kylie cheered.

"Just get out of here before someone sees you," he growled.

"Thanks!" Izzie gripped the envelope tightly as they raced back to the car.

"Think the key to your castle is in there?" Kylie joked when they were back in the car and Hayden was discussing with Brayden where they should go to get something to eat. They had missed the dinner course at the ball.

"Let's find out." Izzie ripped the seal and pulled out a letter. Something was jingling inside. She flipped the envelope over and a ring fell out. Brayden turned on the car light so they could get a closer look. The ring had two small stones. One looked like a diamond, but the blue stone was clearly her mother's birthstone, a sapphire.

"Is that Grams's wedding ring?" Kylie asked, staring at its unique shape in awe.

"No. She hocked that years ago to pay the heating bill one

winter." Izzie looked at the ring from all sides. "I don't know what this is."

"Maybe the letter explains it," Kylie suggested.

Izzie unfolded the yellow paper. The letter was written in her grandmother's chicken-scratch script. It felt weird to see her handwriting now that she was gone. It was almost a gift in itself. Izzie started to read.

Darling Iz,

I'm not one for too many words, but I can feel your granddaddy yelling from the grave—tell her the important stuff before it's too late! We all know I'm not going to be around forever. You heard that diagnosis just like I did. I'm losing it. If not today, or tomorrow, then it will be the next day and my ghost will be angry that I never said what I needed to. So here it goes.

I've found your daddy.

When you read this you'll already know that, but I want you to know the hows and whys of this happening. When I got sick,

I worried about what would happen to you. I knew you had to have family out there somewhere, and your mama's journal, which I found in the basement, confirmed it.

You're going to be upset that I didn't tell you straightaway, but things have to be wrapped up quickly. All I'll say is that if Bill Monroe is anything like he presents himself to be, I can see why your mama liked him. I'm proud of you, toots, and he will be, too, when he sees how much you're like our Chloe. When the time comes, and I'm gone or don't know my own name anymore, don't you dare cry for me. Just go with him. Leaving me is what you're supposed to do. You're a fighter, just like your mama was, and you'll make your new life shine.

While I'm dishing, one more thing: When I'm gone, you may find out that I was keeping a secret or two. I'm talking about the fact that you also have an aunt—

Zoe Lauren Scott, your mama's baby sister. I didn't tell you about her, because I knew you would obsess about where she's been and why she didn't want to know you. What you need to know, honey, is that it's never been about you. I hope she finds her way to you one day, though. She'll tell you the story, I'm sure, and it will hurt hearing it—how I asked her to be your guardian when your mama died and she said no. I would like to think she turned me down because she knew you and I needed each other. Raising you has been the highlight of my life.

I hope you can find it in your heart to forgive me for the lies and the secrets. Families can be messy, but at the end of the day, they're all you got. That's why this ring is in here—to remind you. This is my engagement diamond. It's not worth much, but it's real, like your mother's birthstone I got her for her sixteenth birthday. I took both the stones and had them put on this ring together. It was a tad showy for my taste in the end, but now it's yours. I hope you'll wear it and think of me, your cranky, old grandmother, and your mother, a wise, strong-willed woman gone before her time.

We'll be watching you, honey. I know you'll make us proud.

Love always,
Grams

Izzie choked back tears as she slipped the ring on for size. It fit on her middle finger. She and Kylie stared at it in awe. Her mother and grandmother really were with her, after all.

Grams, Izzie thought. *You were full of surprises right up until the end.*

Twenty

Mira and Izzie stood at the top of the stairs in the great hall and watched their sweet-sixteen party unfold in front of them beneath brightly colored green, blue, and purple papier-mâché lanterns. One hundred of their closest friends, family, and parents' friends were trickling into the converted rice plantation on the outskirts of Emerald Cove, and Mira wasn't down there to greet any of them.

"You know, if Lover Boy doesn't turn up soon, you and I are going to miss our whole party." Izzie held her masquerade mask up to her face. It was antique gold and had hand-sculpted scrolls and rhinestones glued above the eye line. It was much more ornate than her simple but elegant green chiffon dress. "If you think about it, it's kind of funny because I never wanted this party to begin with, but you've been waiting for this your whole life. Now you're going to miss it because of a boy."

Mira glowered at her. "You only have to play watchman for a few more minutes." She checked her watch again. "He'll be here." *He was coming, wasn't he?* Mira removed her mask to get a better look at the crowd. She had opted for one on a stick because it was more elegant. Hers had a black-and-white toile pattern over the left eye and shimmery silver feathers that complemented her black lace and satin dress perfectly. But removing the mask did no good. She still couldn't tell one person from the next, because their own masks concealed their identities. She watched as Charlotte, Nicole, and Violet took theirs off to stick their heads through one of three masquerade ball cutouts that people could pose with. Mira could feel Izzie staring at her. "What?"

"Nothing," Izzie said, but Mira could tell it was *something*. "Okay, I just can't believe that our roles are now reversed— you're the one sneaking around and lying, while I'm a picture-perfect EC role model." She teased, grinning. "Our plan for people to make donations instead of bringing gifts will even look good for Dad's campaign. *If* Grayson Reynolds reports it right."

Mira thought she was going to be ill. "Don't say that name."

"Hey, you're going to be hearing it a lot, don't you think?" Izzie asked coyly.

Mira stared at the crowd instead of answering. Savannah had just walked in with Millie. Mira was still a little miffed that Izzie had invited her. "No."

Izzie sighed. "Fine. I'll stop. It's your birthday party, too, and if you'll enjoy it more with him here, then I'll cover for you." Mira hugged her. "But take it from someone who knows—the lying will eat at you. Just come clean, Mira. How mad can they really be when you explain things?"

"I've already tried," Mira said with a sigh, thinking of all the crying and shouting she'd done the last few weeks trying to get her parents to see that Landon wasn't his dad. It hadn't worked, which was why Mira had resorted to Plan B: seeing him behind their backs. Landon was the best thing that had happened to her this year, and she was going to fight for him.

"There you two are!" Mira jumped at the sound of her mom's voice. Her parents walked toward them in their black-and-white patterned masquerade masks.

"What are you guys doing up here?" Mira asked, sounding nervous. "I thought you were supposed to be greeting guests at the door."

"So are you," Mira's mom said with a laugh. "Or did you forget how to be a hostess all of a sudden? Someone said they saw you two hiding up here, so we decided to come up and see what was going on. Everyone is asking for you. Are you okay?"

"We're fine!" Izzie covered for her. "Mira just wanted to touch up my makeup before we made our grand entrance."

Mira knew she had a tendency to be paranoid, but she suddenly had the sneaking suspicion her parents knew what she was up to. She started to perspire, which was not a good thing when her makeup was flawless. "Is something wrong?" Mira asked, her voice tightening.

Her parents looked at each other. "Do you want to tell her or should I?" her dad asked.

"I think you should," Mira's mom said firmly. "I never had a problem with that nice boy. You did."

That nice boy. She had to mean Landon. Her parents must have found out he was coming. Izzie actually looked nervous herself. But Mira was not. She had prepared a speech in case she ever needed to give it.

"If this is about Landon again, I don't want to hear it. I like him, okay? I can't help it," Mira said, her voice rising. She dropped her mask to her side. "He is a great guy, and you should be happy that I found someone like him. He treats me well and makes me laugh. We have fun together, and he thinks about others before himself." She thought of Art Equals Love and the way he always defended her against Selma Simmons. "And if that's not enough for you guys, then—"

Mira's dad cut her off. "Are you finished?" His voice was calm. "Because your mother and I have something to say, too." Her mom nodded. "We're sorry we didn't trust your judgment about Landon. He is a remarkable young man, and if you care about him half as much as he cares about you, then we're sure we can all get along no matter what his last name is."

Mira was so flabbergasted she almost fell over. She felt Izzie nudge her. Landon was walking up the back staircase behind Mira's parents, and he was headed toward her. For a moment, Mira felt as if her throat was going to close up. This wasn't what they had planned! Mira was supposed to meet him outside, make sure his masquerade disguise was decent, then usher him off to hang out with Charlotte for the night just so he could be there at the party. And now he was blowing his whole cover…and yet he didn't seem bothered by that. He was actually smiling.

"Hi, Mira," Landon said. He was wearing a dark gray suit and holding a large silver mask in one hand. In his other hand was a small corsage box. "This is for you." Mira took it wordlessly. She didn't understand what was going on. She watched as Landon turned to her parents. "Good evening, Mr. and Mrs. Monroe."

Mira's mom shook his hand. "You look very handsome tonight, Landon. Thank you so much for coming."

"Landon," Mira's dad said as he gave him a strong handshake. "Thank you for agreeing to escort Mirabelle at her party."

"I wouldn't miss it, sir," Landon said.

Mira stared at them all incredulously. "Am I missing something?" Izzie laughed.

Landon and Mira's dad looked at each other. "The three of

us had a nice talk the other evening about you," her dad explained. "Landon gave the same passionate speech you did, Pea, and that's when your mother and I realized we were being too hard on you kids." He smiled. "This is your relationship, and we want you to be happy. It's going to be hard, but we're going to try to keep politics out of it. Grayson and I spoke as well, and we're going to do our best to keep you two a separate issue."

Mira couldn't believe what she was hearing. She hugged both of her parents fiercely. "Thank you," she said, trying not to get choked up. She couldn't believe how much lighter she felt in just a matter of moments. "This is the best birthday present you could have ever given me."

"Does that mean we should return the matching necklaces we got the two of you girls?" Mira's mom asked with a wink toward Landon.

"Well, I wouldn't want you to have to go through the trouble of making a return," Mira said, trying not to smirk. "Izzie and I would be happy to keep them anyway." Everyone laughed.

"We should get downstairs, Bill," Mira's mom said. "Our guests are waiting. I think Brayden is, too." Izzie took their dad's arm and let him lead her to the staircase. Mira's mom squeezed Mira's shoulder. "Happy birthday, sweetie."

"Thanks, Mom," Mira said. She could hear her favorite Katy Perry song drifting up from downstairs. It was time to join the party. She crossed her arms and looked at Landon. "So...you faced my parents alone, huh?"

Landon pulled Mira toward him. "I had to. No offense, but I didn't think your great big disguise plan was going to work. He used one hand to put his mask on. "Did you really think your parents wouldn't guess I was under here?" Mira laughed. "The mask is very *Phantom of the Opera*, I'll give you that, but it wasn't going to fool our state senator." He pulled the mask away, and his face was serious again. "They had to know you were going to try to sneak me in here, and I could just see how this whole thing would go. Making our relationship all cloak-and-dagger sounded exhausting. So I decided to talk to your parents myself and tell them what I told my own dad—you are a girl worth fighting for, and I'm not going to stop till they realize that."

Mira felt her arms begin to tingle. "You really said that?" she whispered.

Landon's eyes searched hers. "I really said that. I was not going to miss you blowing out the candles on your birthday cake." He leaned in for a kiss, and the two lingered there for a while. They only separated when Mira heard the next song the DJ started playing. They both laughed.

"Taylor Swift?" Landon smirked. "That never gets old with you, huh?"

Mira shook her head. "Never. I think I requested three of her songs tonight just in case you want to sing along."

Landon took her hand. "Maybe we better get downstairs to enjoy them."

Mira smiled. She couldn't think of anything she wanted to do more.

~

After the food, the dancing, the pictures, and more food, Izzie and Brayden lingered on the dance floor for a slow song even though most of their friends were taking a break. Brayden wound his arms around Izzie, and she could smell his coconut shampoo. It reminded her of the beach, summer, and surfing. Who could believe all those things were right around the corner again? So much had changed since the last time she had dipped her toes in the ocean.

"What are you thinking about?" he asked as they swayed to a Maroon Five song. As much as she liked him dressed down, Brayden always looked good in a suit.

"Summer, you, me, EC, Harborside," she said.

Brayden suppressed a grin. "That all? Next you'll be telling me we need to look for summer jobs."

"I already applied for a Harborside Beach lifeguarding position," Izzie said. "My aunt and my dad said I could get my job back."

"Then maybe I should look for something there as well," Brayden said. "This summer is about you and me being together." He spun her around. A new song had started that was up-tempo, and it was hard not to dance. "So are you ready for your present yet?"

Izzie stopped dancing. "No presents, remember?"

Brayden looked offended. "I made a donation, but if you think I'm not giving my girlfriend a gift at her birthday party, you're crazy."

Izzie liked hearing him call her his girlfriend. "Okay, but you didn't have to. I have everything I want already." And she meant it. She stared at her grandmother's ring on her right hand. Just looking at it reminded her that life was finally starting to make sense again.

"Hey! Fellow birthday girl," Mira called to her. Landon was standing beside her, and they both looked happy. "Ready to have everyone help us light the candles on our birthday cakes?"

The one thing Mira and Izzie weren't sharing at this party was cake. Mostly because they couldn't agree on one. While Mira's was a shimmering pink tower with elaborate silver decorations concealing each layer of red velvet, Izzie's was a vanilla sheet cake with buttercream frosting and raspberry filling. Her mom had made something like it every birthday when she was little. Grams had tried to re-create it later, but she wasn't the best baker.

"What exactly do we have to do again?" Izzie asked. The candle-lighting ceremony had been Ms. Mays's idea, but since Izzie never attended meetings, she felt out of the loop. All she knew was that Mira had made her make a top sixteen list of important people.

Mira gave her a look. "I told you—the DJ will announce we're lighting our cakes. Then we'll alternate asking groups of friends and family up to light our candles. Then everyone will sing 'Happy Birthday' to both of us, and we'll blow out our candles."

"And we couldn't have just lit our candles ahead of time why?" Izzie gave Brayden a quick kiss before heading with Mira over to the gorgeous cakes on display in a corner of the room.

"Because it's more fun this way!" Mira said as if it should be obvious.

"And now we invite everyone to join us as Mirabelle and Isabelle light their sixteen candles," Izzie heard the DJ announce, and immediately a crowd started to gather.

Ms. Mays was waiting by the cake display. "The DJ already has your lists, and since some of the people match, those groups will be called up to light both cakes at the same time." Mira and Izzie nodded and took the long candles from her.

"First up for these sisters is their family! Bill, Maureen, Hayden, and Connor—come on up, guys!"

Their family walked up and lit candles on each cake. Then the DJ had Mira invite up her mom's parents, who had flown in for the party, and an aunt and uncle. Next, Izzie lit candles in memory of her mom and her grandmother, and Aunt Maureen read a note from Zoe and lit a candle on her behalf.

Both girls had a few separate candle-lighters after that, with Izzie picking Brayden to light one, of course, and then they called up their mutual friends.

In his suave voice, the DJ announced: "Next up, Mirabelle and Isabelle would like to invite up Charlotte, Kylie, Violet, and Nicole. Come on up, ladies!"

Afterward, they each had only one candle left.

"I thought your top slot was going to Brayden," Mira whispered through a tight smile since everyone was still taking pictures.

"Nope," Izzie said, smiling wearily as well. "I thought yours was Charlotte."

"Nope," Mira echoed, and they both looked at each other.

"I know I'm not all warm and fuzzy like you are, but my top-dog slot could only go to one person," Izzie admitted, "and that person is you."

Mira smiled. "Really?" She squeezed her like a lemon. "I'm so glad you said that because I made you my top spot, too! Guess sisters really do think alike."

Izzie liked the sound of that. "I guess so," she said softly.

"For their final candles, Mirabelle and Isabelle have chosen each other for the honor," said the DJ.

The girls took their final candles from Ms. Mays, lit them, and handed them to each other as flashbulbs went off like fireworks.

"And now, we invite you all to sing 'Happy Birthday'! On my count: one, two, three!"

The song was so deafening, Mira and Izzie could barely hear. Mira put her arm around Izzie, and they sang the song to each other.

At the end, the DJ crowed, "Make a wish, ladies!"

Mira and Izzie looked at each other and knew they were both thinking the same thing. Who needed wishes when they already had each other? Sixteen was going to be a great year.

Acknowledgments

Belles is ultimately a story about family, and I couldn't have created this series without my publishing one, Little, Brown Books for Young Readers and the team at the Poppy imprint. Cindy Eagan, the original champion for Mira and Izzie, you may be gone, but your mark will never be forgotten. To my editor, Pam Gruber, who has deftly handled each and every turn in the Monroe/Scott landscape with a keen eye for detail and a big heart that loves these characters as much as I do. High fives also to Elizabeth Bewley, Ames O'Neill, Kristina Aven, Christine Ma, Jodie Lowe, and Andrew Smith.

I'm so thankful to have Laura Dail and Tamar Rydzinski from the Laura Dail Literary Agency in my corner. Thanks for being my fiercest champions.

The YA community is a great family to have as well, and

mine wouldn't be complete without Elizabeth Eulberg, Kieran Scott, Sarah Mlynowski, Courtney Sheinmel, Joanna Philbin, and Julia DeVillers. Falling under the writing heading is also Mara Reinstein, a trusted friend and critical first reader (I need that!), and my awesome copartners in the Beach Bag Book Club: Larissa Simonovski, Kelly Rechsteiner, Jess Tymecki, and Pat Gleiberman.

None of this would even be possible without the readers, librarians, and bookstores that have been so kind to me and my books all these years. I'm forever grateful to all of you and to my family and friends for all their love and support.

Finally, a huge hug and kisses to the people I call my home: Tyler, Dylan, Captain Jack Sparrow (yes, the Chihuahua helps, too!), and Mike, who knows me all too well and pushes me to be bigger and better each and every day. Thanks for the nudge in the right direction.

Fifteen-year-old Harper McAllister thinks her summer plans are ruined when her parents receive her latest heart-stopping credit card bill and ship her off to camp at Whispering Pines. Suddenly Harper is at the bottom of a social ladder that she can't climb wearing wedge sandals and expensive clothes. She seems to be winning over supercute camp "Lifer" Ethan, though, and if she can manage to make a few friends—and stay out of trouble—she just might find a whole new summer state of mind.

Head off to sleepaway camp with this
sneak peek of *Summer State of Mind*.

AVAILABLE APRIL 2014

1

Confessions of a Shopaholic

Harper McAllister @HarperMc
SCHOOL. IS. OVER! Can't wait to hang w/ my friends
@KatetheGreat & @MargoDivine at our home away
from home...the Americana!

THIS IS HOW I Was Meant to spend my afternoons. Standing in the middle of a big, bright store filled with all my favorite people—Emilio Pucci, Stella McCartney, and Chloé.

Not behind a Bunsen burner wearing supertight plastic goggles that leave red marks on my tender skin.

As I flip through the racks at Intermix, I can feel my stress level drop, much like that piece of plastic that accidentally fell into my Bunsen burner during my second-to-last science lab. (The lab *still* smelled this morning, even after I secretly spritzed Vera Wang Princess perfume in the air.)

"*Eeee!*" I look up and see Margo racing toward me waving a long electric-blue halter top like a flag. The glittery straps are so blinding I shield my eyes. "This is that top I saw in *Lucky*!" Margo pins it to her tiny torso and spins, which sends her long black hair flying. "I've been looking for it everywhere! Isn't it cute? I could wear it as a shirt! Or a minidress! Or as a beach cover-up if we go to Cancun!"

When Margo is excited she talks so fast that I wish I could rewind her. The girl loves to shop even more than I do. "It looks like something you'd wear for a dance competition," I say with a laugh. Margo starts to pout, so I add, "But if we do go to Cancun, we'll just have to go dancing so you can wear it."

Margo squeezes me like a lemon.

"What do you mean *if* we go to Cancun?" Kate teeters over on four-inch cork wedges, towering over us like a giant. She practically trips into me, and her dirty blond hair smacks me in the face. "I thought the trip was a done deal."

I backpedal. "Did I say *if*? I meant *when*."

Kate looks at me harder. "Are you sure?"

Sometimes Kate cross-examines me like they do on those legal shows my grandma watches in the middle of the afternoon. "Yes!" I say brightly. She continues to stare me down, and I crack. "The thing is I haven't exactly asked McDaddy about a date yet." Kate gives me a look. "I tried to bring it up the other night, but he was meeting Rihanna for dinner and was stressed 'cause he couldn't find his keys. I'll sort it all out tonight."

Kate smiles with satisfaction. "Okay. I don't mean to hound you. I just want to tell my parents when I'm going to Atlantis so they can go to Barbados the same week." She wrinkles her nose as if she just got a whiff of rancid sushi. "I hate Barbados."

"Atlantis?" Margo and I repeat at the same time.

"Harper's dad said he is taking us to Cancun," Margo reminds Kate, speaking slowly in case the fumes from my Bunsen burner incident the other day are having some lasting effect on Kate's memory.

"That's right!" Kate hits her forehead. "*I* was the one who suggested Atlantis." She thumbs the fabric of a pair of dark wash jeans on a table next to her. "I just thought it would be more fun to swim with sharks and celebrity watch than worry about being kidnapped in Mexico." She sighs. "But it's your choice, Harper. Margo picked last time."

"Yeah, because my dad paid." Margo's mood goes from a shopping high to a discount-bin low, and I feel my heart race with alarm. Kate and Margo step toward each other, and my thumbnail goes to my mouth. I start to bite it. "I don't recall you being that bent out of shape about skiing in Park City, Utah. Harper!" Margo swats my hand away from my mouth. "Stop biting your nails!"

"Sorry," I say sheepishly. I asked Margo to keep me in check about my nail biting. My disgusting habit seems to get worse in high-stress moments like this.

"Actually, now that I think about it, we picked Park City because Harper wanted to go there. I suggested Aspen, remember?" Kate clicks the heels on her cork wedges loudly and looks at me.

Okay, I did say I've always wanted to ski the white powder in Utah, but I didn't know Margo was going to book our winter break trip around something I said. We usually do what Kate wants. She picks what table we sit at for lunch, what movie we see on a Friday night, whose party is worthy of us attending. The three of us have been tighter than super-skinny jeans since I arrived at Friends Prep almost two years ago, but sometimes I still feel like I'm on friend probation with Kate. Margo says that's because Kate thinks I've moved above her in the hierarchy of our friendship. All because a few people—including the lunch lady—have started asking for my advice instead of hers.

"Should I get the Greek yogurt or Yoplait for lunch today, Harper?"

"Would you button this top or leave it unbuttoned, Harper?"

"Harper, what is the square root of 364?"

Honestly, I have no clue what the answer is to that last one.

I don't want Kate to feel threatened by me. If it wasn't for her, I wouldn't even be popular. When my family moved to Brookville almost two years ago, I didn't know a soul. Thankfully, Kate rescued me from lunch-table no-man's-land. She spied me in line wearing my pink Hunter rain boots and said she knew I was "one of them," which in Kate's book meant "destined to be popular." I was an overnight success, just like my dad when his wedding video company produced an unknown rap star's low-budget music video and the song became record of the year. McDaddy Productions was born soon afterward, and we went from a tiny house in middle-class Mineola to a mansion in JLo country (she and Marc Anthony used to own the house across the street from ours). Some days I am still getting used to how different my life is here.

"My dad has his heart set on Cancun," I tell Kate apologetically. "But the good news is he said the resort is secluded and five-star. I think Beyoncé told him about it."

That makes Kate smile. "Well, if Beyoncé goes there . . . You're *sure* we're going?"

"Absolutely!" I insist, but the truth is, I'm not sure McDaddy remembers promising to take my friends and me away for my fifteenth birthday. He was shooting a video with the hottest pop star on the charts, London Blue, on my actual birthday and promised to make it up to me. He also arranged for me to get a shout-out from London Blue online that got over a hundred thousand hits on YouTube. I don't want to disappoint my friends, though. Margo has taken us away twice, and Kate keeps promising to bring us on a trip next winter. Mom finds the group-trip tradition kind of strange, but she chalks it up to being a North Shore thing. Going from the middle of Long Island to the North Shore really was like moving from Antarctica to Los Angeles. There are a lot of cultural differences. Don't even get me started on the Truvia versus real sugar debate.

"And the best part about Cancun is that we don't have to worry about getting eaten alive on an excursion," I tell Kate. "Swimming with sharks at Atlantis has *Good Morning America* lifestyle piece written all over it. 'Almost high school sophomore eaten by sharks on summer break,' " I say using my best reporter voice. "I'll be darned if Josh Elliott reports on me, and I'm not alive to see it."

"Amen," seconds Margo, folding her hands in prayer for a moment before slipping the blue halter over her head to try it on, much to the chagrin of the nearby saleswoman.

"I guess you're right. Again." Kate pulls off the cork wedges dejectedly.

I quickly look around the store of brightly colored designer pieces to find something that will cheer her up. "Ooh, Kate! Isn't that the Chloé shirt you were looking for the other day? They must have gotten more in."

Kate rushes over to the rack and squeals. I breathe a sigh of relief.

"It's the shirt!" she announces, a smile replacing the scowl on her face. She holds up the tee. It has nylon flowers around the collar, the Chloé logo written across the front, and a stick figure drawing of a girl on it. I don't think it's anything special, but Kate is acting like she won a private fitting with the designer herself. "Isn't it sweet?"

"Yeah," I say, because that's what she wants to hear.

"If we each get one, we'll look like triplets!" Kate pulls me in front of the nearest mirror and holds the tee up under my chin. She and I do look somewhat related. We have the same dirty blond hair and brown eyes, but she towers over me in the height department while I have her beat in the bra-size category. "We have to buy them. This will look great on you even if it is a bit snug in the chest." She opens her slouchy leather bag and retrieves her wallet. I open my mouth to protest and watch her eyes widen in horror. "Seriously! My credit card is in my other wallet." She sits down on one of the velvet ottomans in the store, and Margo walks up next to her. "I was going to buy them for us as last-day-of-school gifts. They'll be gone tomorrow." She drops her bag on the floor in disgust. Her eyes narrow as she stares at the front door. "Cassie Anderson is probably hiding behind one of the racks trying to steal them from us as we speak. Some last day of school this is turning out to be. First no Atlantis, now no Chloé tee that I have wanted forever."

She's laying the guilt on thick. "I'll buy them for us." I gently pry the shirt from Kate's hands, and the saleswoman swoops in to take the tees up to the register.

Margo follows us. "H, no! You bought us the Swarovski crystal flip-flops last week and MAC makeup the week before that. It's too much."

"So? You bought us facials at Red Door Spa a few weeks back." I pull my credit card out and hand it to the salesgirl. "Friends do things for each other, right?"

"Right!" Kate seconds. I notice she's still holding the cork wedges she tried on earlier. She stops a salesgirl walking by, and I hear her whisper: "Can I put these on hold for tomorrow?"

On hold. I suddenly wonder why Kate didn't do that with these shirts, too.

"That will be three hundred sixty-eight dollars and forty-two cents," my salesgirl says and swipes my credit card before I even have time to hesitate.

Three hundred and sixty-eight dollars isn't that bad, is it? I sign the receipt with a whimsical signature I have been perfecting, making a giant loop around the *H* and *A* for Harper Avery McAllister. Usually signing my name and getting handed a cute bag full of new clothes is my favorite part of shopping. But when the salesgirl hands me my receipt this time, I can't help but think about everything I've bought lately. There was that Nikon 1 camera I needed because for a split second I wanted to become a photographer, the pair of skis I've never used but had to have because they were on sale, and the Prada dress for the spring fling that looked like the one Amanda Seyfried wore to an awards ceremony. Those three items add up to about eight hundred dollars and that doesn't include any of my Starbucks runs or dinners out with the girls. Gulp.

I'm sure I have nothing to worry about, though. McDaddy is the one who gave me the AMEX and told me to consider it my "fun money."

"Here you go." The saleswoman walks around the counter and hands me three bags. One for each of us. I start to cheer up as I pass them out like candy.

TWO SOUTHERN BELLES
AND ONE LIFE-CHANGING SECRET

Don't miss **Jen Calonita's** BELLES series!

More juicy novels by
Jen Calonita

Secrets of My Hollywood Life

The fabulous (and not-so-fabulous) sides of being a hot teen star in Hollywood.

Sleepaway Girls

Turns out you can't hide from high school drama—even in the wilderness!

Reality Check

A TV exec picks four normal girls as THE next big thing in reality TV. Can their friendship withstand the spotlight?

Belles

A brand-new series about two very different girls and the secret that will change their lives forever.

poppy

Available however books are sold

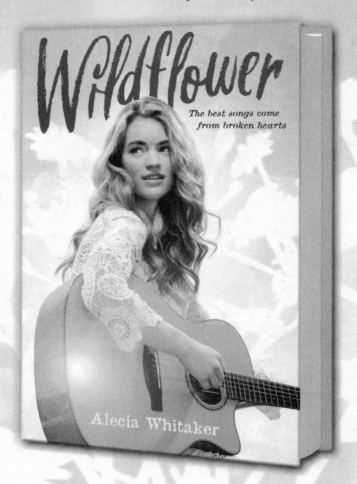